Underlying Crimes

Joann Mead

Underlying Crimes
©2012 Joann Mead

To Aunty Mary

And to my beautiful husband, family and friends (they know who they are), thank you for your illuminating ideas, edifying insights and infinite patience.

Prologue

They hired the hit man to kill little Jo
Hired the cops to cover the crime
That never occurred
When the garbage men came that day
To dump the little pogy
Into the bay

I am the man
Who doesn't give a damn
My names are many, my motive the same
Whether corporate upperworld
Or criminal underworld
We are all to blame

All the same in the name
Of malice and evil
All complicit
With the underlying crimes
We all commit, we weave and spin
So we all win

Unless the pogies arise from the bay
Some day
And the children, one small little child
And all the dogies
As they frolic in the fields
And play in the dirt

Where the soil and the wetlands
Rivers and drains, sewers and sludge

Carry the virulent stew
The soup, the sauce
To permeate, attack
And make them weak

The haunting pogies
Silver bellies up in the bay
And the day
The poor little dogies began to die
Swollen brains, bursting with pain
The poor little child dies in a day

Overshadowed and obscured
The stealth chimera
Inadvertent creation
Your bioterror error
Sown by the complicit guilt
Of your underlying crimes

How dare you politicians
Complicit
Sell yourselves
As the cheap whores you are
And the pogies and dogies
Are the price you pay

The pogies, silver
Belly-up in the bay
And the day the dogies
Swollen brains, bursting with pain
The poor little child
Dies on a winter day

When others sicken, chronically ill
Overshadowed and obscured
The stealth chimera, inadvertent creation
Your bioerror terror
Sown by the complicit guilt
Of your underlying crimes

J. J. Mead

Part 1 Confusion

Chapter 1 Bent Plates

A DARKENED ROOM drapes drawn, but outside it was bright daylight. The room was lit only by luminous blue screens and tiny flashing red and green lights. In the hazy glow of computer light, Jo's olive skin gave off a shiny bronze hue; her long, curly hair, a mix of chestnut and yellow-gold framed her small oval face. Intent on finishing, she pecked away at a computer, immersed in the rebuttal for her lawyer.

To Jo's right, a wooden-pegged rack full of Sofia's ice skating medals hung on the wall, cockeyed from their weigh. The gold, silver, and bronze Jo's daughter Sofia acquired over the past fifteen years. On the wall behind Jo, late 1970's Soviet communist era posters donned the walls. Glory to work! *Zclava rabotayet!* Workers of the world unite. The vivid red scarves on peasants wielding hammers and sickles contrasted starkly with the glitzy scarlet and gold clad skaters of Holiday-on-Ice. Glamorous show posters from "Fantasy" and "Hollywood" were interspersed with the Soviet memorabilia Jo and her husband Jeremy had collected while living in Moscow in the late 70's and early 80's.

Jo thumbed through a litter of paperwork, alternately typing on the keyboard. Her binoculars were propped nearby on the desk.

Startled by a loud buzz at the front door, Jo hesitated, froze, and listened.

The buzzer grated again. The diminutive Jo

heard a gruff male voice coughing, a throat clearing gurgle that made sure he was heard. He pushed the buzzer a third time.

"Oh crap!" Jo muttered just above a whisper. "Who's that?"

Jo waited a few moments, grabbed the binoculars and crept quickly to the shuttered window in time to see a hunched, stocky, bald-headed guy disappear down the walkway. Moments later, a gun-metal gray van drove past, exiting on the circular drive. Binoculars in place, Jo peered at the license plate, but could not get it in focus.

"Damn!"

Across the circular drive on the grassy commons, Jo spied a man in the distance with his dog. *Familiar*, she thought. She noticed the two earlier that week. The leashed brown mutt and his master disappeared and reappeared, meandering in and out of the thick bush leading to Harrison Road.

Jo opened the front door and peered hesitantly around the corner. An envelope lay on the doorstep with a scrawled "By Hand Delivery". It beckoned her to open. It read, "This letter is to confirm that you are instructed to attend a meeting at Allbio New England on November 29th with Lance Steadman and myself. Your refusal to attend is not acceptable. We are scheduling a meeting with you tomorrow at 1 pm. Failure to attend this meeting will be considered insubordination and will result in disciplinary action up to and including termination of employment."

"Humpf! Rizzo, you HR rat!" Jo emoted, thinking that tomorrow morning she and Jeremy would show her lawyer the letter. Jo unraveled the rhetoric, thinking of militaristic consequences. *Insubordination! What are they going to do, execute me by firing squad?*

Jo added the Allbio letter to a stack of papers. Restless and unsettled, she paced and set down the binoculars on a side-board in the tiled entryway. Grabbing a steno pad, Jo sat on a loveseat and wrote down what had just transpired and her take on it. Some time went by before a grinding, braking sound and loud engine startled and pulled her attention away. As if she were hiding her thoughts, Jo tucked the steno pad under the cushion of the plum colored loveseat. Jo peeked with the binoculars through the drawn drapes to see the back end of a noisy white truck.

Pumped up and adrenaline laden, Jo anxiously worried aloud, "Allbio...uh-oh! More goons, I can't let them get me!"

Binoculars in hand, she grabbed the handset from the kitchen telephone, and darted out, closing the back patio door behind her. After dialing 911, Jo asked for the police, but the telephone died as she jogged away from her condo. Moving through the common area past the patios of neighbors, Jo knocked at a neighbor's back door but no one answered. Further on Jo found an elderly woman she met once, pruning in her rose garden.

"Hello, please may I use your telephone to call the police? My phone has died." Jo gestured waving her telephone hand piece. "There's a problem at my condo... a big truck outside." Jo gasped, hyperventilating.

"Why certainly!" The frail, white-haired neighbor led her inside.

"Will you please come to 29 Circular Drive in Willow Dean? I'm calling from my neighbor's phone. There is a large truck outside my condo and I'm being harassed."

"This is dispatch. We are sending the police now."

Jo thanked her neighbor and left through the front entrance. Feeling less anxious and slightly relieved, Jo returned carrying her kitchen telephone and binoculars. As she came around the corner, she flinched with surprise when she saw a Bayside police car had pulled up into the dead end where the large white truck had been. At the end of her condo walkway, Jo found two police patrolmen standing at her door.

Jo greeted the cops. "You got here quickly. I just called from my neighbors. There was a truck here, where you are parked."

"We got here in one minute. We were nearby. A garbage truck was parked out front when we arrived," said a round-headed cop.

Both were bulky-framed cops, one with a round moon-face, the other with a block-like head attached directly to shoulders. Neither cop appeared to have a neck.

Jo recalled her conversation with Ted, her next door neighbor, earlier that morning. He told her that the garbage truck usually arrived before 8 am but today they were very late. Ted, retired, observant, noted the daily routines of Willow Dean.

Jo mused and asked herself why the garbage truck would linger as long as it did. *Not normal, that's unusual*, she thought. To Jo, the timing of everything seemed off. *How could these cops get here so fast?* Jo wondered, bewildered.

Jo felt she needed to explain to the cops, "We'll that wasn't the *usual* garbage truck. And someone else came... earlier a bald, thuggy-looking guy in a gray van. He banged loudly on my door. He left a threatening letter from Allbio. They have been harassing me. I thought the truck was them again. The company has been trying to intimidate me."

The front door was locked so Jo excused herself to walk around to the back. She opened the front door, invited the cops in and showed them the letter from Allbio.

Patrolman "Square-head" looked quickly at the letter and summed up, "Well there is nothing going on now. All they did is send a courier to deliver this letter. So we'll be going." The cops left to walk to their patrol car and Jo followed.

Surprised by their dismissive lack of concern Jo asked firmly, "Wait! Can I see your identification?"

Officer Square-head smirked and gestured ape-like with his hands curved inward, pointing towards his uniform and badge. "Round-head" followed suit, mimicking the same simian gesture. They continued to saunter towards their patrol car but Jo insisted, enunciating each word, *"No! I want to see your ID."*

Neither cop replied. Patrolman Roundhead pointed at the patrol car, presumably to show the obvious. Both walked towards opposite sides of the police cruiser.

Jo fumed. She desperately wanted to see identification and rashly thought, *I know what I can take as identification!* Jo grabbed the rear license plate firmly with both hands. It was bolted on tightly but the plate bent outwards on the upper corners as Jo tried to pry it off. Her grip slipped. Losing her balance, Jo stumbled and stepped back to steady herself.

Pulling out handcuffs, Square-head barked "Okay that's it. *You're under arrest!*"

Jo backed away and adamantly blurted. "But I didn't *do* anything! *All I did was bend your license plate!*" She felt embarrassed by her impulsiveness.

Jo panicked and attempted a run but Squarehead quickly lurched forward, grabbed her wrists and handcuffed them in front of her as she squirmed, struggling to get away. Jo's immediate thought was that these cops were *not* ordinary police. *Why wouldn't they show me their ID? Or tell me their names?* She suspected that they were contracted by Allbio. Jo howled loudly, "You're not the police! You're from Allbio! You're the Allbio police! *You're the Allbio Police!*"

Ted, the next door neighbor, had been standing on his front walkway watching the tussle. Jo, handcuffed but still struggling, turned towards Ted and shrieked again. *"Help! They're not the police! They're the Allbio police!"* Patrolman Squarehead grabbed Jo's forearms hard with a heavy-handed vice-grip and lifted her a foot above the ground, her legs still running in place. As he transported her to the driver's side rear door of the police cruiser, Squarehead dragged Jo's legs against the rear right of the patrol car, scraping her tennis shoes up against the cruiser's fender.

Roundhead pulled open the door to the back seat. Squarehead then shoved Jo's head and shoulders into the prisoner cabin. Lying across the seat, Jo's rigid legs hung stiffly out the door as Squarehead pushed at her unbending legs. Jo was relentless and still yelling when she felt the door slamming, repeatedly, against her legs. Four dull, pounding wallops, the muted sounds of metal against bone. "Thump, thump, thump,…thump!"

Jo instinctively tried to pull her legs into the cab but only the left knee bent towards her chest. Then the next, more forceful round began. "Thump, thump, thump,…thump, thump!" Squarehead whacked even harder on her limp, inanimate right leg. Silenced from the unexpected beating, Jo did not resist as Squarehead pushed in her lifeless, anesthetized leg and seated her upright. After Roundhead helped manipulate the harness over Jo's head, he disappeared behind the patrol car and walked back towards the condo.

Squarehead, now seated in the driver's seat, turned around. Jo's eyeglasses were askew across her nose from the melee. Squarehead peered angrily over his shoulder, gruffly reached back, grabbed Jo's glasses and he viciously popped his middle knuckle into her right eye. Jo was stunned in disbelief but the sharp, stabbing pain convinced her of his intent. She felt as though her eye dislocated, as if it were pushed deep into its socket. Jo cowered but knew she must somehow save herself from this malicious cop.

A few moments passed before Jo turned her neck around. Her vision was fuzzy but she could just make out her neighbor still standing in his walkway. "Help me Ted! They're trying to kill me!" And again she bellowed. "They're not the police! They're from Allbio! *They're trying to kill me!*" Jo's voice diminished, hoarsened from her screams, she pleaded an insipid, "Help me, please help me."

Jo feared for what might happen next. She was afraid the police would try to dump her somewhere, perhaps in the Narragansett Bay. Her inner monologue echoed, *they've already hurt me, next they will kill me. They've been bought off by Allbio. They will get rid of me, dump me in the bay.*

Squarehead opened the rear door, tightened Jo's handcuffs and squeezed them tight, to punish. Returning from the condo, Roundhead was holding Jo's sheepskin jacket. They drove away in their cruiser towards the Willow Dean entrance where another patrol car had already arrived. Jo noted an inaudible conversation going on between the new cops and a man who was on foot. As they passed by, Jo looked out the window at the man's face which appears palsied. His eyes were fixed somewhere distant in a twisted, frozen stare. Jo wondered to herself. *Did he see what happened? Wasn't he the man walking the dog?*

En route, Jo twisted and squirmed; the

harness loosened. On the Ocean View Road, the patrol car rounded the corner where two state troopers were stopped at the street light. Unable to see their faces clearly, her right eye throbbed and felt ajar, but she recognized the car markings as state police. She twice mouthed a barely audible plea. "Help me!"

Squarehead, also eyeing the state troopers, blurted out a question and answer, "Why are you yelping at them for help? *We're police!*"

Jo groaned a mere whimper and sunk lower in her seat. The harness was so loose she slipped her head sideways and freed herself, carefully, so the two cops beyond the screened divider would not catch on. Jo's thoughts turned to escape; still afraid her ultimate fate would be at the bottom of the bay, down by the docks where she would become fish food. Confused and seized with fear, she was intent on jumping out of the police car. *Who cares if the car is in motion? They will kill me anyway!* Jo elbowed and nudged, pushing the door with her left shoulder. She wished there were a door handle or a button to unlock, but prisoners are not allowed that liberty.

Chapter 2 Chinese Coolies

YOU CAN SEE the Allbio water tower from Aunty Mary's house. The enormous mushroom-like water tower sprouted on the hill near the biotech industrial site. It was just two weeks before Jo's arrest that she and Jeremy drove to the family gathering for Thanksgiving dinner.

Jo wittered drolly to Jeremy, "Is that mushroom an edible white Agaricus or a Death Cap? Maybe it's a common puffball? Or is it a Destroying Angel? How it can hold water and not topple over is a mystery to me!" Jo had always been interested in mushrooms, dragging Jeremy through the woods to look at them, even getting lost a few times.

At the rambling old two-story house, the usual loud banter of Italian Americans, second, third and fourth generations, resounded over two dinner tables. The youngest were anxious to have it all over with so they could run off with their friends. Remnants of turkey, ham, roasted potatoes, red peppers and spinach calzone littered the table. Jo and Jeremy helped shuffle plates to make way for the usual choice of pumpkin, apple and blueberry pie. There is something to suit everyone's taste.

"Hey Jo, I was talking to a couple of guys from Allbio who came into the auto shop the other day." Twenty-five years ago, Cousin Vin and his mom, Mary, had opened Stella's auto repair shop in the town of Tuxet, a bedroom community adjacent to the new monolithic Allbio site.

"These guys got fired from Allbio. Apparently they were working in engineering, outfitting the new plant. All five guys got fired. They said they were just doing their job, just doing what they were told to do." Vin wondered why.

"Ya know, I heard something about those guys." Jo said, "Something was done wrong, some filters were put in upside down or inside out, I don't know the details."

Jeremy fondled two cigars he brought with him. "Vin, we can smoke these later out on the patio."

Jo grimaced and stuck her tongue out at Jeremy, affirming a long standing argument. "I will never kiss you again!" Jo went on, "Plenty of weird shit going on around that Allbio site! Oh and hey, Aunty Mary, remember Gary Marcus, the Allbio guy who came into Stella Auto?"

"Oh what a house that guy has! I drove his wife home when she dropped off her car. The house had a huge porch with hanging flower baskets. And, god, you should have seen the size of the house!" Mary punctuated with her arms and hands splayed for emphasis.

Jo, fueled by a few glasses of red wine, ranted, "It figures...but watch out for that guy. What a lying sack of shit he is! Don't trust him!"

Mary's eyes widened. "Oh, yeah?"

"Next time you see him...slit his tires!"

Laugher and commotion accompanied the cutting and serving of pie and coffee. "Hey, ya know, Allbio is going to put in sewers here on

Harrison Road next year. If we hang on to this place, that should put the house value up. It would cost us fifteen or twenty thousand dollars to do it ourselves!" Vin could see dollar signs from the potential windfall.

"Well, not for nothing, 'cause Allbio will be filling up your sewers with their CHOs!" cautioned Jo.

Aunty Mary asked with her usual sarcasm and cynical sense of humor. "So what the hell are CHOs, Jo?" amused by her own alliteration.

Vin, his wife Donna, and their eldest son DJ rested their heads on their palms looking mildly curious. They knew next to nothing about what goes on in biotech.

"CHOs are Chinese Hamster Ovary cells, genetically changed. They are these little Chinese cells, with little coolie hats!" Jo gestured with pointed, tented hands above her head. "They put humanized genes into these Chinese cells. You know cheap labor!" Jo said in paroxysms of laughter while the others groaned and chuckled.

"Look out, here she goes!" Jeremy teasingly warned.

Not missing a beat, Jo went on, "What's *worse*, those Chinese Hamster cells now have a foreign gene with scrambled DNA in them. It's genetic engineering. And those cells are gonna go right down Allbio's drains and into those sewers that Allbio is so generously building for you."

Jo raved on over the raised eyebrows and laughter. "But it's OK – the CHO cells should be dead…. maybe?" Jo deviously suggested something more sinister, both to shock and entertain.

Aunty Mary countered, "OK, OK enough! We don't wanna know. Not before I eat my dessert!"

Jo pushed the humor, "So who wants pumpkin pie? Hmmm – looks like the orange custardy media they grow those CHO cells in!"

Jeremy, who hated pumpkin pie, led the groans of feigned disgust. Then Jeremy and Vin retired to the patio to smoke those two cigars. The younger cousins and kids had dispersed leaving Jo, Aunty Mary, Donna and her son DJ still seated at the dinner table. They nursed their coffee trying to wake up after a feast heavily laden with tryptophan.

DJ asked, "How is Sofia doing?" Is she still in Europe with the ice show?" DJ and Sofia first met when they were in their early twenties and both were notably impressed with each other's attractive good looks.

Jo missed her daughter Sofia. "Oh, she's doing great. She was in Marseille last week. She says the show and ice skating cast are a lot of fun."

DJ, having never been out of country but knowing Sofia was in France, grinned. "Not too shabby…"

Aunty Mary rifled through her purse and pulled out photos sent by Sofia. "Wow, what a dish, look at her DJ!" Mary passed around photos of Sofia donned in elaborate and sometimes scantily clad costumes from Holiday-on-Ice.

Mary told DJ, "Well, she is only your *second* cousin, that's not illegal is it?"

15

DJ cringed at the thought of "kissing cousins". Jo and Donna shook their heads disapprovingly as they contemplated the quirky thought of incest in the family.

Mary insisted "Yes, but wouldn't they have beautiful babies?"

Jo, the scientist, pondered aloud "And maybe some weird mutations along with DJ's beautiful blue eyes."

DJ put an end to the weird and wacko conversation. "Not a good idea, Granma."

How dissimilar Jo's family was from Jeremy's. The Blair's were a proper, British "middle class" family that was upper class by American standards. Perhaps those upper class values were the trigger for Jeremy's rebellious and antiestablishment tendencies.

Jo's family of dysfunctional Italian-Americans included Momma, an Ellis-Island immigrant. Mussolini-Momma, a fascist, married a first generation Sicilian with ties to Federal Hill in the little state of Rhode Island. An eclectic mix of painters, artisans and creators of exquisite cuisine, Jo's family spawned eccentricities in preferences, sexually and carnally. All were conflicted with the guilt ingrained from Catholicism.

Jo, looking for origins and order, traced the roots of her father's family to the Romani gypsy, despite the adamant objections of Aunty Mary. "We are Italians! Not Sicilians and how *dare* you call us gypsies!" Aunty Mary was as adamant an Italophile as any ethnocentric "proper" Anglophile. And

Jeremy was just that, despite his misspent youth as a skin-head adolescent with steel tipped shoes. A late blooming long-haired intellectual, he joined the left wing of the Labour Party after flirtations with the British communist movement.

Later in life, Jeremy still dreamed of fast motorcycles, not the big Harley's of the middle-aged bad boys but the demonic Ducati, ultra-fast, twin cylinder. Sport bikes with diabolic slant-eyed headlights. Personification on wheels, lean and fleet, Jeremy, still an avid tennis player, is wiry and tough despite his penchant for fine cigars and an aversion to all vegetables green and cruciferous.

Jo and Jeremy, both lovers of science, rebellious in youth, and here was where their personalities merged. Smart, like the right and left sides of the brain, they completed one another.

Chapter 3 The Behemoth

LIKE A TRIUMVERATE they stood, the Allbio version of Father, Son, and Holy Ghost. The holy trinity here was Allbio CEO Henry Givens, VP of Manufacturing, Ferris Pentanil, and VP of Site Governance and site manager, Bill Bonaducci, emitting an aura of omnipotence. Each took turns speaking to the crowd that had gathered under the big top tent on this carnival-like occasion.

"Welcome everyone! Allbio is proud to present the largest recombinant drug production facility in the world!" CEO Givens paused to magnify the impact. "The world's largest of its kind, right here in the smallest state of the union! We are the biotech leader in manufacturing therapeutic drugs for the treatment of disease. We understand the role of genes and our science focus drives our passion for benefiting medicine and mankind!" CEO Givens spoke to cheers and applause.

Ferris Pentanil seized the momentum. Addressing the crowd, he began with a bellow, "Life! We are working on it!" Dr Pentanil paused as the crowd yelled wildly over their thunderous clapping. This second in the company VP was an Allbio favorite. "We are improving the quality of life with quality products that conform to the highest standards of GMP, Good Manufacturing Practices. We are a company with great people and great scientists." He was himself a scientist and he had been in the trenches during the early advent of genetic engineering and biotechnology. All Allbio workers emulated and admired him for his success and awe-inspiring rise to riches.

"In this great state, we have a highly reliable infrastructure and unencumbered access to resources: electricity, sewers, and water. Especially clean water for production of our blockbuster drug, Quelify."

Dr Pentanil handed the podium over to Bill Bonaducci who managed Allbio's New England plant. "Allbio is revolutionary in its colossal ability to produce bio-therapeutic drugs in unheard of quantities. And today is the last day that the new facility will be open for you to tour before it is locked-down and sterilized." Bonaducci explained, "These twelve enormous bioreactors each hold 30,000 liters and they stand the entire height of this five story building. Behind these walls, everyone will wear full-body white bunny suits. No human skin cells, dust, microbes or air particulates may enter. These huge bioreactors, and miles of pipes and valves will be sealed and sterilized to protect the cell cultures. If bacteria or other contaminants penetrate a faulty seal, an entire drug batch will be ruined. And it only takes one bacteria to destroy everything!"

Jo's mind wandered into her biotech past. She remembered her first biotech tour nearly ten years ago at Gensar. It was a small-scale, biotech development lab. Her job at a start-up company, Gensar Biotech, introduced Jo to recombinant cell technology and the CHOs (Chinese Hamster Ovary cells) that churned out drugs. That was where she first met those CHOs with the "coolie hats" working in reactors. The bioreactors in that early development lab ranged from small milk-bottle-sized 2 liter spinner flasks up to washing-machine-sized 50 liter bioreactors. Those Gensar bioreactors were tiny by comparison to the behemoth bioreactors Allbio built.

In those early years while working at Gensar, Jo's friend and guide, Mike, "bunnied" her up in a convoluted fashion, explaining the logic to the gowning sequence. They wore clean-white gortex bunny suits, goggles, gloves, surgical masks, head covers or "bonnets", and foot "booties".

"Carefully don your gear on the "dirty" side of this line." Mike pointed to the red painted line on the linoleum floor. They sat rubbing shoulder to shoulder on a short bench that straddled the lined demarcation. "Now, avoid contact with the floor and swing your feet around to step over the clean blue line."

Amused at the gyrations, Jo chortled "This is just like playing a game of contortionist twister!" She giggled at Mike who now resembled Peter Rabbit with floppy white ears. He had strung a second hair bonnet ear to ear as an improvised cover for his beard, like a masquerade at a ball. A microbiologist, Mike emphasized the importance of sterility.

"We wear the bunny suits so there is no contamination from microbes…bacteria, fungi, *mycoplasma*, especially *mycoplasma*! You don't want them in here. Once the microbes get in, that's it! The batch is contaminated, destroyed. And you've got to toss the whole batch down the drain."

Jo's mind often wandered. Her memories sparked reflections on what biotech was like ten years ago and what it had become now. Her thoughts and attention shifted back to the present as she and Jeremy toured the massive new Allbio New England structure, unencumbered by bunny suits. They gazed at the maze of piping and the dozen enormous five story bioreactors.

Jeremy mumbled a quip aside to Jo. "With these huge vessels, it looks more like a gigantic dairy. Where are the cows? Those vats could be used to culture one hell of an expensive yogurt! After the two billion dollars Allbio invested in building this place, you would expect something more elaborate and sci-fi."

Jo taunted Jeremy as they strolled across the sprawling campus to tour the brand new Allbio New England corporate offices. "So you're not impressed, Jeremy?"

"I am just disappointed that after all the money they spent, it looks about as interesting as a dairy factory. But I guess they will make a few bob." Jeremy was not impressed but he goaded Jo all the same.

Jo came around to Allbio's defense. "Sure, these biotech companies are raking in the profits from some of the world's most expensive drugs. They capitalize on "unmet medical needs", rare diseases and devastating illnesses. So if you are really suffering, these drugs might be your only chance. They aren't cures, but they sure can improve your health and the quality of your life."

"OK, gotcha Jo. I still think it looks like a dairy, but according to Allbio it's all about fighting diseases and improving mankind."

"And it gives us a paycheck. Right, Jeremy?" Both nodded yes.

Jo and Jeremy stopped talking as they joined the queue to tour the brand new Allbio New England manufacturing plant. Quotes of inspiration donned the cream-colored walls that led to the corporate offices. Faintly inscribed were familiar, well chosen words to encourage high achievement or perhaps to uplift the dispirited. As they walked the wide corridors, Jo was enthralled with the quotations. Some were favorites she herself used in slide shows and training sessions. The translucent quotes faded as they disappeared into the walls on which they were stenciled. They were intended as subtle suggestions to guide employees in their daily work life.

Jo read one quotation to herself. *"No bird soars too high, if he soars with his own wings."* ...*William Blake.*

Jo's thoughts drifted to her daughter and the artwork Sofia painted on a corridor wall in her high school, a William Blake reproduction of the Ancient of Days. Sofia adored Blake, his art more than his poetry, but she knew all his verse. As an ice-skating chorus girl, Sofia soared with wings, eighteen pounds of blinking multicolored electric lights, that unfolded in a spectacular fashion as she glided onto the ice for the grand finally of "Hollywood". Jo and Jeremy had visited friends living in Vienna where they trouped en masse to the Holiday-on-Ice skating performance. She kidded Sofia that now she truly soared with her own wings like William Blake's prose.

But on the corridors of Allbio, Jo thought the fading quotations had an Orwellian feel of platitudes and justifications, as if to infer there were no limits. Regardless of the means, you can get as high as you want to go. *No bird soars too high unless you fly too close to the sun, and your wings are held together with wax, Icarus.*

Chapter 4 *Sfogliatella and the Rules*

"WHY DIDN'T YOU buy the sfogliatella?" Aunty Mary was feeling her usual critical and ornery self. "These cannolis are so damn rich and so expensive!"

Jo and Aunty Mary sipped coffee and nibbled on the ultra sweet and cheesy tubes of pastry. Jo bought the cannoli at Napoli's Bakery, a pricey but popular Italian-owned shop around the corner from Aunty's place. It wasn't unusual for Jo to stop by for Aunty's insular insights and indulge in facetious chatter.

"Oh, so *that's* the appreciation I get!" Jo kept up the pace and encouraged the sarcastic banter.

Aunty Mary always had a new story to share. She knew her local community and the Ocean State, its people, politics and the myriad of small business owners better than anyone. She knew who you could trust to do business with and who you could ask for a favor. She also knew when to be leery of people and who to avoid.

"Oh, here's a good one for you! My son Vinny was having a sausage sandwich at New York Hot Dogs, you know, down by the infamous nightclub with the strippers?" Jo nodded to Aunty's scene setting. "Well, two guys from the Town Council were at the next table. They had a cryptic conversation going on."

"Cryptic? Were they speaking another

language?" Jo's attempt at being clever was usurped by Aunty who was always miles ahead.

"No. More like vague innuendo, if you know what I mean." Aunty smirked at her own playful use of words. Jo grinned broadly and raised her eyebrows waiting for more of the taunt.

"One of the guys pushed a manila envelope across the table, sort of slid it slowly. Vin thought it looked a bit pouched, like something green and crumpled was in it."

"What? Money?" Jo asked.

"Hey, don't be stupid. What else would it be? And Vinny heard him say something like 'There'll be more, when we get everything. Just keep it up'."

"So is this the way people do business in this state? Greasing palms?" Jo had finally gotten it.

"Hey, it's one hand washes the other. Payola is the standard operating procedure in this state! *Pay to play*. You've got to play by the rules of engagement! Jo, don't you know the three Rhode Island rules?"

"What rules? Hey, I didn't grow up here. I didn't know the rules were different!" Jo prodded, wanting to know more.

Aunty Mary quickly pulled a cigarette from her pack of Newport lights. She waved her finger at Jo to wait a minute, lit up, drew deeply and blew a steady stream of blue white mist above Jo's head.

"Let's start with rule #3." Aunty leaned forward to emphasize the rule. "Ask people in your government for help. You ask those who *make* the rules to help you. They are the same ones who *don't live* by the rules. Rules are for everyone *else*."

Jo quipped up. "It's the Golden Rule". *He who has the gold makes the rules*. So whoever has big bucks or has deep pockets. Maybe big corporations like Allbio?"

"Yes," said Aunty "the people with the *gold* pay the guys who *make* the rules and it's the rule-makers in the government that we put our *trust* in."

"So what do you think was going on with the guys from the Town Council that Vin saw, Aunty?"

"Town Councils, building inspectors, water meter readers, all the way up to the state house politicians. Anybody who can do something for you, its pay or *be* paid. Want a permit for your business? Just pay the price to whoever calls the shots. They will bend the rules or even make new ones."

"Yeah now I get it. And for the corporations, like Allbio? They need water, so maybe they'll pay the law makers to give them a guaranteed amount? They've got to make sure that they don't run dry; even if the wells do. And what if Allbio wants someone to look the other way while they dump their crap down your sewers? So what is that shit they are dumping down the drains?" Jo quizzed Aunty to see if she remembered.

"It's those damn thirsty Chinese "coolie" Hamster cells you were telling us about!" Aunty Mary exclaimed as if she were riled. They both howled and hooted.

"So who are you going to tell when you know people are doing something wrong?" Jo asked.

"Nobody! You keep it to yourself! Cause if you rat, then they will come after you!" Aunty Mary warned, more serious than in jest.

"So I can't tell on Allbio?" Jo smirked a twisted smile as if she were resigned to the fact.

"Hey they're going to build a sewage line and tie us in! I'm sick of this old septic system! And besides that, there is Rule #2. Don't Rat!" Aunty coughed as she laughed.

"So I can't rat, snitch or tattle-tale?" Jo egged Aunty Mary on.

"What are you gonna do, tell on your boss at Allbio? Hey, they pay you handsomely honey." Aunty was emphatic that Jo follows the rules.

"So don't ask, don't tell." Jo added a corollary to rule #2.

"Don't be a fool. Just bite your tongue, because someday, someone from Allbio will come back and bite you in the ass. And after all, those dumped Chinese cells won't take our jobs!" The rant spilled over into a cascade of laughter and snorting.

"But seriously Jo, you never, ever bust your compatriots. You have to be loyal to those who do for you."

Jo thought about it and asked, "So what is rule #1?"

Aunt Mary's eyes widened as she fired back. "Be loyal! You aren't listening! Rule #1 is "Be loyal!"

"But who can trust anybody when trust is trumped by loyalty?" Jo queried in exasperation.

Disillusioned, she answered her question with a question.

Jo drove home thinking about the state's history of corruption. The state had a culture where criminal transgressions were rewarded and encouraged with a wink and a nod. A culture where it is all up to the individual person to follow the state's three simple rules. First and foremost, loyalty. Be loyal to the ones who rule. Take care of the people who take care of you. The rule arises naturally, especially in a small place with a dense social network. A small state where very low degrees of separation prevailed. Not the notorious six degrees of separation but seldom more than two degrees, where people are only two steps removed from anyone else. Secondly, don't be a "rat". A snitch. A tattle-tale. And thirdly, ask the local and state politicos to help you.

Jo thought about Aunty's three rules. Did the rules add up to a culture that accepts lies and deception? A culture that could accept bribery? Influence buying? Was it a blind acceptance of pervasive corruption? In a culture where the loyalty trumps trust, who can you trust when trust is trumped by loyalty?

No one.

Sometimes referred to as the family of "bosses", Jo, Jeremy and their daughter Sofia each thought they knew best. They were a self-righteous bunch that seldom agreed and who argued over minutia. But on larger issues, politics or war, they were more closely aligned. The family's ethical role model was Jeremy. Sofia listened and learned but in practice would bend the rules when influenced by the Italian-American ethics of Jo, not so squeaky clean and honest to a fault as Jeremy. Jo was accepting of little white lies, as long as no one is hurt. But all three were equally sure about their thinking and insisted on fair-play.

Professional ethics was at the center of Jeremy's intellectual existence. In his thesis on the "Teaching of Ethics in Medicine and Business", the latter, business ethics, he insisted was an oxymoron. He read the philosophers. His interests were in Wittgenstein, post-modern ethics and Foucault, but Jeremy had little interest in the theologians. Morality existed for him outside of religious dogma. Not enforced through the fear of sin, hell, fire and damnation.

In contrast, Jo's Roman Catholic upbringing emphasized sin, hell, fire and damnation and gave her rules meant to be broken, especially when it came to men and sex. Being naughty hurt no one. Right? "The heart does not feel what the eyes do not see." An old Italian expression.

Jeremy, not emotionally expressive, he seldom said "I feel..." Wittgensteinian philosopher at heart, metaphysics and ethics transcend the limits of human language about feelings. Jeremy didn't see the world in microcosm like Jo, but took a global vision.

Jo would taunt Jeremy. "Why don't you ever say "I feel..."? How do you ever expect me to know how you feel about anything?"

Jeremy thoughtfully explained how using

language to describe how you "feel" is fraught with difficulty. He agreed with Wittgenstein that describing feelings in language is a bewitchment. Jeremy expounded on post-modern thought by Foucault, "Language is too often used to control people, to elicit their emotions, to manipulate them, to mold them, to put them where you want them."

Jo echoed. "So you are saying that words are used to exert power over people?"

Jeremy and Jo both viewed words with suspicion but arrived there by different roads.

"Yes, like the three bigwigs, the Allbio Holy Trinity, using words to influence their audience just as Foucault wrote about, language and physical design built to show power. 'We are the *largest* in the world...we are the *leaders*...we are *great* people with *colossal* ability...' The language they used made it clear that they had the power over everyone, everything, the workers, the scientists, the state, and other resources." Jeremy said.

Jeremy continued. "At the tour of the plant that day, they showed the sheer power of their *behemoth* machines. They showed how they could use the *massive* scale of pipes and *oversized* vats to make *enormous* amounts of money. They even used language for power on those quotes in the corporate offices."

"Now *you* are using words to add to the bewilderment!" Jo exclaimed.

For Jo, bewilderment added to life mysteries. By today's standards, Jo would be diagnosed as borderline autistic. Too often staring out a window, or off into an unfocused distance, her

30

left eye would wander eccentrically looking for the netherworld. Jeremy thought her oblivious to social subtlety of language, her social development somewhat compromised and immature. She did have a puerile sense of humor; appreciative of the lewd and ludicrous. Their conversations met as captivated by the absurd and bizarre; they played a language game. Jeremy and Jo played by posing ideas in bizarre ways and absurd or extreme conclusions. Jo loved Kurt Vonnegut, a favorite in her youth.

For Jeremy, bewilderment added to intellectual puzzles. *We are bound by the limits of our linguistic ability. Language can't capture reality. There is no way of connecting words to sensations and reporting true feelings, making a lot of psychology for Jeremy a real problem.* "There is a tiny box in all of us, whose owner can only observe the feelings in that box. You cannot describe it accurately to others because you have to use words." And Jeremy stored the contents of his box deep within.

Jo always tried to create a pattern, an orderly way of cataloging, grouping and making a rationalized sense of logic; putting everything in the tiny box. Continually perplexed but when Jo did not know the answer, she made it up. A fact Jeremy often called her on. She was mathematically deductive but incapable of adopting traditional methods. She created her own "if-then" reasoning and ability to manipulate numbers. Adept at chess and memory games, winner of math awards, but during puberty she lost interest in mathematics.

Arrested development in adolescence left her emotionally stuck at age thirteen. But always a collector, ordering, categorizing, coins, stamps, plants, mushrooms, rocks. She collected anything animal, vegetable or mineral, and men, Jo had her collection of men.

Chapter 5 In Cahoots

IN CAHOOTS, PERHAPS it comes from the French, *cahute*, a small hut or cozy cabin implying as close as two people can get in a small place? Or maybe from another French derivation, as in *cohorte* or the far sexier *cortège*, anyway it all means they are in it together.

Allbio CEO Henry Givens made it clear from the start what he wanted. Unfettered access to resources, primarily water, electricity and sewers. CEO Givens, VP Ferris Pentanil and Bill Bonaducci, his leading man at Allbio New England, set the ground rules when they lunched with the state governor and his *cohorte* of senators and state house reps. Givens couldn't help thinking that in no other state did he have such easy direct contact with the top deciders and legislators.

The meeting venue was unique in itself, a grandiose Newport mansion on Belleview Avenue. The lavish castles and palaces built by top architects of the day were once the so-called summer "cottages" of industrialists and financiers, The Italian Renaissance-style villa with its 18th and 19th century French décor ostentatiously displayed the wealth of the past robber barons. The railroad and coal industry magnates were now replaced by political and corporate dons who cahooted as always.

Henry Givens, Ferris Pentanil and Bill Bonaducci were greeted by the private owner, a developer and businessman, in the foyer. A grand white Italianate spiral staircase caught Henry Given's eye, a metaphor he hoped for today's meeting as an upward spiraling relationship. Bonaducci, Allbio New England plant manager, focused on the 19th century French striking clock, a gilded bronze elephant holding a dial with white enamel Roman numeral chapters. He collected antique clocks and he knew them well. Atop the dial, a gilded bronze cupid stood poised, bow flexed, ready to shoot his arrow. Bonaducci rubbed the elephant's patina bronze forehead and commented, "This elephant's trunk is lowered. If it were raised up it would signal good luck." The host assured his guests that this elephant was crowned with a bowed cupid who brought love and romance to all who entered. The romance began. Cupid fired his arrow.

"It is obvious to me that you guys really care!" CEO Givens was seated at one of two tables along with the governor, two senators, his right-hand science man Ferris Pentanil and the host. The jovial mix of corporatos and politicos were served a seven course meal starting with clam chowder, a choice of creamy New England white, Manhattan red or Rhode Island clear. For the seafood adverse, creamy wild golden chanterelle mushroom soup or Tuscan white bean soup, were options. Quahogs, raw or steamed clams, cherry stones or the more succulent littlenecks unique to the ocean state, traditional clam "stuffies", crab cakes and calamari were sampled by nearly all. Whatever the guests fancied was laid before them in all senses, plus there was an abundance of pastas and antipastos for

34

the less adventurous or shellfish allergic. There was sea bass, lobster and filet mignon padded on the serving table. Fresh vegetables and melt in your mouth bread-and-butter corn. Nothing spared. All washed down with copious amounts of the best French and Tuscan wines.

"What a great state you have here. And a great place to do business!" Givens effervesced like a bubbly soda. Easy access to politicians and far less hurdles than other states, he thought and he told them so. The animated senators joked that in this small state there are only two degrees of separation. Not the usual six degrees of Kevin Bacon lore.

"After all, this is not a big place!" State Senator Egregio laughingly remarked.

In Given's eyes Egregio was the solution for Allbio New England's problems, he knew what the senator wanted. The dark and handsome, wavy haired Senator Sam Egregio; his district covered the six towns surrounding the Allbio New England compound. The senator was a paradox; a contradiction in terms of his notable good looks and stature. His name is a double entendre. In Italian his name "egregio" means distinguished. But more apropos, he was egregious in his double dealings and slimy as a raw Rhode Island quahog. His veneer of the honorable senator, a distinguished and prominent financial leader, investment analyst and trusted official came with elevated privileges and business opportunities which he cultivated. Senator Egregio mulled over his plan as he slurped down a dozen cherrystone clams.

After lunch, the *cortège* of public servants

tailed the governor and CEO as they retired to the greenhouses, seaside pavilion and manicured grounds. The group splintered. Givens and Egregio crossed the gardens to stroll along the cliff walk with its spectacular view of the Atlantic Ocean. It was prime oceanfront property.

"Anything and I mean *anything* you guys need." Senator Egregio did not mince words. "Believe me, you can trust me to get things done."

Givens knew that *quid pro quo* was expected and he could barter like a pro. In this Rhode Island game, pay to play was the *modus operandi*. In pay-to-play, Allbio, the payer with its deep pockets of gold could buy whatever it needed. Givens knew that whether it was legislation or regulation, special access or other favor, Egregio had the power to get it all done. Egregio was a master at the game of legalized corruption.

Senator Egregio had negotiated the new sewers months ahead of schedule. The senator called in favors where needed. The company was already ahead of Allbio's ramped up production schedule. The cost of building the sewers split 80:20 by Allbio and the neighboring towns. It was seen as a win-win game for all concerned. But Henry Givens needed more.

"We need water!" he spit out. "Allbio needs enough clean water to produce our drug Quelify. Biotech is a thirsty industry."

Egregio's razor sharp mind cut to a deal. He knew that the state would do back flips for Allbio. He was a 'cirque de soleil' contortionist when it came to bending over backwards for the big players and payers in the tiny state. They desperately needed investment and Allbio was a rare jewel, a finely cut blue diamond, no gem in the rough start-up that might fail.

The diminished jewelry business in Rhode Island, once robust, had been in decline for decades and many jobs went with it. High tech jobs, good wages and tax revenue to stimulate growth were a necessity in the state's downward spiraling economy. More than kudos came with attracting pharmaceuticals and biotech like Allbio, but not without a price to pay.

"Water is critical. Our scale of drug production is huge. We have the world's largest scale facility." Givens doggedly repeated. "Our need for clean water supersedes any ordinary industry."

Senator Egregio knew where the conversation was going. "I realize the water board refused your lawyer's request for a water guarantee. I've been working with Allbio's lawyers trying to push an agreement through. But it looks like we need to kick it up a notch."

"Where will you kick it? What ball do we need to kick?"

"No ball, just balls, *coglioni!*" said Egregio grabbing his own crotch. Givens laughed at Egregio's gesture and use of the Italian vernacular.

"We've poked the water board for a guaranteed daily amount of water but got nowhere. They'll need a cattle prod to move, *not* just a poke. Senator, can you provide that prod? Of course, we would make a large contribution to your political action committee when the water deal goes through."

"That would be helpful to cement our working relationship. I can bring the request to the General Assembly." As a legislator, the senator held the trump card for the three rules -- the law. "My lawyers can draft the legislation. And it will guarantee however much water Allbio needs and force the obstructive water board to reverse their earlier decision. I myself will introduce it to the general assembly." Senator Egregio flashed his "trust me" loyalty smile.

"And what can I do in return? What's in it for you?" Givens whispered as he leaned in close to Egregio's right ear. He suspected that the senator was fishing for something else.

Senator Egregio kept cool despite his proclivity towards hot-headedness. With his cohorts and underlings he could be vicious, an attack dog. But Givens, as CEO of a major company like Allbio, needed special handling. Egregio knew he had the upper hand. In this card game the stakes were not paltry. What was in it for him could be substantial. "There is so much more I can do for you, Henry. Everything is negotiable. Certainly the Allbio PAC can support my political campaign." Egregio referred to the corporation's political action committee. "But there is something else; something *very* big in it for you and me personally."

Givens' eyes nearly popped in anticipation. Not just a win-win but where was the senator's innuendo going? "Tell me more Senator." They had wandered far along the cliff walk and were clearly out of earshot. Their conversation would be lost in the strong breeze blowing off shore.

"Spot stocks."

"Spot stocks?" Givens stopped walking.

"I am a stock broker and an investment analyst. Legislators in this state are all part-time. My full time job is with Global World banking. We advise on corporate finance and Allbio is one of our biggest clients managing your retirement and pension schemes in the state." To answer the big question Egregio explained, "Stock options that can be delivered 'on the spot' are a relatively new invention. I can help you create something that will benefit many. It's a way of rewarding your most esteemed loyal people, a way to benefit many, including yourself if you want."

"And for you Senator?"

"I take my percent." Egregio was blunt he had got Givens where he wanted him. He explained how it worked. Using a supply of "easy to back-date" stock options, a slush fund of stock options is created. I can hold these spot stocks in a fund for you in my investment company. A fictitious list of employees will hold the spots, just placeholders. "The stock options can be doled out to whoever you like, your most trusted people, just like the luncheon buffet we just had, whatever the palate desires. I like to call them 'Spot Stocks' because they are handed out on the spot by management people at Allbio New England you trust. I will handle the transactions to change the fictitious stock holder to the real person in the company who has the stock awarded to them." Egregio explained how it was certainly one way to build a reliable devoted cadre to expand the operations at Allbio New England. Secrete away millions in stock options at Global World, back-date them and award bonuses that could be exercised immediately. Egregio's Global World would benefit from the infusion of Allbio 'cash' created by holding the Allbio stock and on the commissions for stock trades. It seemed like a no-brainer. Hidden stock options held under fictitious names, they were buried gold.

Givens agreed. Like pirates they conspired to bury the hidden treasure.

Booty boys. Loyalty cemented the pair together. Everybody wins, keeps people loyal and nobody can rat, a perfect following of the Rhode Island rules of the game. Givens had a final incentive to offer as a show of loyalty to Egregio personally.

"Sam, we have a lot of extra people as we are running two factories at the site. The old one will not be needed once we have full production of Quelify at the new plant we built. Shedding employees would be bad for your upcoming reelection. I can slow the firings and make most terminations happen after the voting."

"Henry that would be a very good thing. I don't need any opponent using those Allbio firings as ammunition during the campaign."

On the way back to the plant, Henry Givens told Pentanil and Bonaducci that he had an agreement that would get Allbio New England the water they desperately needed. He went on to explain the "spot stock" scheme and its benefits.

40

Bonaducci was quick to see the advantages as he could use it as a tool to reward where he wanted. It mollified his concern about Henry's agreement to keep people on payroll at his plant that he no longer needed. He knew that Henry Givens would cover him if people asked questions about financial losses and lack of efficiency. He would not ask too many questions; after all he had been in the state long enough to know blind loyalty keeps you moving up the corporate food chain.

Chapter 6 Team Cha-ching

JO HELD THE RIFLE tightly against her shoulder, holding her breath with each shot, she spotted a target, focused, pulled the trigger. She paused only long enough to find a new target, line it up in the viewfinder, steady, aim, inhale, and fire. Fifty shots in close succession....fifty hits scored.

The Allbio team building event was underway at the popular arcade and gaming venue, Jillians. The locale had shooting galleries with pop-up targets, flying ducks, hopping bunnies and pecking farmyard chickens. Blow away everything that moves! Old carnival games with hoops and rings and bowling pins next to high-tech multi-player Formula One racing cars. Group games meant to bond and cement the corporate team into one perfectly unified and coherent working machine.

"Aha! Perfect score." The board lit up, not a single target missed. Jo and her team mate, curly-headed Chrissy, high fived each other. "Go Q-Team!"

Noticing the commotion Jo's boss, Lance Steadman, sidled up looking inquisitive.

"Fifty!" Jo said proudly with a big grin spread across her face,

"So where did you learn to shoot like that?" Steadman asked, his buggy blue eyes directed elsewhere around the arcade. Lance never looked anyone straight in the eye, unless he was looking through you.

42

Jo retorted straight-faced, "We had a rifle when I was a kid. We used to shoot beer cans." With a faked hillbilly drawl, she facetiously added, "Out back behind the trailers."

Lance Steadman stood expressionless, his face deadpan. He did not appear to pick up on Jo's humor. He nodded benignly and wandered off to join his team. Jo and Chrissy smirked with muffled chuckles at each other. They shrugged their shoulders at Steadman's typical distant reaction. Rolling their eyes in amusement, Jo and Chrissy playfully colluded. They wanted their Quality Team to win, to show the guys on the Production Team that they could win and they *would* win. So look out! Chrissy, Jo and their Q-team mates were fiercely competitive and lit up like firecrackers while playing the games. They pressed on to the arcade speedway, acing the Formula One race car event.

Later that evening, Jo told Jeremy about the Allbio "team building" activities and her glib comment to Steadman. "I think he might have believed me about living in a trailer park."

Jeremy quipped, "Yes, he probably took you seriously. An inbred Italian hillbilly!"

Jo spontaneously twanged an inflecting banjo tune "Ner, ner, ner, ner... ner, ner...ner, ner... ner" reminiscent of the "Dueling Banjos" in the movie "Deliverance". She alternately thrust her arms up and down, swiveling her plump hips in an exaggerated sexy motion. Both Jo and Jeremy cracked up laughing during the musical jig and gyrations. With the images they conjured up, they continued their banter and repartee as they fell into bed.

"Rumpy-pumpy?" Jeremy suggested his favorite British euphemism. Playfulness became foreplay leading to an exhausting sequence of thrusts and groans of delight.

On other evenings, Jo and Jeremy often shared stories of the workplace; what they called the "daily funnies". These conversations, along with the more mundane trials and tribulations of the workplace, highlighted the absurdities, anomalies, comedies of their work day and anything that had exasperated them -- often, the people.

Jo had little love for her co-workers, in particular the Allbio managers. She loathed and distrusted her colleague, Gary Marcus, who blatantly lied at every opportunity. Marcus represented the Production Team for Steadman's group. Jo told Jeremy about Marcus and his outright mendacity during "mock" FDA audits. "What a pathologic liar!" Jo gasped. Jeremy rejoined, "Devious bastard, don't ever trust him!"

Jo worried her Q-team would pick up the wrong message from Marcus. She warned them that deliberate lying to the FDA was probably *not* a good idea. When the tall, pompous Marcus strutted around the office, Chrissy would stutter and cringe like Scooby-Doo, whispering softly, "Be afraid, be really afraid!"

On one afternoon, Jo joined Steadman and

Marcus in a small conference room in the corporate training center. Steadman, a vegan, nibbled on a plate of tabouli, humus and pita bread, while Markus speared summer melons and grapes. They were waiting for everyone to join in on the teleconference phone line. During monthly calls with corporate headquarters, there was frequent muting of the telephone line. Steadman and Marcus would smirk and make fun of the corporate director who droned on to excess. The corporate director tried to validate people at the plant she thought due for recognition. Jo would nod along with the group's ragging. But on that particular day, Steadman had something else on his mind.

Before the meeting began, Steadman remarked "Oh those "spot stocks"! He peered over at Jo who automatically feigned preoccupation, as though she were lost in her thoughts.

Marcus unclipped his usual appendage, a mobile phone headset that adhered to his sandy brown hair. As if planned or rehearsed, Marcus replied, "Yeah, what do you think of those spot stocks!"

Both looked inquisitively at Jo to see if her curiosity would be tweaked by the lucrative sounding "Spot Stocks".

Jo thought about it. She interpreted "Spot Stocks" as "on-the-spot" stocks given by management. She surmised it must be a perk, something she was unaware of. But it smelled faintly of something illicit, maybe a bribe, and she was reluctant to act too interested. To Jo's relief, the lardy, fat-faced Dickerson entered the room with a plate full of soggy, greasy French fries.

Jo could not resist. She broke her silence with a one-word wisecrack. "Vegan!"

The diversion worked. They all chuckled.

Dickerson fingered his flaccid fries, lowering each into his gaping distorted mouth. Marcus kept fiddling with his headphone, while Steadman appeared to be having a meditative moment. Jo made imaginary notes on a steno pad as she pondered their earlier innuendo.

Jo wondered, was that a test of her loyalty? Was she being baited? Are "Spot Stocks" a lure, something to entice Jo into Steadman's web? Did those "Spot Stocks" create indebtedness to the people doling them out? Or were the stocks a reward for loyal people who are part of the "team"? A dangling carrot, a sweetener, or part of team building? In her mind, questions about the "spot stock" motive persisted.

Since when were company stock options offered "on-the-spot"? Jo thought it best not to ask. She decided to just play it like she was oblivious. This was Jo's usual ploy when she did not want to be read by those she did not trust. She frequently resorted to an aloof, glassy-eyed daydreaming state of confusion. Oblivious to what was going on around her. The conference phone trilled and the meeting went ahead.

Earlier, before Jo arrived to the meeting, Steadman had mumbled to Marcus in a hushed interrogative. "Will Jo bite?"

"WIIFM. What's in it for *me*?" snarled Marcus as a way to explain how he saw those spot

46

stocks, accentuating the "me" as he always did, "*Most* people are motivated by money, Jo should bite."

"And "Spot-stocks" are an unexpected wind fall!" Steadman gloated, his eyes popping out on stalks.

"Yeah, Dickerson is gonna buy himself a brand new SUV – luxury edition!" Marcus nodded his head rhythmically with his delivery.

"She'll see the advantages of being part of the team." Steadman, pokerfaced, finished with a self-assured "Huh!"

Later, much later, Jo read about similar "Spot-stock" fabrications by corporate executives in a software technology company, Comverse. One night, she mentioned them to Jeremy. The software company had given a fictitious stock holder a moniker, "I.M. Fanton", it was a slush fund invented to hide extra stock. The software company used these stock grants to dole out to favored employees. It was simply an illegal way to cook the company accounts.

Jo's care around Gary Marcus was well-founded. On more than one occasion, Jo listened quietly as Marcus criticized people, especially women, for whatever reason. "Oh that Kathleen Weathers! I'm gonna get her." He curled his lip and snarled in his shrill effeminate voice, laced with a southern lilt.

He went after many others. "Deborah Donovan, she has a performance problem!" Name calling and setting up women as a target of his spite were his forte. He would purposely denigrate and attack people that others might admire - a skilled corporate character assassin. His target could be anyone, even people who were supposedly on his team, if it furthered his position and made him look better.

Gary Marcus was the whole corporate shark package; artful, deceitful, selfish and arrogant. At thirty-something, he was driven by big ambitions for himself. Marcus was sterile; his un-descended testicles left him with a high-pitched voice that broke when unguarded. Unable to have children, he adopted a Third-World daughter. But when the young toddler squirmed on his lap, trying to break free from his restraining vice-grip, he bellowed, "I'm gonna get me a boy!"

His wife was always nervous, jittery with an icy-cold, limpid handshake.   Strong, capable women reminded Marcus of his sexual inadequacy. Only his timid wife could avoid his wrath, or so it appeared.

Jo chose to forget Marcus and his attacks most of the time until one occasion when he was unhappy with Aunty Mary's Stella garage. Marcus grumbled with a surly threatening gesture, shaking his head, "Humpf, I need to speak with your Aunty Mary!" A vague but obvious threat directed at Jo's favorite aunt who ran the accounts at cousin Vin's auto repair shop. Jo remained quiet, unresponsive, pretending not to notice. Unsettled, she quietly clocked the remark and thought it was "dangerous" for her and Aunty Mary.

As Jo's boss, Steadman's initial reaction

was to sneer at Marcus's audacity and his obviously venomous attacks. But Steadman knew who would collude and who he could control. A foot shorter that Marcus, Steadman's had a bug-like appearance with two large round blue eyes. His small stature, five foot two, and a thin, stick figure reflected his vegan diet.

Jo thought Steadman was like a Chihuahua with his furrowed brow, premature shaggy grey hair and oversized eyes that always avoided contact as he had at the team building event. Even at their interview, several months before, Jo found him odd, distant, restless, unable to focus on the person sitting across from him. His office always looked barren. It revealed nothing of his inner turmoil, only a miniature zen sculpture of sand and rocks.

Jo noted during an unguarded moment how Steadman swaggered, not with arrogance but with distain, for everyone and mostly for himself. Shuffling his feet, toes kicking outward, side to side, as if uneasy with how he judged the world to be from his contemptuous outlook. Steadman was a contradiction who seemed tormented, perhaps self-loathing at the persona he had built in the work world. He tried desperately to hide his self-contempt, annihilate his uneasy work persona and reinvent himself as a vegan-minded urban guru. He used catch phrases from the "hot" management books as a perfect façade for hidden flaws.

Later that summer, the monolithic Allbio plant was primed for full-scale production of the newest miracle drug, Quelify, a drug that quells overactive immune systems. But as things too often go, the early production batches failed.

"Yep, three in a row." Marcus creepily confided one-to-one with Jo in low, muted tones. There was a problem in purification, the wrong filters were used. They would all need changing, retrofitting. Marcus left off the information or did not know that the original guys installing those filters were all fired.

Jo threw out a smoke screen, "I don't know much about that." Jo thought, don't appear too knowledgeable, remembering how Vin had told her about the filter problem and firings at family Thanksgiving dinner. Jo felt her adding the extra knowledge would make her collude with Marcus in sharing inside secrets. It was time to play "oblivious woman" yet again.

And then the investigations began. Jo and her staff were busy with the obligatory training that biopharma legally required. Good manufacturing practice (GMP), assured the safety, quality and purity of the product.

The water contamination problem, Jo thought, came from those wrongly installed filters. But the plant manager wanted Jo's team to "train" people to rectify contamination from another source. Water testing showed positive for "Total Organic Carbon" or TOC, the quality lab acronym. Speculating on the cause of the contaminated water, the plant manager and some "quality" people thought it occurred with too much spraying of the disinfectant alcohol. But the microbiologists weren't too sure and neither was Jo who remained skeptical of the alcohol explanation that pointed the blame at clumsy production people. It all seemed to be a convenient way to justify money for useless production worker training. Jo suspected that this was a "red herring" and that the superfluous training would increase the Q-Team's budget which was always under fire from corporate.

Recently, Jo had accomplished a coup in her Q-team training department. A federal grant she got her hands on for "Investigative Skills" training, to find out the "root cause" of the contamination problems. And she was eager to tell the big honcho, Bill Bonaducci. She would have her chance.

In the fall, Jo and the other managers touted their team's accomplishments to the site vice president, Bill Bonaducci, and other senior people visiting from corporate headquarters.

"GMP training is now up to 97% complete at the site, up from 40% just six months ago." Jo bragged about her Q-team's achievements. "We are the first in the state to tap into federal funds, a grant of $150,000 for training." Jo operated the imaginary cash register keys. "Cha-ching!" She grinned broadly, wide-eyed, and smug with humor. "So, with the new "Investigative Skills" training, we will be able to get to the bottom of the TOC water challenge."

Jo looked at Bill Bonaducci, the site VP as she said, "After all, we would not want a repeat of the FDA warning letter for our "failure to investigate", do we?" At that moment, Bonaducci flinched and threw his head back. Jo, noting his reaction, thought it a positive affirmation and directed her next comment to him, "Yes, I see that Mr. Bonaducci agrees that we must get to the real root cause of our batch contamination problems."

Jo surmised that since the FDA warning was written to Bonaducci when he was head of a West Coast plant, he would certainly want to avoid the same thing from happening again. Jo was satisfied with her presentation and full of herself. She took pride in being proactive on Allbio's behalf. Jo would prevent those repeat hand slaps from the FDA. But the air began to thicken and cloud in that room, there didn't seem to be the "feel good" atmosphere at the meeting. And at the time Jo was oblivious to what transgression she might have made.

Marcus followed up on the successes of the production team and clearly contradicted Jo's work with words that the company wanted to hear. "Over half the world's production of bio-therapeutic drugs and we'll be up and running at full production by 4th quarter. Contamination problems in the batches have been addressed and solutions are in place. We expect to beat our timelines and to satisfy the expanding demand for our blockbuster drug, Quelify." The "feel good" atmosphere returned to the room.

Two days later, Jo received an e-mail from the visiting corporate director praising her for the GMP program and investigative work. On the same day, Steadman began drafting a performance document, depicting Jo as "not a team player".

According to Steadman, she was inept and incompetent. She did not focus on "high-impact" projects. But another week went by before Steadman called Jo in to his office with the precursor to what Jo felt would be an inevitable firing. Jo had forgotten Aunt Mary's Rhode Island rules, especially rules one and two, loyalty and don't rat. She had misread the room and the company's reaction to her work. Dumping the failed batches down the sewer was a cheap alternative to finding any real cause.

Steady, aim, inhale, and fire.

Chapter 7 Moscow Dreams

JO AND JEREMY dined in an upscale restaurant, noted for its Kobe beef carpaccio and flambéed berry with liquor crepes. Sitting at a table near the piano bar, their eyes lit up with the flaming preparation of melted butter, sugar, peach brandy and Curacao.

Although it was their wedding anniversary, neither was joyful. They held hands intermittently, as they talked over coffee.

"I'm just trying to make sense of everything you are telling me. You had all these successes, the training program, the federal funds....and now your boss is trying to get rid of you? And it looks as though he will fire you before Christmas. So, Merry Christmas to us." Jeremy paused before his muted expletive, "That bastard!"

"It really doesn't make any sense...but *something* must have triggered this. Things were going well, the grant money, the water investigation and the accolades from corporate. People took notice, especially the investigation skills program. I had set up a way to delve into production problems, finding the root cause. Allbio people called it 'CSI: Rhode Island'. They thought it was very cool."

Dejected and confused, Jo sighed, "Jeremy, I just don't get it. I know I'm not the most agreeable person, but.."

Jeremy interrupted seeing that they were getting nowhere. "But tonight's our anniversary. How many years?"

"24!" Jo piped up switching gears.

"And here's to our life together, and to Moscow memories." Jeremy reminisced.

"Nazdarovia!" they both chimed in.

"And to our lovely daughter Sofia. Our little girl skating in "Fantasy-on-Ice!" Jeremy kept trying to cheer Jo up. "Where is the show tonight, in Geneva?" They both adored their Sofia.

"Yes, but now she wants to get into the show 'Dreams' with her new boyfriend." He's from Moscow, but he's not Russian. Armenian, I think. Armand something, one of those long I-A-N names. Sofia says this new show is the best one yet, and the star is the French Olympian, Philippe Candeloro. If she does join that show, can we go in the spring? Please, pretty please?"

"We'll need to see how things pan out. Without your job, we may be a little strapped for cash." Jeremy, sensing disappointment, conceded affectionately, "Ok. Call Sofia tomorrow, you haven't spoken to her in a whole week!" Grinning at Jeremy's sarcasm, Jo nodded.

A few days later, Jo and Jeremy munched a breakfast of tea and toast before running off to their jobs. Agitated, Jo grumbled, "I keep asking for the paperwork, the so-called 'complaints' about me. I think they're most likely from that lying shit, Marcus, and his lapdog Dickus," making Dickerson's name in line with the Monty Python movie.

Jeremy chuckled, "Allbio has hired characters from the Monty Python movie? The Life of Brian?"

Pissed off and incensed, Jo gave a quick smile at Jeremy's humor before ranting, "That bastard Steadman. I've bugged HR rat Rizzo everyday this week. Steadman has given her *nothing*. He's full of crap. And *nothing* will stop him from booting me. Rizzo had the nerve to suggest that I resign and take a buyout!" Jo fumed.

"OK, calm down." Jeremy took his cell phone from the charger and strapped it to his belt. "I talked with my friend George at work. He's giving me the names of some high-powered Boston lawyers. In the meantime, get yourself a cell phone so we can stay in contact."

Later that morning, Jo called Jeremy from her office telephone. "I'm feeling exhausted. Tomorrow I'll call in sick and go pick up that cell phone."

"Well, if you think so. Buy a cell phone with a PDA, so you can have a calendar, other functions." Jeremy paused. "Maybe we shouldn't talk about it on your work phone."

"Yeah, you're right. But right now I really don't give a damn." Jo groaned, "Hey, I love you."

Early the next morning having taken a sick day, Jo thought about different cell phone stores she'd seen. Verizon? Cingular? The store on Main Street was closer but always crowded, so Jo took a longer route to the Coast Road store. "Damn, they're not open yet, I'm too early." Jo thought. The donut shop across the road beckoned her to coffee and a French cruller. Jo watched the morning news on the donut store's TV until it was time to return to the mobile phone shop. It was now open for business.

As she pushed open the door Jo overheard a podgy sales guy talking to a young Asian salesgirl. "Things are going on at the head office. Apparently some things are changing, maybe the buyout by AT&T." He told her he'd been sent there from regional headquarters. The salesgirl shrugged and nodded as he spoke. "Podgy" walked towards Jo as she neared the display counter.

Jo chirped up. "I'd like a PDA cell phone, do you have model 210z?" Jo asked for the one Jeremy suggested.

"I don't think we have that model, I'd have to order it. But here are the cell phones in stock." Podgy waved his hand across a row of a half dozen models.

Jo mumbled. "I'd like to get one today, I need to make calls on it right away."

"While perusing the selection, Jo noticed another customer, a younger, well-dressed guy browsing at the phone accessories in the spacious shop. She clocked his brilliant green eyes, immaculate white shirt and plain blue tie.

Podgy was in no hurry to get Jo out of the store. Jo overheard "green-eyes" tell the salesgirl he wanted to activate an old cell phone for his wife. He nipped out to his car, a silver Grand Prix, to look for it.

Jo chose a cell phone from the limited selection available, a plain black and grey nondescript piece. Podgy seemed to take forever keying in numbers to activate the new cell phone, but Jo waited patiently for him to get it up and working. When he finally stopped poking at the tiny keyboard, Jo asked, "How do I know that the phone is activated?"

Podgy answered, "I'll call the store telephone number." He dialed and the store phone rang. Podgy hung up and nodded to Jo.

"And my number is? Please don't say it out loud." Mr. Green-eyes came through the shop door, as Jo said, "Security, you know." Jo glanced over as Green-eyes startled. Did he flinch at her words? Jo wondered. Why?

On the sales slip, Podgy wrote down the cell phone number and his name. Dan Rod.

"Thank you for choosing Cingular. Let me know if I can be of further assistance."

Why did the podgy sales guy take so long to set up her new phone? Jo was upset and saw trouble everywhere.

Chapter 8 Officer on Duty

FROM HER BEDROOM dresser, Jo piled a stack of papers into a canvas bag, a freebee from a Biotech convention. In her confused state she hoped someone could help her, nothing seemed to make sense. She drove, canvas bag in tow, to the local police station; a small building near the North Road.

Once inside at the front reception desk, Jo asked to speak with the officer on duty. Officer Ken met Jo in the miniscule waiting room and brought Jo into a tinier office. He sat behind an old wooden desk.

Jo, still standing, was agitated. "Someone's been in my home, they've gone through my paperwork and I think they may have taken things. I don't know, but I think they may have tapped my home telephone too."

Ken looked at Jo in disbelief. "Now wait a minute, you're not making much sense here. You seem upset."

"Look, I know I must look like a bag lady that's come in off the street, but I'm not. I am a professional. I make $94,000 a year as a manager at Allbio. This morning, when I went to buy a cell phone, I was followed back from the Cingular store on Coast Road. I think they've been in my home, gone through my paperwork while I was out. Allbio is behind this harassment. They are trying to intimidate me, to get me to leave."

"I don't know how we can help you." Ken's comment was more like a question.

With her cell phone in hand, Jo explained. "After I bought this cell phone, I was followed by a silver car, a Grand Prix. The guy was in the store browsing. He must have followed me out. I saw his car turn left on a street behind me, through my rear-view mirror. He cut across on a parallel street. I pulled off on another side street, and saw him pass by in my mirror. I took down his license plate number."

"And you say that Allbio is behind it?"

"Look, Allbio can do *anything* it wants. They *own* this place, they can hire *anyone*."

"This sounds like something out of a book or a movie!" Ken shrugged his shoulders and chuckled.

"I need to call my husband." Jo fumbled with her new cell phone. "Jeremy, I'm at the police station. I think someone has been in our condo, rifling through my papers in the bedroom. I think they took the proposal for the grant money I got for the investigation training, the Allbio CSI course. And Jeremy, somebody followed me when I left the cell phone shop."

"What? Wait." said Jeremy confused at Jo's agitation and accusations. He was really worried about involving the police and decided to take a different tack to calm Jo down. "I have a lawyer for you, Courtney Hill; she comes highly recommended by George. Call her now!" Jeremy was emphatic.

Officer Ken pointed at the cell phone. He wanted to speak with Jo's husband.

"Yes, we'll check out your home with your wife."

On the next call, Jo reiterated the current situation to the lawyer who had already been briefed by Jeremy on Jo's problems at work. They planned to meet on Monday. Jo went on. "I think someone has gone through my papers…"

Courtney interrupted. "Stop! *Don't* say anything else." Jo, perplexed, paused.

"Don't say anything now, wait until we meet on Monday, 10 am. But think about your situation. Think about what you need to tell me."

Jo mused over what transpired, about what had just happened. How the cop reacted to her story, her phone call to Jeremy and his advice on the lawyer. *She thought, this lawyer, Courtney Hill, knows where I am and yet she wants me to shut up, so what is going on?*

A moon-faced cop had been standing at the intake office door, conversing with Officer Ken. Ken gestured to Jo, "Ms. Blair, we'll meet you at your condo in Willow Dean, right?"

Jo echoed. "Yes, we'll meet there."

The two cops followed Jo as she opened the front door to her condo. Leading them to the bedroom, she gestured towards a stack of papers. The bedroom walls were plastered with framed communist era posters from the late 1970's and early 80's; Lenin statues, laborers with hammers and sickles, Komsomol youth with red bandanas, and over the bed headboard, portraits of Vladimir Ilyich Lenin and his wife Krupskaya.

Jo focused only on the stack of documents. She did not register the impact the stark Soviet

61

Socialist Realism had on the provincial cops.

Pointing to the pile of paperwork on the bedroom dresser, she questioned their disarray. "I'm sure these are out of order....perhaps some items were taken? I won't know which ones until I go through them."

Jo finally noticed the moon-faced cop, his brows furrowed, closely inspecting a poster of Vladimir Lenin with a group of stylized workers, muscular and robust.

Jo stepped down the hall to a den that doubled as an office. Officer Ken trailed behind. Inside were an assortment of computers, an eclectic mix of more communist posters, carved wooden African masks, Russian Matryoshka dolls, vintage Holiday-on-Ice posters and Sofia's rack of ribbons and medals from her competitive ice skating days. For Jeremy and Jo these possessions represented a record of where the family had been. When the moon-faced cop joined them, he scrutinized a Soviet propaganda poster with missiles and dollar bills that alluded to American financing of the war machine.

As Jo walked to the kitchen, Ken and the moon-faced cop followed. The kitchen was decorated with Russian folk art; Alexander Kalugin's multicolored "Chicken" and gold, red and black Khokhloma utensils.

"This phone, I think the telephone is bugged, it sounds different." Jo reflected out loud.

"And you think your home phone is bugged by Allbio? Hmm."

Jo defended her assertion, "Allbio could get

it done."

"I don't see any evidence of breaking in. So how could someone have gotten in?" Ken pressed on. Jo's eccentric foreign décor suggested questionable credibility to him.

But Jo insisted she had an answer. "They could easily have cut a copy of my house keys in no time. Allbio is like a city. I'm out of my office constantly and my house keys are on my desk. Just last week we were all at a three hour meeting, they could have had a key cut. My boss is trying to fabricate things, trying to set me up. And his boss, they both want me out because I know something that would embarrass them. Allbio is worth billions, they have a huge investment here and incredible influence. They are the biggest thing that has come to this state in years."

"This all seems like quite a story – but even if it were true, there is nothing we can do with no sign of a break-in. This is a quiet neighborhood. My colleague and I will ask the neighbors if they've seen anyone suspicious around."

Unsettled, Jo watched as the officers left, closing the door behind them. That didn't go well thought Jo. I wonder if I did the right thing, the cops didn't seem interested in anything I said.

Chapter 9 Something Else

AS JO AND JEREMY walked across the spacious plaza of Government Center, Jeremy warned, "Look Jo, now let's get this clear, *don't* get sidetracked on this. We're here to sort out your employment issues." Jeremy had been unsettled with the visit by the police at their home.

Jo protested "Ok, OK but.."

"No buts, just *don't* go off on your suspicions or about break-ins. Show Courtney Hill the counseling document from your boss. Tell her about your repeated requests for the supposed e-mails that show the complaints from colleagues." Jeremy was emphatic. "And *don't* go off on your visit to the police station and people following you. Stick with the problem with Allbio and your boss."

"Ok, got yah. I'll stay focused." Jo conceded.

It was raining gently as they ducked into the tall skyscraper. Jo and Jeremy rode the elevator to the 17th floor. When they arrived at the office, an assistant escorted them to a conference room. The tall, svelte impeccably dressed Courtney Hill, a partner in the Boston law office, got quickly to the objective.

"Now, although your husband is here, you are my client Jo, not Jeremy. Here is the hourly agreement and retainer amount. And we agree to develop an exit strategy and negotiate a severance package."

Jeremy agreed. "Yes, I understand, Jo has

64

brought the documents, I am just writing the check for the retainer."

Jo gave the papers, graphs and materials to Courtney. "Here is the counseling document from my boss. Notice the date on it. Two days *before* Steadman wrote this, I gave a talk at our department meeting. The site VP, Bill Bonaducci, and directors from corporate headquarters were there."

Jo handed Courtney a Power-point print out of the presentation. "I talked about what I considered to be accomplishments: the success of the GMP training program, the water investigation. Both were noted as "best practice" by the corporate training director. I got an email from her praising my work. And that I tapped into federal grant money, $150,000 for site training on investigation skills, getting to the root cause of problems at the plant. There was plenty of kudos and groundswell on that one. And yet, when I expected accolades, my boss, Lance Steadman, slaps me with walking papers two days after what I thought was a good presentation of my department's accomplishments. Go figure?"

Courtney explained. "Yes, but it's *not* against the law for your boss to make decisions, bad or otherwise. He can decide what he likes." Courtney paused and queried. "But *maybe* there is something else? Something else you might know?" Courtney tilted her head waiting for Jo's response, but Jo shrugged her shoulders and slowly shook her head, not knowing what else she could know. She thought briefly about it. What else could have prompted the fallout from what she thought was a meeting that showed her success? It just didn't make any sense to her.

Courtney instructed Jo. "I'd like for you to collect information, e-mails, other contradictory information from colleagues, clients...and think about *what you might know*. Continue to ask for those e-mails about complaints and conversations that Steadman listed here. Ask HR for what they have. They've had plenty of time."

Later that evening the telephone rang. It was Sofia. "Hi dad, did you get my e-mail? I just arrived in Monaco with my friend Lucienne."

"Monaco? Are you in Monte Carlo? I didn't know the ice show was going there." Jeremy remarked, handing the telephone to Jo who nosily nudged his arm, angling to listen in.

"OK, here is your daughter!" Jeremy said exasperated with Jo's impatience and persistent "Gimme, gimme!"

"Mom! I'm in our room at the Hotel Meridien. It's fantastic, a 5-star hotel. I can look out my balcony and see the ocean. Lucienne is in the shower."

"Lucienne?" Jo queried at the unfamiliar name.

"Mom, I'm still in shock, I can't believe I'm here. Why she chose *me* to come with her is a mystery to me, but we just started talking backstage, between chorus numbers, and she asked me to come with her to Monaco. Her male friend is a sports promoter and he is footing the bill for everything. And we are going to the World Soccer game tomorrow. Box seats! VIP seating. Oh, dad will be so jealous. We'll get to meet some of the team!"

"It sounds too good to be true. Are you sure nothing else is expected from you?" Jo asked.

"There had better not be!" Jeremy had been listening in next to Jo.

"No, nothing! Tell dad not to worry. We drove here from Nice. This is a promised vacation for Lucienne, and I was invited as her little friend to come along. The ice show is on hiatus this week. No shows."

"Hey honey, enjoy the lucky vacation…and send us photos." Jo said with some hesitation.

Sofia heard Jeremy in the background. "She'll probably send us a tee-shirt that says 'My kid went to Monte Carlo and all I got was this lousy tee-shirt'."

Sofia giggled. "I'll e-mail you with all the details."

"Hmmm....." Jo and Jeremy wondered how this trip had come about. And Jo in her agitated state wondered much more. Something is going on. Something sinister. Something retaliatory. Was someone protecting our little girl? Whisking her off to a safe haven. Away from the goons that Allbio can muster up anywhere in the world. Allbio would do anything to unnerve their adversaries, their disrupters, those who might reveal their cover-ups and dirty secrets. Their dirty water filled with failed batches from Allbio. They would go after Jo by threatening her family, putting her daughter in harm's way. Seized with paralytic fear, Jo said nothing about what she feared to Jeremy.

Chapter 10 Rizzo Human Resources Rat

INTENT ON GETTING hold of the disparaging e-mails that her lawyer pushed for, Jo arranged to meet with HR Rizzo in her office. Jo and Jeremy often joked about the sadistic Dilbert Character, Catbert from HR, who took great pleasure in torturing and abusing employees. They would mimic the illogical repartee and the "evil dance" of Catbert and the pointy-haired boss.

Jo poked her head around the corner of the HR Rizzo's office and feigned a friendly greeting. "Hi, it's been a while since I was here last."

Rizzo scowled and officiously countered. "You were out for two days."

Jo ignored the jibe and fired back abruptly. "I heard that Chuck Ludlum was fired." Ludlum headed up the investigation on the water contamination.

Rizzo hesitated a moment before sniping back "He wasn't fired. He resigned for *family reasons*."

Incredulous, Jo blurted "Oh *come on now*, everyone knows that Ludlum was *fired*."

"Who told you that?"

"Marcus. He told Dickerson and I last week." Jo was ready for combat.

Miffed, Rizzo grimaced and shook her head disapprovingly. "He shouldn't be saying that."

Jo registered the comment. She wondered what *else* Marcus could be orchestrating. She suspected he must have been up to his usual jiggery-pokery trying to unsettle Jo, his potential rival for advancement.

"Do you have those e-mails and information I asked for? You said you would have them last week." Jo prodded Rizzo.

"I have some of them but Lance Steadman still needs to give me a couple more."

Pressuring Rizzo, Jo demanded "Well I *must* have them tomorrow. I've asked Steadman to give them too you."

Relenting, Rizzo acquiesced. "OK, I'll ask him again today for them."

Later that afternoon, Chrissy, hyper-ventilating and anxious, appeared at Jo's office. Breathless, she spewed forth. "They are dropping like flies in Micro!"

Jo looked up from her computer to see Steadman lurking a few feet behind Chrissy, listening in on the conversation. He had taken to hanging out around the water cooler in the hallway where he could keep an eye on Jo.

Chrissy, not noticing Steadman hovering behind her didn't wait for Jo's reply. "They fired Manuel *and* his new boss, the Micro lab manager. His boss just started working in the lab three weeks ago!" If only Chrissy knew that Steadman wanted her head to roll; he concocted excuses to sack Chrissy just two weeks ago and tried to co-opt Jo in the plan as Chrissy's manager. Jo had refused. Clearly agitated and rattled by the spate of firings, Chrissy was unaware that Jo too would probably be given the pink slip.

Jo calmly replied "Oh my, really?' Her knuckles curled in a fist against her lips. Jo was surprised about the microbiologists being canned but she half expected that others besides her were under fire. She couldn't help thinking. *Are the dominoes falling?* All that time and money spent in finding these experts, bringing them in from all over the country, stealing them from other biopharm companies and now they are being chopped for what reason? Could it be the problems with producing the drug Quelify? All the failed batches? How about that group of guys that were fired for installing the wrong water filters? *And what about the water, what really caused the contamination?*

That afternoon, Jo met with Eva, an internal investigator, who told her that Bill, the lead investigator, was leaving Allbio. Eva, uneasy, wide-eyed and ruffled said she might also be leaving soon. Her husband wanted to go back to Puerto Rico. *Wanted* to go back? Jo knew they were both US citizens and they were looking to buy a house. So add two more who were working on the failed batch problem, why were so many people scurrying like mice? Eva knew more about the water and batch failures problems than *anybody*.

Both Eva and Jo were on edge, but neither confided with the other as to why.

Jo wondered why so many people involved with the investigations were disappearing. Together they would all fade away into the corporate walls like Allbio's stenciled platitudes. Disappearing epitaphs etched on graveyard tombstones. Their epitaph would be inscribed "Allbio *desaparecedos*", having disappeared for various contrived reasons; sucked up by the corporate vacuum. There were just too many unexplained events and unanswered questions for Jo and no clear answer.

Eva and Jo spent the afternoon redacting the identifying facts on investigations, customizing them for use in "CSI Investigator Training". They broke for coffee in the cafeteria where Jo noticed a bulky butch-cut woman following them. The woman lingered near Jo and Eva although she had no reason for standing so close, for hovering so near. Were they being tailed, or was it only Jo's imagination? Was she a security detail, a watcher? Maybe she was keeping tabs on the duo? Jo was not sure.

A persistent, relentless Jo returned to work early the next morning and stood at the door of HR Rizzo's office. Poking her head in, Jo forced a smile and greeted Rizzo with a query. "I thought I would drop by to pick up the info."

Rizzo shook her head, "I don't have them all yet."

Jo, starting to anger, said, "Look, you said you would have them today." Jo became adamant, insistent. "I need them *today*!"

Rizzo shrugged her shoulders. "Sorry, I don't have them."

Jo, glowered at her and in a steady determined tone said, "I must have them *now*. I know there is a computer network outage scheduled for tomorrow. Otherwise, how do I know the documents won't be invented?" Jo's anger had made her reckless and she was tired of all the prevarications by Rizzo and Steadman.

Rizzo looked bemused and repeated "Invented?"

Jo thought for sure that Lance Steadman would take advantage of the network outage to craft some nasty emails criticizing Jo.

Enunciating every word, Jo punctuated emphatically. *I must have them now – today! Or I will take action.*

Without waiting for Rizzo to reply, Jo quickly turned and walked down the hall and out the building. Within a few minutes she was back in her office where she fired up Outlook. A fourth e-mail reminded everyone of the network outage that would take place at noon the next day. Jo thought, "What an opportune time for Steadman to fabricate complaints about me. Get me booted out and then Marcus and Dickerson could grab my grant funds, my clients and my training staff. This would be Marcus orchestrating the downfall of a rival; he had no qualms about lying if he thought it was in his best interests"

Realizing it wasn't all about her, Jo mused. "What else is it? There must be other reasons for executing a network shutdown? And why are all these other people who were working on the batch problems disappearing? Fired? Resigning for "family problems"? What about Ludlum, he has four young kids! Why would he resign? What is it about the water and batch failure investigation? Why is Chrissy so agitated that "they are dropping like flies" in microbiology. Isn't Manuel the analyst who's been delving into the water problem? Why did the new Microbiology lab manager get fired too after only three weeks on the job? And why was Eva so on edge? Is it because her department is falling apart with her boss's departure and her thinking about leaving too?

Jo knew she needed to protect herself from Steadman, Marcus and Dickerson. They would make up incriminating lies that would condemn Jo. They would probably fake emails to build a case against her.

Jo thought she must act swiftly. She knew there must be more to it. Maybe they wanted to purge some of the data on the water investigations? There is no date-time stamp, no audit trail when the network is down but as Jeremy told her someone can "work" on any server direct and not leave a network trail. They could even stop any audit trail on the server until the changes in the data had been made. How strange that the water problem was miraculously resolved the last week, according to Marcus in his presentation, while the microbiologists and investigators were being eliminated; purged from the employee ranks.

It all began to add up. Jo looked at her meeting notes from the previous week on the water testing about faulty stoppers on the test tubes. So the stopper had tiny holes, "porous septa". They were perforated. How *could* they be full of holes? Someone invented a story that the alcohol sprayed to disinfect everything made its way into the test tubes through tiny pores in the rubber stoppers marring the water quality. Such was the explanation for the "excursions", the failed test results on the water quality.

Or so we were told at the monthly meeting, Jo cynically thought. The water samples tested for contaminants miraculously went from 303 positives to 3 once the brand of rubber stoppers was changed. It looked more like corporate machinations and invention.

Jo's thought. *If it seems too good to be true, it probably is.* Jo's deduced that if indeed it is a lie, someone will want to purge any information to the contrary. So that makes sense. Someone must want some sins expunged to clean up the records. Maybe Allbio was going to clean out any email about the water problem and batch failures to fit this false explanation about test tube stoppers and alcohol?

Jo quickly drafted an e-mail and sent an alarm up the chain of command. Steadman and Bonaducci were purposely not included. Making sure she stopped short of the top brass at corporate headquarters; Jo included all the people who should know about a potential breach in the integrity of Allbio's quality systems. She sent a warning to her trusted cadre all the way up to the head of corporate compliance. Jo now suspects that she *does* know some of the answer to Courtney's question about *what else Jo knows, knowledge she shares with others who are leaving the company.*

Jo headlined the e-mail "CONCERN FOR DATA INTEGRITY DURING NETWORK OUTAGE". Jo thought, its 9:30 am EST here; people will soon be waking up on the west coast.

74

Lars Franklin, head of corporate compliance will have this e-mail in his in-box when he arrives at work this morning. Jo had forgotten rule two – Don't rat!

Chapter 11 Flashing Amber

SHORTLY BEFORE NOON, Jo startled at the "bing" from an e-mail reply and thought, "Well it looks like the corporate people have woken up in California." Franklin, the head of compliance, asked Jo why she suspected information might be compromised during the network shutdown.

Jo answered that the site investigations might be at risk and perhaps her boss was also fabricating complaints about her. Franklin replied that IT security at Allbio New England assured him that the network outage was necessary for upgrading the systems. He suggested she meet with her boss to discuss her grievance with him. Jo started to wonder if she went too far with her e-mail alert; that perhaps Franklin didn't understand that something smelled strongly of fish.

Lunching at the cafeteria, Jo eyed again the heavy-set woman with the butch-cut black hair. Having never seen the woman before, she thought it conveniently odd that the woman would show up again twice in such a short time.

When Jo returned to her office, the red voice-mail light was on. She retrieved the message from HR Rizzo. "You will have the information tomorrow morning. I'll leave it under your door."

It was nearly 5 pm as Jo drove off the compound past the new Allbio construction and headed towards Atek Way. It was early winter, the road was as dark as slate; it looked as though the lights had gone out. As she neared the main intersection, the stop lights were not working and cars cautiously made their way on to Hollow Road. Jo made the journey down the I-95 to her home. She listened to a voice message from Jeremy, "I'll be in later tonight, after tennis". She fed "Kat", and made a short meal of tomato soup and grilled cheese. Unsure of things that transpired that day, Jo decided to go back to her office. It was 7:30 pm and she still had time to print e-mails and to check if there were any other replies. It would be 4:30pm on the west coast, so she could make phone calls too.

It was only a short drive to the Allbio plant, but Hollow Road was also curiously dark, no street lamps were alight when Jo came to the T intersection. Atek Way was eerily deserted. It was as black and murky as squid ink. Jo's black Turbo 6 beamed the only headlights on the small dirt road. Spooked by the darkness, Jo could see amber colored overhead lamps on perhaps three or four trucks parked on the site. A few men stood near some spot lights at the Allbio entrance. As she drew closer, Jo noticed that none of the buildings were lit. Jo pulled her black turbo discreetly into an unattended construction exit and parked next to her office building. She swiped her security badge then gingerly crept through a hallway to find her office dark and her computer down. There were no signs of life anywhere in the building. Returning to her car frustrated, Jo made a tight u-turn back on Atek Way and headed towards the I-95.

Jo entered the onramp heading south, a near 360 degree turn, as a bright yellow glare lit up her rear view mirror. It was an electrical truck with amber overhead lights stretched across the top of the cab. On the curved ramp Jo shifted from 2nd to 3rd gear and accelerated hard. But the truck lights continued to shine annoyingly in her mirror, tailing her much too closely.

"What the fuck are you doing!" Jo yelled unheard as the intrusive driver closed in on her.

Both vehicles entered the right lane of the I-95 southbound. On this particular evening, the traffic was thin. Jo tore through the gears with the gas pedal nearly floored... 65-70-75. Jo moved one lane to the left and was followed by the amber lights. She accelerated to 85-90, noticing the 55mph limit posted on that stretch of the highway. The truck barreled down, as Jo changed lanes; a lane to right, back to left, back and forth over the next two miles. Jo stayed focused. She thought. *This guy is trying to ram me! Or is he trying to scare me for driving on the dark Allbio site? How long will he chase after me?* One more lane change and a mid-sized sedan mysteriously appeared behind her. Jo could see the amber lights of the truck, behind the sedan. Slowing from 85 to 80, Jo pulled across to the far right lane. She braked sharply, decelerating from 80 to 50, and exhaled with relief as the truck passed on her left. She was nearly home. She exited off the next ramp.

With halting, gasping, breaths, Jo wondered aloud "What the hell was *that*?" Unnerved by what had just transpired, Jo slowly drifted home in dazed bewilderment. She fell into bed exhausted and dozed off before Jeremy came back from playing

her, sat a few moments, peered at his license plate number and jotted it down on a scrap of paper. Jo continued to look at the man who continued to look at her. Wide-eyed, she mouthed to him, "Stop following me!"

Jo peeled out on a circuitous route, u-turning recklessly on Five Mile Road. At the stoplight, a late model hatchback pulled up on her right. Askew in the window was a hastily applied, hand-scrawled sign that read "Dangerous". The back seat of the hatchback was filled with very large, clear plastic bags of bread-rolls. Jo wondered if the message was intended for her, or if delivering bread rolls is somehow dangerous? Jo unnervingly thought. *It is all very odd and everything is beginning to get to me.*

Jo climbed the stairs to Aunty's apartment on the top floor of cousin Vin's house.

"So, what's going on? What is it, honey?" Aunty Mary asked with a worried grimace on her face, her coal-dark eyes looking for an answer.

Jo held her stack of papers, "Can I leave these here?" Jo asked and then blurted out, "What a pack of lies! They made it all up last night. There was a power outage at the Allbio site last night."

Taking note, raising her eyebrows, Aunty added, "The power was out *here* last night, across the road, all the shops on Route 77 as far as the corner drugstore. It was totally blacked-out till after 9pm."

Jo elaborated. "The street lights were out on Hollow Road near Allbio too, and on Atech Way. The entire site was powered down, except for some trucks and spot lights. Look Aunty Mary, they want to get rid of me, so they created a load of bull-shit lies."

Jo noticed a telecom truck out Aunty's front kitchen window. The lineman, a woman with a hard hat, hurriedly did something to the overhead phone lines.

Aunty Mary, not noticing the activity, asked "What are you going to do?"

"I've got a lawyer. I'll talk to Jeremy. Please put these papers away for me. I'll come back for them later."

Chapter 13 Under Fire

JO LEFT AUNTY'S house and hopped on the Interstate for the one exit jaunt to home. A small truck followed much too closely. But now Jo was really worried at where things were heading. "Is this all really happening or am I seeing connections that don't exist?" Jo pondered. Aunty Mary seemed to suggest the power outage was widespread and not just Allbio.

Nearing the off ramp, Jo pulled over to the right shoulder and put on her emergency blinkers. The truck slowed behind her, but Jo angrily waved the guy to go ahead of her. The face is familiar, she thought, "Where have I seen him before?"

Jo exited the off-ramp, pulled behind some medical office suites and called Jeremy from her cell phone, telling him what transpired that morning.

"Jo, do *not* go back to work today. I'll leave early and be home around four. I want to look at the documents; we'll need to show them to Courtney Hill." Jeremy is now really concerned about the pressure on Jo.

When Jeremy arrived home in the afternoon, he kissed Jo on the cheek. "Let me change up and we will go get the papers at Aunty's".

Moments later, the phone rang, it was HR Rizzo. "You haven't been in your office. You cancelled your meeting with your staff. Your last ID swipe was at 9:20 this morning."

"No, no, no. Listen, you're wrong. I moved my car in the parking lot to our assigned places at 9:20. I left the site for lunch around noon. I had car trouble and now I'm on my way back to Allbio. My husband arrived home and I'm taking his car."

"No, don't come now. Our meeting scheduled for Monday is moved up to 8 am. We'll discuss client concerns and the supporting documents. Steadman will be with us, we'll meet in my office."

Jo abruptly said, "Fine, good-bye", and hung up. The conversation at least confirmed that the two blondes watching her must have lost her, after she gave them a scare in the parking lot. Little did they know that she had not left the Allbio site but merely moved her car to the back lot, hence Rizzo had got wrong information from them.

"And, what did Rizzo have to say?" Jeremy inquired.

"Looks like they'll fire me tomorrow. Would you mind coming with me, 8 am? Just wait in the car while I'm in there?" Jo groaned, her lower lip jutting out, eyes downcast.

"Yes, of course Jo. I'll go to my office after."

After retrieving the paperwork from Aunty's place, Jo and Jeremy dined at a local bar and grill. They found a remote table.

"Not much substance here. Looks like Marcus and Dickerson threw something together rather hastily." Jeremy opined.

"Jeremy, it's absolute crap, waffling and

illiterate…a real rush job. And the 9:47pm e-mail about Jason's 'complaint' from Rizzo must have been written after the blackout last night."

Jo paused and continued. "Last night while you were playing tennis, I drove to Allbio just after 7:30. Everything was dark except for a few spot lights and electrical trucks with bright yellow-orange lamps. My office lights were out too. It spooked me so I got the hell out of there. When I got to the I-95, I saw these bright amber overhead lights in my rear-view mirror. The truck followed me fast, even as I went full throttle up that 360 degree ramp and accelerated to lose him. He chased me, back and forth in the lanes. I was going 85, maybe 90, and he was right up my ass! And this morning, two blonde chicks followed me. One tailed me upstairs to Jason's office. Jason wasn't in."

"Calm down, Jo." Jeremy, worried about his frantic wife, wondered how much was real, exaggerated or fantasized.

"I know this seems crazy, but Jeremy, they *are* following me and like Courtney said, there must be a reason why. Maybe it's the investigations about the water and the filters? Or something else that I just don't know, because *you don't know what you do know*." Jo continued with her musings. "Maybe they're afraid I'll go to the FDA? I need to get those investigations into a safe deposit box. I'll call Jason tonight as I didn't get to talk with him today. I have to let him know what's going on!"

"Jo, are you sure? I don't know if you want to draw anyone else into this."

"Jason wouldn't say nasty things about me. Neither him, I would swear to that, nor his boss, Kate Sheppard. She sent the e-mail praising me for getting the federal grant money for investigator training, look I have the printed email."

"That's good. Show that to your lawyer. Courtney will want to see that."

That evening Jo, sitting in the front patio, called Jason at his home. Initially, Jason was confused about the alleged complaint. He was well aware that there had been a power outage. Jason told Jo that Lars Franklin, the corporate head of regulatory compliance, flew in from California that night. Jo was surprised that her network outage "concern" email to Franklin had prompted enough interest for him to catch an evening plane out.

"Monday morning at 8am they are going to walk me right out having fired me. Look, I don't expect anything from you. I just want to let you know what's going on. For all we know, you could be next." Jo warned Jason that people involved with the water problem were being fired.

Jeremy joined Jo on the patio as she flipped off her cell phone, "Are you sure you didn't rant? You're in such a state. Maybe Jason thinks you are totally off the wall!"

"Jeremy, you have to believe me. He listened. He understands. I told him I didn't expect anything from him, it was an FYI for him."

"Jo did you tell him that HR Rizzo said there was a complaint from him to Steadman about your department's work when you saw him earlier?"

"Yes, yes. He seemed genuinely taken aback. He did not make a complaint; he didn't have a clue where that came from."

Jo hesitated, reluctant to go inside their home, "Please Jeremy, no discussions about this in the condo. I still think our home is bugged. *Somebody's* been in…when I went to the police I thought someone had gone through my documents at home….and the phone too is probably tapped."

"Look, we'll do what you want – get a home security alarm and I can ask the security company to run a sweep for electronic surveillance in the house and our phone. Phone taps of private houses need a court order and I cannot see Allbio wanting to make this public by involving a judge. We will do whatever it takes to make you more …comfortable. I know you are under a lot of pressure. But why we can't talk in our own house is beyond me!" Jeremy really worried about Jo's fragile state.

Sunday morning Jo and Jeremy had walked to the corner mini-mart for the newspaper. Still riddled with anxiety, Jo explained "I just want everyone to be ok, to be safe." Jo's concern grew fretful. "Is Sofia ok?"

"Yes." Jeremy assured her "She is *surrounded* by people – you know that. She's been with her friend Lucienne in Monaco."

"Please, please don't talk about it in the house. We mustn't talk about things—they'll know—*they'll try to hurt us*." Jo paused. "Is Aunty

Mary ok? The phone truck was there...last Thursday when I brought the papers to her. And I was followed. I got the license number. And the car next to me had a sign "Dangerous" in his window. And the car was full of bread rolls." Jo's anxiety increased along with the pitch of her voice, "Please Jeremy, "I've been followed...and I'm worried about my family...our Sofia..."

The Monday 8 am meeting at Allbio was not quite what Jo expected. Jo and Jeremy went unnoticed by Allbio security as they drove through the gate in their aging Honda. As Jo promised, the meeting would not take long. But to Jo's surprise, Jo was *not* fired but placed on "administrative leave". Unsure of the implications, Jo was satisfied to delay the inevitable chopping block.

Lance Steadman sat in silence during HR Rizzo's brief overview. Rizzo asked Jo and Steadman not to discuss anything when she left the room to make copies of documents. In Rizzo's absence, Jo and Steadman engaged in an adolescent stare-down, with Steadman eventually losing the game. He relented by walking out of the small windowless office.

Jo amusingly relayed the story to Jeremy as they drove off the Allbio site.

"Your staring him down was absolutely puerile! In the meantime, you had better get to work on that rebuttal that Courtney Hill wants from you. You now have time to get things straight for Courtney to help us. So please *stay focused*. Get the story organized. No rambling on about flashing yellow lights or being followed!" Jeremy sternly reprimanded Jo.

"Ok, ok, that I can do." Jo cowered and brooded pensively as they drove home in silence.

Chapter 14 Frantic, Manic and NIN

THE BLINDS WERE DRAWN although it was daylight out. Jo sat at the computer in the darkened room typing her rebuttal; her papers piled in relative order. Jeremy called Jo's cell phone to see if all was going well.

"Yes, I'm working on the response for Courtney…just about finished! Thanks, I love you too."

After Jo's goodbye, she played with her new cell phone, looking at the received calls, then the dialed calls. She scrolled down on the menu to #1, the first call dialed.

"Hmmm, I don't remember calling that number…" Jo thought. She fired up her browser and googled the number 1-666-234-5678. "Allbio Security Switchboard" was the first website to come up on the computer screen.

Jo flinched, emoting "Holy shit! What's this number doing here? I've never called this!"

Impulsively, Jo shut down the computer, pulled the rebuttal paper from the printer, grabbed her keys, purse and cell phone, thinking "Somebody needs to see this number. I need to show Jeremy after all my wild talk of being followed and watched. Maybe if I show Courtney she can help."

Jo wasted no time and she was soon en-route on the interstate to Boston. Jo noticed two cars keeping pace with her. As she drove on she could see the same two cars in her rear and side view mirrors. She thought, could they be following? Is this Jo's second Mr. Toad's wild ride?

A few miles on Jo noted a sign to the central MBTA station. She decided to take the train to Boston. As she exited the downtown ramp, the same two cars follow her to the station. Jo pondered. *How curious, something strange is going on.* She pulled to the curb, letting the two cars pass, then circled the station and headed back to the interstate towards Boston.

Jo knew it was no coincidence that the two cars were again on the interstate. "No way!" Jo growled and slowed down. The newer silver saloon car passed on her left. Dark grey plastic obscured the license plate number. Jo grumbled. "Too dark to read, why do they allow that?"

A few more miles and Jo neared a smaller train station of the MBTA. As she veered right on to a rural road, the older brown sedan followed. Jo erratically pulled a quick u-turn, turned her head and looked over her shoulder to read the crooked plate of the older model sedan. "AT-76", a dealer license plate. Jo surmised. Easy on, easy off plates. Slap it on for a quick change of identity.

Both cars slowed. There wasn't much traffic that morning, and both cars u-turned to follow Jo's black turbo. Jo headed towards the small town center, turning chaotically, trying to lose the two tails. She cranked up the volume of her CD. Something manic was playing...pounding full of angry emotion. NIN, Nine-Inch-Nails. The industrial rock built to its signature crescendo, as Jo drove randomly, turning frequently, determined to confuse and obfuscate with her messy motion. It was a heart pounding, frenzied ride reminiscent of her first Mr. Toad's wild ride; disturbing, bewildering and perfectly framed by the abrasive lyrics of NIN.

After a dozen senseless, maze-like turns, Jo could no longer see either car. She was relieved to think she finally lost them. But only moments later, directly ahead of her was the crooked plate of AT-76. The music blasted full volume and with the same anger and rage, Jo screamed a menacing rant. "I will fucking kill you!"

Jo could see reflected in his dashboard mirror the face of the young guy in the old brown sedan. As though he could hear her, he made a quick right turn and sped away. Jo wondered if he was frightened that she would do exactly what she promised.

The song ended in concert with her threatening expletive. In the quiet pause that followed, Jo felt relieved. She exhaled, grinned slightly and said aloud, "So *there!*"

Jo turned off the music and drove on in silence, all the rest of the way to Boston. Her eyes panned the road for familiar cars, license plates. So many had magnetic ribbons, commemorating the support for the troops and other good causes; yellow ones, red-white and blue ones.

Trekking across the expanse of Government Center, Jo rode the elevator to the 17th floor law office. A paralegal greeted her.

"Courtney is out of the country, in Europe,

but I can have her call you."

"Here is some information for my file." Jo handed over a short stack of papers. "Could I use a telephone to call my husband?"

"Yes, you may use the one at the front desk."

As Jo telephoned Jeremy, she watched people popping in and out of the elevator. A UPS man stepped one foot out and he looked at Jo and stepped back into the elevator. A telephone repair man with a set of tools clocked Jo as he walked by. Jo scowled at them both suspiciously, as if they are stalking her. She thought perhaps they were.

When Jeremy arrived, they met up in the conference room. "Jo, I took the "T" here, what is it? Why aren't you at home working on your response?"

"I *was*! But I noticed something unusual on my cell phone. The first number dialed." Jo showed Jeremy the number, 666-234-5678. "I didn't recognize the area code or the number, so I googled it. It's an Allbio Security number! I *never* called this number...but the fat guy who sold me the cell phone in the Cellular store must have."

Jeremy hit the redial, called the number and listened to the recorded greeting. "You have reached the Allbio Security Switchboard....."

"Hmm...interesting." Jeremy commented.

Jo's brown eyes widened like bullet points, "Could they be listening to my calls? Did they bug my phone?"

"Probably not listening, but *tracking* them." Jeremy fiddled with the cell phone menu. "Well

97

there's a "call forward" to this number, so your cell phone calls are routed through Allbio Security. They *monitor* your calls."

Alarmed, Jo began to ramble, "Jeremy, I was followed today on my way to Boston....a number of cars."

"What? Who followed you? This isn't more of your paranoia, is it? How could Allbio have a whole fleet of cars following you?" Jeremy asked frowning skeptically, his thick eyebrows rose. "But your cell phone *could* be used to track your whereabouts."

"Jeremy, I know what I know. And maybe it's what Courtney keeps asking me about. I thought it was the investigations, but now I know it is one investigation in particular... the water contamination....the organic carbon problem. They blamed the source of the carbon on the disinfectant alcohol being sprayed around. They said that the alcohol got into the water samples through small holes in the test tube stoppers. But the data they reported didn't make any sense to me."

"And they fired their investigators, like Ludlum, and the micro analyst; you said his name was Gonzales?" Jeremy lit up like a light emitting diode.

"Yes. *Anyone* and *everyone* who questioned the lab data. They've dumped *huge* batches of contaminated product into the local sewer that they had helped build. And that's a lot of money lost on a multibillion dollar drug." Jo paused and deduced, "That's why the big boys, the insiders, were selling off their stock in October. That's when they found out that a shitload of contaminated drug had gone down the drain."

"So, what do you want to do? Go to the FDA?" Said Jeremy was now convinced that things were awry.

"No, not the FDA. Their visit to Allbio this year was insipid. Everyone in QC said FDA sent their lightweights. Either they were inexperienced or bought off. Just like the three monkeys. See no evil, hear no evil and speak no evil." Jo gestured with her hands cupping her eyes, ears and mouth.

"So you're saying they don't look deep enough." Jeremy confirmed. "But we *talked* about this---you said you didn't want to go that route. We called it plan B."

"But now with the cell phone bugging and all the tailing by goons we have got to do something now. Look, I called the FBI, they are located just across the square from here." Jo pointed in the general direction.

"Are you sure you want to do this? I thought you wanted to stick with plan A... work with Courtney on a rebuttal." Jeremy reminded Jo and argued the point.

"But we are *right here*. We can talk to the FBI *directly*. They said they have intake agents. They take inquiries." Jo walked over to the window. "Look out across the square, you can see their building!"

Jeremy, still resistant, laid out the conditions, "Fine, but promise me, no flashing yellow lights!"

Nodding yes, Jo wrinkled her brows and

stared back at Jeremy with an affirmative promise.

"What you just told me about the contaminated water and the insider trading sounded convincing but, *please*...focus on that and that alone!" Jeremy pleaded.

Jo and Jeremy walked hand-in-hand across Government Center toward the FBI field office. In the building foyer, isolated men stood loitering or talking on cell phones. Jo thought, "Are they agents in training? This must be how undercover agents practice. They loiter around as information gatherers, watchful observers or they roam around buildings dressed up as blue-collar workers, electricians and postmen."

In the outer office at FBI headquarters sat a disabled young man with a cane, who appeared to have a crippling leg injury. Jo and Jeremy registered at the front desk and were given a report form. Jo wrote a synopsis of what transpired. How Allbio "bugged" her cell phone, their contaminated water investigation, their insider trading, how she was tailed by people she suspected were Allbio.

To Jo, what was going on in the foyer seemed staged. A young FBI agent sat next to the articulate, slender, disabled man with a rehearsed sounding story, something about the people responsible for what happened to him. He was vague on detail but asked the FBI to look into the matter for him. An injustice prompted him to seek their help. To Jo, it just seemed too theatrical to be real. Unintentional voyeurs, Jo and Jeremy were the lone audience to the unfolding story, an obtuse telling of what transpired to maim the unfortunate fellow. The slender young man rose awkwardly from his chair and relied heavily on his cane as he limped out the door.

When the FBI agent eventually appeared at the intake window, Jo presented herself with Jeremy hovering behind. The intake agent, also very young, asked them to pass through a security metal detector in the office. He came back out to the small reception area.

"You are fine. We can talk in this office here if you like. The gentleman who was here had metal in his leg and didn't pass the metal detector so we talked in this office. We have a secure camera surveillance room, if you prefer, but we can talk right here."

Jo, anxious for privacy, asked "Can we go into the secure room?"

The intake agent buzzed Jo and Jeremy through to a small room devoid of furniture. The agent reappeared behind a counter with a sliding glass window. A curved surveillance mirror was mounted in an upper corner; a camera for recording the encounter was installed just opposite.

Jo estimated the age of the agent at late twenties and noted his good looks and blue eyes. Briefly she verbalized her suspicions of insider trading at Allbio and the problems with water contamination. Jeremy stepped forward to give the name of his friend in the field office. All was just matter of fact.

"They tracked my cell phone calls, and followed my car." Jo continued.

The young agent said "I don't think this is a federal matter. This is a local issue, in Rhode Island." Jo was miffed by his dismissive, her shoulders stiffened.

Taken aback, quick to anger, Jo fired away, "Yes it *is* federal! I was followed today in Rhode Island *and* in Mass.."

Embarrassed by Jo's outburst, Jeremy took a few steps back and looked down, his hand cupped over his mouth pensively. Jo could see Jeremy reflected in the curved surveillance mirror.

"How long have you been with the agency? What is your experience?" Jo lashed out frustrated at the agent again.

"Three months...but I can't give you my background information." He quickly replied.

Jo thought it odd he would actually confirm his inexperience. She impulsively pulled out of his hand the scrap of paper with the scribbled Allbio security number.

The agent quickly retreated, returning with a seasoned agent who scolded, "You have to leave, we've already spent thirty minutes with you."

Jeremy, embarrassed, frustrated and fuming blurted at Jo. "Let's go!"

Jo's eyes were brimming with tears as they exited down the elevator and out the building.

"You were fine, and then you went off. Look, *they did not believe you*! Especially when you went on about being followed. You should have stopped. And then you went after that agent!"

"He's a plant." Jo accused.

Jeremy was on the attack "No! Don't you

102

worry, you saw the camera, and they recorded everything. He told you, you can call for the report...that's done...now back to plan A, right?"

Jo countered, "But...he didn't understand it was federal!"

"He didn't believe you! Especially when you attacked him and *his* credibility. Jo *really*! We need to go back to Plan A. This informing the FBI plan's done!"

Humbled by her outburst at the FBI office and still unsure of recent happenings, Jo continued to write her rebuttal early the next morning. Her cell phone called her to the tune of "Hello Loco". A European country code lit up. It was Courtney Hill.

"Jo, my assistant said you came to the office and you seemed agitated."

"Well, yes. It's my cell phone. I called you from the police station the day that I bought it, the day I was followed. The first number dialed on my cell phone seemed odd, a 666 number. I didn't remember calling it so I googled it. It's Allbio Security Switchboard. I *never* dialed that number. Jeremy said my phone calls were forwarded, probably routed through Allbio Security."

"Stop!" Courtney interrupted abruptly. "Don't tell me anymore." She went on, "*Don't* discuss your case with my partners or *anyone*. I'll be back in Boston soon."

Chapter 15 Noah's Ark Truck Park

IT WAS TUESDAY morning. Outside the day was bright but Jo and Jeremy Blair's condo was as dark as a bat cave. The curtains were drawn, the blinds were closed. Jo talked with Jeremy on the telephone.

"No cell phones, I'm on the land-line; I don't trust my cell phone." But Jo was really wary of both. In fact since Mr. Toad's Wild Ride and the cell phone redirection, Jo had a sense that everything could be a threat or could be read that way.

"Your cell is fine. I removed the Call Forward and the Allbio security number was kicked out." Jeremy assured Jo. "And by the way, did I leave my palm pilot at home?"

Jo spotted the small green and black zippered case, "Yes, it's next to the server."

"Not a problem, I have today's schedule on my computer calendar. Please just work on the Allbio response for Courtney, and stay focused! We meet with her Friday."

"I'm getting there. There's just so many inconsistencies, so many lies." Jo complained, closing with, "I love you. See you this evening."

"Love you too."

Jo poked at the keyboard, trying to wrap up the details of the rebuttal for Courtney. She downed a quick instant coffee then pulled out her bird watching binoculars from their case in the hallway closet. From behind the living room curtains, Jo took a curious peek with her binoculars, scanning the grassy meadow and Harrison Road in the distance.

Back at her desk, a few moments passed when she heard a repeating "bip, bip, bip" beckoning her to Jeremy's PDA. Jo unzipped the case and on the calendar display was an appointment reminder for 9:00-11:00 am. The lit screen glowed with what looked more like a warning, "Razor's Edge".

Jo's brows knitted as she mumbled curiously, "Hmmm, that's weird. What could that mean?" She thought of a multitude of possibilities. Maybe Jeremy is going somewhere dangerous like a perilous place? Or maybe it referred to the type of situation Jeremy was in-- like walking a precarious, razor-sharp fine line? If you slip up, the consequences are deadly, you're sliced and diced, or perhaps your throat is slit? Jo's imagination made her thoughts turn to increased fears for Jeremy and the safety of others. Her constant brain chatter gave her the heebie-jeebies. She zipped up the PDA, set it aside and returned to writing her response.

Later, pleased with her progress on the document for the lawyer meeting on Friday, Jo took a break and drove to Main St. She parked at the pharmacy and walked to Anna's Café. She ordered a light breakfast of poached eggs and toast and then looked up as a greasy-haired man in a brown bomber leather jacket entered and sat nearby at a center table. Jo thought him oddly familiar. Another tall, thin man came in, sat on a café barstool, ordered coffee and greeted the bomber jacket fellow saying, "Hello, how are you?" A brief encounter, they exchanged little else between them. They continue in isolation with their respective coffee cups.

Jo glanced sideways at the small center table. The brown bomber jacket guy appeared to be shielding his hands behind the plastic stand-up menu. "Why?" Jo pondered. She could tell he was aware of her gaze. Jo concluded to herself that both these two casually dressed men had something to hide. This is all part of their job. Spooks, she speculated. This isn't Moscow and the USSR so she discounted spies. Jeremy would call them "Minders" in Cockney slang? Maybe, or are they street watchers sent by Allbio to watch for their interests? Perhaps, with all that had happened and Jo's fragile sense of security she was often suspicious of the motives of others.

Uncomfortable with her thoughts, Jo paid her bill and walked out past the restaurants and specialty shops. On an impulse and wanting to send something to her mother, Jo bought a tiny teddy bear with "Mom" embroidered in a heart. As she walked out of the store even Jo wondered what had compelled her to make such an unusual purchase for her. Continuing on her stroll down Main St, as she neared the bank, the man with the brown bomber jacket stood, adopting a thug-like pose and observing nothing in particular. She hurried passed him towards the bank, but then he made a move as he sprinted past Jo. She opened the bank door, there is the leather jacketed thug standing in the teller line. He briefly said something to a teller, a short phrase or sentence, then turned and exited the bank. Jo's fears were now close to the surface. What did the man say to the teller, he obviously did not make a transaction like everyone else? Maybe I am not wrong to be wary of people, Jo thinks, and it was related to me coming in to put more evidence against Allbio in the safety deposit box.

The same teller, "Jonathon" on his nametag, took Jo through to her safety deposit box. The box key needed coaxing to work. Eventually Jonathon led Jo to a tiny, private, closet-sized room. From her purse she retrieved folded investigation notes and scraps with license plate numbers collected in her two Mr. Toad's Wild Rides that included the chase up to Boston. She stashed them in the long metal box.

Jo drove home and as she entered Willow Dean, a Fedex truck was pulling away quickly from her condo. Jo followed the truck around the circular drive to Harrison Road as it sped into the adjacent industrial park past one story buildings with a dearth of signage. They entered another parking lot with what looked like hangers or garages. Jo caught up with the FedEx truck as the driver hurriedly backed his vehicle into one of the hangers. She pulled up close enough to get a glimpse of the front license plate number, scribbling it on the corner of an old mapquest search to somewhere with a stubby pencil she kept in the cup holder. The driver looked straight at Jo as he backed in. He must have seen her chase him from Willow Dean.

As Jo y-turned she noticed the parking lot

had a mix of trucks, seemingly one of every kind. A Stan's Heating oil truck was parked along one side, a Coca Cola truck behind it and another white truck with lettering Jo was unable to read.

"Very strange." Jo observed aloud. She questioned herself as to why the FedEx driver who had just delivered a package to the house was in such a hurry to tuck his vehicle away. Why are there were so many differently branded trucks in this remote location. She coined it the Noah's Ark Truck Park.

Jo returned home to find a FedEx package on her front porch. The return address was unfamiliar to Jo. Wary of the contents, she gently carried it to the garage and placed it in an old pressboard cupboard. That afternoon, Jo worried and imagined twisted, sinister plots of Allbio commandeering postal carriers to deliver exploding letter bombs.

When Jeremy arrived home from work, Jo was in a very anxious, unnerved state. Agitated, Jo started from nowhere, "Why is there a package? Fedex brought a package, but we can't open it."

Perplexed and somewhat aggravated from this unprovoked verbal assault as he walked in the door, Jeremy asked "What package are you talking about?"

"Please come for a walk –we can't talk in the house. If they bugged my cell, I know they have bugged our home. Please let's talk outside."

"This is absurd, but I'll indulge you. Okay, let's go for a walk." Jeremy changed his sport jacket for a heavy fleece.

Jo hyperventilated, full of angst, as they walk toward Harrison Road, "Across the road, over there, I followed the FedEx truck, there's one of every kind of truck in the lot over there. They are hidden away and when I followed the FedEx driver he sped into this area and hid his truck. He looked at me for a long time."

"So what would *you* do when someone looks like they are following you? So *what,* Jo?" Jeremy queried.

"It's a sham. Jeremy, I'll show you." Jo was increasingly frantic as they approached the industrial park entrance.

Jeremy halted. "I'm not tromping through there with you." Jeremy grimaced and snapped angrily, "*I've had it with your paranoia!* There is nothing odd or unusual here." He pointed to the sign at the entry, "*Look*, that sign says 'private property'. Why did you go in there?"

Jo cowered and whined, "But Jeremy, they are trying to hurt me, to hurt us! Will they hurt Sofia, are you sure she is alright?"

Jeremy shifted from anger and tried to alleviate Jo's panic. "Sofia is fine, she is with lots of people, she is *surrounded* by people. She has been in Monte Carlo with Lucienne. She is well looked after."

Jo, still agitated, pleaded. "Is my family okay? My mother? My sister? Your parents? Can anyone hurt them? Are they alright?"

Jeremy, trying to calm Jo's irrational fears, reassured. "Yes, yes they are *all* fine. And our daughter is fine."

Jo lowered her eyes dejected. Clearly distraught, she frowned, looked up at Jeremy and shook her head from side to side. "Maybe we should move away from here? People at Allbio will try to hurt me...to hurt *us*! I need to leave!"

Jeremy gripped Jo's arm as he led her home. Gently, firmly, he said "No, we are not leaving here. You *must* stop with the paranoia!"

Troubled with Jo's fragile state, Jeremy implored, his voice heaving with emotion, *"I don't want to lose you!"*

Jeremy felt that the world was closing in on them and he was really concerned with the deterioration in Jo. Jeremy looked at the package that was frightening Jo stashed in the garage. As he did so he saw a customs declaration that showed it was an early Christmas package from his sister in Australia. "It can wait; I have other things to worry about." He didn't know how true this was or what would happen to Jo next.

Chapter 16 The Cop Shop

THE NEXT NIGHT, Jo was incarcerated.

After bending the cop car's number plate and being arrested the patrol car arrived at the police station, the cops half lifted Jo out of the patrol car. The duo was miffed with Jo's ability to get out of the restraints. "How did she do that?" Roundhead (Officer Decker) mumbled at Jo's Houdini trick with the restraint harness.

"See, we are at the police station," Squarehead said to Jo, "Where did you *think* we were going?"

Jo walked cautiously keeping her right leg straight, her knee radiated a piercing needle-like pain. The cops brought Jo through a tiny reception to the intake room she remembered from her last visit with Officer Ken. As he seated her, Roundhead cuffed her left arm to the chair, leaving her right arm free. Her eye still smarted from Squarehead's blow but at least it felt back in its socket.

Both cops stepped into the hallway and Jo overheard a comment, "...but she had her binoculars and telephone." They returned to the intake area; Roundhead held her fleece jacket and said, "I brought your jacket and cell phone. I thought you might need them." But Jo was surprised to see her cell phone in *Squarehead's* hand. Wary of why and how Squarehead got hold of it, Jo recalled that although her fleece jacket was in the front entry room, her cell phone lay in her basket of silk scarves *on her bedside nightstand*.

"You can call your husband." Squarehead tried to hand the cell phone to Jo.

"I'm not calling from *that* phone. It's been *bugged* by Allbio. They've put their security switchboard number into it." Jo rashly replied.

Squarehead impulsively fired back, "*That could never be used as evidence. You could have put that number in there!*"

Jo, surprised and unsettled at Squarehead's out of place comment, looked to her right at the police station telephone sitting on a table. She said, "I'll use this phone. I'm not using *that* phone" pointing to her cell phone. "I'm entitled to a phone call, aren't I?"

Squarehead (Sid Borrelia on his name tag) placed Jo's cell phone on the counter behind him. He crouched down on bent knees in front of Jo, his face just inches away from hers. Jo defensively cupped her right hand in front of her eyes but could see him between her fingers. She was worried the beating had not finished. Surprised at her own calm, Jo feigned sobs, trying to appear weak, emotional....vulnerable. Squarehead glared intently, taking his time, closing in, almost touching his forehead to hers. He peered deeply between the slits of her fingers, suspicious of her crocodile tears.

Jo's mind was racing. *Evidence on the cell phone?* Why would he even *think* to bring that up? Why should he be concerned with evidence implicating Allbio? Why would Squarehead want to defend them? Why should he *care*? What's *he* got to do with it? There were too many questions, too

112

many inconsistencies in Jo's mind. She thought that perhaps these guys really were Allbio police, maybe contracted on a special security detail. Squarehead did not linger and soon disappeared from the office.

Jo coughed a nervous cough, and oddly enough so did Roundhead. Both hacked repetitively. Anxiety in the room was infectious. Roundhead instructed, "You can dial the number for your husband," gesturing to the telephone next to her. "Tell him to bring $50 in cash to give you, for your bail."

Jo dialed slowly, as though trying to remember, attempting to appear more unnerved and upset than she actually was.

Jeremy picked up his office phone, "Hello, this is Jeremy Blair."

"Jeremy, this is Jo. I'm at the West Bay police station. I've been arrested." Jo calmly stated, not wanting to sound alarmed.

"Are you alright? Jeremy hesitantly asked, trying to make sense of the situation.

"Jeremy, I'm fine. Please don't worry." Jo paused. "You'll need to bring $50 cash for bail."

"I'll be there as soon as I can, but it will be a while before the next train."

Roundhead took hold of the telephone saying, "I need to speak with your husband."

"This is officer Decker." For the first time Jo registered his name. "We have arrested your wife. Do you know where the station is?" He continued with the details.

Once off the phone, Decker commented.

"Your husband sounds English."

"Yes, he is." Jo confirmed. "He will be awhile; it could be an hour or two at least."

In the interim, Decker wrote up a report on the computer. Jo squinted at the screen, barely able to see a photo of a police car and asked, "What is that?"

"It's a photo of the license plate you destroyed." Decker answered matter of fact. Jo looked down at the floor and did not comment.

After a short while, Decker tried to take the edge off. "Look, we're nice guys; Officer Borrelia didn't try to hurt you. We're just doing our job. You don't want to go to the hospital emergency room or anything. They'd keep you waiting for four or five hours." Playing the "good cop", he emphasized that this was his story.

Jo answered in a deadpan monotone, "I'm not hurt. I'm fine." trying to disguise the painful pangs in her legs, her throbbing, aching knee, the sharp stabbing in her sore eye. She tried not to divulge her emotions through carefully exercised restraint and her inner wariness.

"We'll need to take fingerprints." Decker removed the handcuff from the left chair handle and clasped the cuff on her right wrist. Jo stood gingerly keeping her right leg straight while walking. It took only a few steps to the fingerprinting table. Decker very slightly pulled up Jo's sleeves, to steal a peek at the tiny lacerations and reddened wrists from Jo's struggling and from being squeezed so tightly.

After a few more steps across the tiny room,

Decker clicked a hand-held camera for mug shots; placing Jo's ID in her hands and slipping her glasses on and off for a few shots. She walked the few paces back to her chair where, on sitting, her knee gave out and she buckled, falling back into the chair. Trying to hide her weakness, Jo murmured. "Oh, I just tripped…I'm ok."

"I'm going to have to put you in the holding cell. Its late shift and we may get called out. There's only one person, the girl at the front desk, and I can't leave you in here. I need to remove your shoes." Decker advised.

"No, please don't. Why?" Jo objected. She did not understand the need.

Decker removed her shoes without a reply. Jo rose tentatively from the wooden chair, keeping her knee as rigid as she could, she walked slowly, precariously to the holding cell with its concrete bench and polished metal toilet.

Jo balked, hesitating to go in. "I'm claustrophobic; please don't make me go in there." Decker led her in and she sat on the cold, hard concrete. "It's *cold*." Jo whined. Decker brought her a thin grey flannel blanket.

Jo pulled her legs up into a fetal position. Holding her knees with her arms she could feel her right knee throbbing, beginning to swell. Intent on gaining pity, Jo blurted, "Please let me out!" Rubbing her sore, pulsating knee, the burning pain intensified. Jo groaned softly.

Time passed at glacial speed as Jo rocked gently, combing her fingers through her long curls. Feeling threads between her fingers she noticed that clumps of hair had fallen out in her hand. She plucked the strands of entwined rusty brown hair from her fingers and layered them floating in the shiny metal toilet bowl. To leave a memento, she did not flush. As if to say, "See what you've done to me. I will leave you a subtle reminder."

"Your husband is here." Decker unlocked the cell. "He is very upset." Jo looked up at Decker's apprehensive moon-shaped face.

After posting bail and the usual formalities, Jo, relieved and at last un-handcuffed, walked in short baby steps towards the front reception.

Jeremy was visibly distressed; tears as evidence that he had been crying. He gently cupped his hand behind Jo's head, brought her head against his chest. He lowered his head to kiss her crown, while trying to restrain his sobs. Jo gazed up, connecting directly with his reddened dark eyes she tried to calm his worries. "I'm fine, Jeremy. Let's go home."

Both saddened by the sorry state of unusual circumstances, they drove home in silence.

While Jo soaked in the bath, holding her bent knee against her chest; Jeremy sat on the toilet seat lid, his mind full of questions.

"I think I'll be okay. My wrists are sore, there are little cuts. Is my eye okay? How does it look? The cop poked it hard with his fist, it felt like it was pushed in. Things are still blurry."

Jeremy inspected her eye, "It looks alright, just a bit bloodshot."

116

"My whole body is sore. Oh, but *my knee, oh it really hurts!* It gave out, buckled at the police station - but I pretended to trip. My joint has ballooned up quite a bit. The cruciate is gone - maybe the medial collateral too." Jo self-diagnosed from her medical past.

"One ligament or two? Shall we make a bet?" Jeremy attempted humor now that they were home, settled, trying to make light of an incongruent, unfathomable day.

"At least the ACL can be repaired." They both agreed, but Jo's mouth turned to a frown and she added a malicious detail. "But Jeremy, it was *intentional*, they purposely slammed my legs in the car door!"

"In the police car door?" Jeremy asked, and then spun around whispering smugly to himself, "Got 'em!"

Jo confirmed, "Yes, they did…and *this* leg they hit the most," still holding her right knee.

Jeremy, turned back around and wondered aloud, "But tell me, what made you bend their license plate?"

Jo hesitated then explained, "I asked them for their ID. More than once, I asked them who they were. They pointed to their uniforms, their badges and finally to their patrol car."

"Oh, and your obsession with license plate numbers, all those license numbers you've been collecting? Oh, I understand, you wanted their license number to identify them." Jeremy said, thinking out loud.

"Yes, their license number, I wanted it. I

117

needed it to know *who they were*." Jo nodded repeatedly, musing, second guessing. "I don't know, I just snapped. I thought they were from Allbio...and they took my cell phone...from my bedroom. Now why would they do that?" Jo asked, since everything seemed jumbled, confusing.

"What? You didn't have it with you? When you called them, they said it was about a garbage truck."

"Yes, but I took the telephone from the kitchen and ran out back. It died mid-call and I rang from the condo up the hill, where the woman with the lovely rose garden lives. I had the binoculars and the kitchen phone with me when I met up with the cops."

"Did you kick their patrol car?"

"No, no, *I just bent their plates*."

Jo shifted to explain that the Allbio goon had come earlier. He had banged on the door and had coughed loudly to get her attention. "A very creepy guy left that letter from Allbio." Fading, exhausted, shifting thoughts again, "I spoke with Ted earlier, he said the garbage truck was late today."

Both had run out of steam, every bit of energy was completely spent. Jeremy, tired but still focused, gave Jo two naproxen and water. "We will get you to the doctor – we'll call, but *after* we see Courtney tomorrow morning. She'll need to notify Allbio that you won't be attending their one o'clock meeting tomorrow."

Jeremy paused and repeated, "You need to be examined by the doctor...no more self

118

diagnoses." He sighed feeling sapped, completely drained. "We are both exhausted." His voice broke, "Oh my baby, that was the *longest* train ride I *ever* had in my life."

Jo weakly moaned in tumultuous resignation as Jeremy uttered his last words of the day, a day unlike no other. *"Let's go to bed."*

Chapter 17 Shrinkydink One

JEREMY'S SIX FOOT lanky frame towered over the diminutive five foot Jo. From a distance, she could be his elderly mother or a small lame child. Jeremy supported Jo as she limped slowly across the square at Government Center. At the law office, they were greeted by Courtney. "How lucky that I just returned from Europe last night."

Jeremy gave a brief matter of fact account of Jo's arrest the previous night. Courtney gave them the number of a criminal lawyer in Rhode Island. Jeremy returned to matters in hand. He showed Courtney the letter from Allbio. "Here is the letter from HR Rizzo. Note the meeting at 1 pm today with the threat to terminate Jo if she does not attend."

"It's coming up to one o'clock. I'll contact them by fax. As of today Jo, you are on medical leave and have serious medical issues. Get a referral for stress."

As they started to leave the office, Courtney noticed Jo's awkward gate. "It looks as though you're limping? Boy, you must have put up quite a struggle!"

Without going into detail, Jo smiled weakly as she and Jeremy said their thanks and goodbyes.

It was late in the afternoon by the time they got back to Rhode Island. Famished, Jeremy pulled their Turbo 6 into the 99 restaurant and said, "We never ate dinner last night. We need a good meal."

"Ohhh, the pain is getting worse. But the food will help." Jo, exhausted, hobbled to the table, looking around her. Sitting in the reception area, an Asian man, perhaps Indian, watched Jo as she lamely walked past. Jo, grimaced, adrenaline expended she began to sadden. Jeremy, tired but trying to remain cheerful, looked at the menu.

"Have a steak, this one with the blue cheese looks like you." Jeremy grabbed Jo's hands affectionately. Holding both her hands, rubbing and gently messaging them, he told her, "I was very proud of you today…and last night. While you were in the bath tub, you were so strong. You kept yourself together."

Softly, Jo slowly, quietly replied, "I'm so sorry I put you through this. I thought they were going to kill me. But I'm *still here*. I thought they were going to throw me in the Narragansett Bay."

"I understand, I will protect you and we will work through this. Always remember I love you."

The following week, Jo met with Diane Gennaro. She entered the psychologist's office awkwardly, keeping her right leg straight. Inching her way with baby steps, she found a chair with side arms. She held on tightly to keep her knee from giving out.

During their first session, Jo spoke only of her job, her background, her obsession with writing everything down. *Document what you do!* The QA motto. Her need to control….everything. Everything in its place, everything under control. The 5 W's. Who? What? When? Where? Why?

Know it all, every detail. The devil is in the detail. Jo was obsessive-compulsive by nature, by nurture or perhaps by virtue of the job she accidentally fell into.

Jo told her psychologist, Diane, about her past as a science teacher in the diplomatic community. Her work as a natural biologist in Africa -- her passion. A few years in medical education. Then biotechnology, not a passion but certainly the most profitable. A good 401k and stock options to help her and Jeremy to an early retirement. The biology of biotech was not the classical natural biology she taught in schools. It was a window into the way the DNA of genes are manipulated and recombined, to improve the quality of life. Or as ineptly proclaimed in the double entendre, *Life, we are working on it!*

It wasn't until her second session with Diane that Jo explained the cause and nature of her injury.

"It's hard for people to believe me. Most people seem incredulous. After all, I called them…the police. So why would they be so intent on hurting me?" Jo questioned aloud. "How likely is it that you call the police for help and they end up beating you up?" Jo frowned, shaking her head from side-to-side. Getting more and more angry but tearfully indignant, her voice broke, "All I did was bend their license plate! Look at me, I'm a five foot, middle aged woman. How threatening can I be?"

Jo momentarily chuckled at the absurd silliness. Her mood shifted, "But to *handcuff* me and dangle me by my arms?' I still have bruises, circles on my arms, and a huge black and blue mark on my back!" Diane's eyebrows rose as Jo continued. "Who would do that to a shrimpy little distraught woman? They should have been thinking, hey, she's nutty, maybe we should calm her down."

"Yes, they could have left and let you calm down. They could have talked to you later, suggested you get some help." Diane suggested.

"But instead they slam my legs in the police car door...both legs, thump, thump, thump.. thump. Maybe four or five times Then I pulled one leg in, but they kept whacking away on my right leg, very hard...thump, thump, thump...thump!" Jo paused, her voice cracking, she said intently, whimpering. "They broke my knee...the cruciate ligament. Those bastards broke my knee." Dejected, Jo looked down and glumly shook her head.

Sitting in her long skirt the petite Diane looked a five foot replica of Jo, only thinner. With curly brown hair, olive coloring and dark brown eyes; she was obviously Italian extraction. Diane tilted her head puzzled, "It does seem unusual...and does your leg hurt?"

"Sometimes it aches. I used to walk two or three miles. Now I can't even walk to the mailbox. I'll need an ACL reconstruction. I know the surgery well. I spent a few years training surgeons how to scope knees. Now the ultimate irony—I need one myself. I never considered people's pain. I never had much empathy or compassion for the patients till now."

"Did anyone see what happened?"

"My neighbor, Ted next door was outside.

123

But I was on the other side on the police car. Jeremy asked Ted later but he said he couldn't see…bad eyesight. Maybe it was the angle…he's quite old too. All the neighbors are older, 70's, 80's. We are the youngsters in the retirement community."

Diane divulged little about herself, as with any good therapist, she let her patient do the talking. At their next session, Jo talked about events leading up to the arrest. Incidents flowed as if episodes in TV soap opera. The night of the black out. Being followed. How Jo's cell phone was tapped. Her problems at Allbio.

"It's Allbio, and my boss, and his boss. I know what it is. I didn't know why, not at first. But it's the water; it's contaminated…the TOC tests for total organic carbon. They aren't going to produce much product…at least not on schedule. They've got a water problem and they want to keep it quiet." Jo continued to rant, "We were looking at the problem, my staff, Chrissy and the others. We got some recognition, 'best practice', and federal grant money, for investigator training." Jo kept on talking. "And in the meantime, the bosses, the bigwigs are all making millions…hundreds of millions. Selling now while the stock is pumped up before any bad news gets out. There's too much money at stake…billions in share value."

"And you blew the whistle?" Diane suggested.

"Yes and they want to keep me quiet." Jo completed her intimation. "The night of the power outage, I was chased."

"Yes, you said a truck with yellow lights."

"And so many others were involved. Jo listed off the suspects. The fat guy who rigged my cell phone, the guy who followed me when I left the cell phone store, the blonde chick at the Allbio site. My e-mails were misdirected, my calls were monitored by Allbio security switchboard." Jo's mind poured out as if a stream of word associations. "Allbio's security is *huge!* They have many, many "contractors", a few well-placed police, members of the town councils, some state house politicians. Think of the revenue it's bringing to the state—it's the biggest investment this state has seen in years!"

"So the police, are they working for Allbio?" Diane asks in anticipation.

"Yes, the police, and a few incompetents in the FDA. Perhaps the FBI too I didn't get much luck when I went there." Jo could not resist pushing the envelope.

Diane, prying Jo's paranoia further, asked, "And you said before, your mail, you were afraid to open packages and they bugged your home phone and your condo?

"Yes, I don't know any more. I may have been overly paranoid but I couldn't know where they would stop. If they could buy the police, could they go to other extremes?" What about the safety of my family? My daughter in Europe? When I was arrested, the cop asked if I had children. He was asking details. Where was my daughter? What was her age?"

Jo paused, her mind raced as her fears spilled forth. "Would they go so far as to compromise the safety of my daughter in Europe? I panicked! She went to Monaco, was it just a fluke or was someone protecting her? Woosh! Sofia is off in Monte Carlo just as all the bugging and intimidation come on strong. What would they do, the Allbio bigwigs, to protect their stock options? And Steadman and Markus with their "spot stocks" implied that they had something for me. They tried to bait me; a lure to bribe me into joining in on their illicit zero-sum game."

Jo's sessions with Diane continued. Jeremy suggests to Jo that she should be prepared for interpretations she might not like, from her court-mandated therapy. But she needs to "show improvement", to help get the charges against her rescinded.

"I'm not paranoid....I don't think that is the word to use." Jo reacted to Diane's diagnosis.

Diane attempted an explanation to assuage Jo, "I don't mean it as a condition, but as a reaction in this circumstance. You were perhaps overly sensitive to perceived threats."

"Yes, I see." Jo said, forcing herself to agree. "Whatever will work best at getting these charges against me dropped."

"And what did they end up charging you with?" Diane asked..

"Destruction of public property, under $100, it said in the local news."

"In the newspaper?"

"Yes, in the local rag. My husband found it under the 'Arrests'. But the police report said $20 damage, to the license plate."

"Then is that all?" Diane was surprised at the minimal charge.

Jo, rubbed her hands and messaged her thumbs, "No…also resisting arrest…I still have neuropraxia in my thumbs and hands – numbness. I tried so hard to get out of those handcuffs. I was sure they would kill me."

Jo hesitated and remembered, "Oh! And disorderly conduct! They said I grabbed Decker's sleeve, and oh yes, kicked the patrol car. I did neither."

"And they reacted, perhaps over-reacted to the situation." Diane deducted.

"Oh yes, a five foot female must pose a real threat." She smiled as she gestured to herself and Diane. "What a threat, such a *violent* destruction of public property and what threatening behavior! Those *poor* policemen." Jo could not resist the sarcasm.

"Sometimes police can be too rough. Could that have happened?" prodded Diane.

Jo pondered, "Could the police have been too rough? Too rough, yes. But acting on their own? No. I still cannot reconcile the facts: that they beat my legs in their car door, that they purposely went into my bedroom and took my cell phone. It was on its charger, on my nightstand table, sitting in a basket with all my scarves! Decker went in. How did he know where my cell phone was? I called 911 from my kitchen phone, not from my cell."

"Yes, it doesn't make any sense. Why would he go searching your bedroom, unless he just saw it by chance?"

"But at the police station, when Borrelia handed me my cell phone and told me to call my husband. I said, 'No', I told them that Allbio had 'bugged' it with their security switchboard number. Borrelia's automatic reply was '*That could never be used as evidence.*' And then he says, "*You* could have dialed that number." Jo was incensed.

"Hmm, yes." Diane considered the suggestion.

"Why would he even come up with that comment? How could he even *anticipate* that?" Jo answered her own questions. "He wanted to make sure that the cell phone and the Allbio switchboard number wasn't going to incriminate anyone."

Jo asked herself 'why?' and 'for what?' and rambled about the many reasons. At the bottom of it was that the Allbio bigwigs wouldn't want their drug production failures public. Their new biotech plant was highly flawed, costly and they were having a hell of a time getting the local water clean enough. "And in the meantime, they are all cashing in on the stocks high price while the going is good." Jo punctuated. "They are all making personal millions."

Chapter 18 Shrinkydink Two

WHEN JO FIRST met psychiatrist Dr Palin at his office, Jo had been summoned by the state to have a second opinion on her temporary disability. Her knee surgery went as well as could be expected but the stress had taken its toll.

Slumped over on her crutches, Jo's ill-fitting leg brace kept slipping down her leg as she hobbled awkwardly. She tugged at the metal rimmed brace as she made her way across the psychiatrist's overly large office, past the tropical fish aquarium, to a rigid chair opposite his desk.

In less than ten minutes, Jo retold an in-a-nutshell version of her pulling and bending the police car license plate, her tussle with the police, her suspicions of Allbio's complicity, her injuries and subsequent anxious, depressed feelings. She gave little detail as Dr Palin did not delve. He quickly assessed her situation.

"The police hurt you, but you *did* provoke them." He smiled wryly and twisted his neck at an angle. Jo couldn't help but notice his thin pony-tail. She wondered why an older guy with such thin hair would want to show off his sparse strands of gray. Maybe a hip symbol of liberal thought? Or perhaps a non-conformist appeal to the mentally mutable? Or was he just an old hippie?

He mumbled, "Ambio, Albino?" He stumbled over the company name. "I'm not familiar with them."

Discordant, something rang on a false note.

129

Jo thought his odd muttering was reminiscent of cop Borrelia's flip dismissal. *How is it that a shrink, a professional practicing in East Bay would not know about the colossal Allbio biotech company in the next town, West Bay?*

"Look at you, you're obviously hurt. You look pathetic on those crutches. And the cops did this? Slammed you legs in their patrol car door!"

Jo nodded with a defeated but cautious, "Yes".

"But surely, someone took a video of what happened." Dr Palin made a statement rather than ask a question.

"No, I live in Willow Dean at the end of a dead-end street. There was no one around. My neighbors are old, mostly retirees that winter in Florida. Ted, my next door neighbor, was outside but he told my husband he couldn't see anything."

"Still, you've been to your doctor and you told him what happened?"

"Yes, I told the surgeon too."

"Call this lawyer!" Dr Palin blurted without hesitation. He quickly scribbled the name, Walt Maxwell, and a phone number on notepaper and handed it to Jo. "He's a high profile guy, worked on the Station Night Club disaster", referring to the nightclub fire that killed 100 people. "Sometimes he works for the police and sometimes other people. Whoever needs him."

Before Jo could respond he dialed the number. "He's a friend of mind...Hello Walt? There a woman here who was hurt by the police during an arrest. They slammed her legs in the door of the patrol car, broke her knee. She's on crutches. She's been to the doctors. Had knee surgery." Palin paused and listened. "Yes, she has your number. She'll get the medical records."

Palin gave no time for discussion. "OK, go get your medical records from your doctor; you said his office is here in East Bay. Get to the office before they close today and bring the records to Walt."

Jo, hesitant and frowning with trepidation, objected. "I don't know. I'm afraid. If I go after *the police*, they'll come after *me*."

"They won't do that." Dr Palin quickly justified. "Well, maybe they *used* to, but not anymore. Believe me, they can't do that now."

"But I don't want anyone to know about this. I don't want people to know what happened or I'll never get a job. I want to be able to retire here. We bought our home for our retirement."

"No one has to know. Walt will just go after a settlement. And then you won't *have* to worry about a job *or* your retirement. You'll have plenty of money."

Jo reflected and said nothing.

The psychiatrist wrote a prescription for Jo's "depression". Jeremy suggested she have it filled just in case the court checked. Later they thought through what had happened at the session with Palin and together they opened the capsules and poured the tiny chemical beads into the kitchen trash bin. Neither had any time or confidence in what they playfully called "Shrinkydink Two". In some way

131

this simple act started to clear some of Jo's confusion.

The next month at a follow-up appointment, Jo visited the disappointed psychiatrist who apparently already guessed the outcome. He commented to Jo. "You aren't strong enough. Your must still be too weak. Maybe you need a higher dose of the medication?"

"No thank you. I'm fine. I now have the required medical diagnoses so they will dismiss the charges against me."

Jo never returned or called Walt the personal injury lawyer.

Chapter 19 Gambinos and Goombahs

LIKE THE GAMBINO crime family, Jo gave the Allbio corporatos nicknames descriptive of their most "enduring or endearing" traits for Jo. There was Gary "Jabba the Hutt" Marcus, a gluttonous greedy slug, feared and despised for his ruthless attacks on good intentioned people. Jabba often prefaced his decisions and rationale with a reference to Allbio Values, numbers 1 through10. Any employee, who displayed even a whiff of integrity or a whisper of independent thought, would be attacked in a twisted, convoluted diatribe of vindictiveness. Unrelentingly vile, vengeful and rancorous, he left a trail of slime in his wake.

Then there was the evil dwarf, Lance "The Vegetable" Steadman a self-proclaimed zen-vegan, with his sand sculpture and very tiny little rake. Very tiny who could not tower over Jo's small frame. An emaciated golum-smeigl look alike, also known as "Buggy Blue Eyes", or "the Chihuahua"; five foot two, eyes of blue that bulged as if hypothyroid. Steadman suggested a multitude of names, many referring to his Napoleonic lack of stature and megalomania. Jo liked "The Chihuahua" best! To compensate for his innate defects, he needed to feel in total control of others. He ruthlessly got rid of anyone in his way. He blamed others for his shortcomings….in his watery eyes he yapped about the incompetent, the weak. He preyed on the vulnerable. But for those who outsmarted him, stared him in the eye…. he would inevitably blink first.

During his first year at Allbio, through carefully orchestrated outmaneuvering, Steadman got rid of his first boss at corporate headquarters. His second boss didn't last long, fired by the site VP at Steadman's behest.

Steadman read the trendy management books about breaking all the rules. He carelessly admitted that he avidly watched Trump, to help with his management style. "You're fired." He practiced his Trump-style with his two former bosses. Now his boss was the head of Allbio New England a situation that he felt comfortable with. He glibly memorized all the newest buzzwords and corporate speak. At first, he impressed. He spoke of his brothers and their relentless pursuit in outdoing each other. Their competition and sibling rivalry spurred him to greater efforts. That's what drove him.

But then he disappeared, for three weeks. Was he gambling in Vegas? He came back with disappointment in his eyes. Jo happened to see Steadman in a hallway. Shuffling and pouting like a little boy, feet kicking outward. Something has happened. He said he liked the tables, black-jack, poker? Jo mused. Maybe he's a high roller?

Eye contact went from minimal to non-existent. Hunched, his shoulders tight, but watching, patrolling the water cooler, looking for signs of weakness and defection. Paranoid. Scared. Ruthless….like Trump.

But how far would Steadman go, when after a string of firings, he found his nemesis in a five foot "plate-bending" woman. Always suspicious. Even paranoid herself. But Jo focused with an internal mantra, *I will not let you hurt me! Or anyone!* The corollary, *and if you try, I will go after you with a vengeance,* her own Sicilian blood coursing through her brain!

Steadman's droning monologue hounded him. *Jo can't be trusted. She wouldn't bite on the spot-stocks. She's ventured into territory that alarmed my boss Bonaducci. The investigations. The water. And whatever else she knows that could compromise us.* She's easy prey. She's got to be the next to go. I've managed to get rid of two bosses, a bunch of my staff, and she'll be the first of my managers. Marcus and Dickerson want her federal funds, her money. This will be easy. Write up the bad performance review. She's gone.

But who would have known. The erratic, the eccentric, are never predictable and are often beyond control. Eluding, thwarting and circumventing, quick acting and outwitting, Jo pushed Steadman against the Allbio corporate wall with her unpredictable, impulsive actions. One of them, Jo or Steadman, would have to disappear, like those stenciled epigraphs that faded into the walls of corporate Allbio.

Steadman worried obsessively. *But she can shoot. Maybe she'll come after me? Staring me down in Rizzo's office! How much does she know?* Will she rat on the spot stocks? She's upset my boss. Bonaducci, the plant manager, wants her gone. All the talk about failing to investigate in her presentation pissed him off. The little conniving bitch never told me what she was going to say. She made me look the fool on front of my boss. Skirting around me when she sent that e-mail about data integrity to corporate, blowing the whistle! Tracking her cell phone wasn't enough. And then what happened with that stupid cop we hired? All the scare tactics sending her hand-delivered mail? And his plan to fire her and shut her up with HR's help for performance issues? How did she know? How *could* she know? Now it's even more complicated.

When the cop bungled his role, Steadman followed the casual but vicious advice of Marcus. "Get rid of her, she knows too much." And with their customary smugness, they hatched a plot with an equally anxious cop. They knew the cop, Borrelia, feared prosecution for battery of a little woman who bent his license plate and tried to run away. *He's afraid she'll go after him for what he did to her. We can use that.*

Gollum. My precious.

Sid "The Smurf" Borrelia, no one was really too sure how the cop got his nickname. Certainly not from the obvious reference to the cute and endearing fictional characters, the tiny blue, half-naked forest gnomes. Nor was he a smurf brain as in someone simple-minded. Could there be a connection to smurfing in the computer world, where high tech attacks deluge and flood computer traffic? Or as farfetched as rudely defined in the urban dictionary, smurfing, the act of hitting someone across the face with one's penis? Or could it be smurfing as in the act of money laundering? No one knew for sure. Perhaps he is a smurf amalgam -- a simple-minded, body bashing, attack dog and money laundering assassin.

Off duty, Sid Borrelia met with Lance Steadman at a park and ride lot a few miles from the Allbio New England site. Steadman came with cash. A job transfer meant he was on his way out of New England. He would soon join Bonaducci and Marcus at Allbio West where another potential blockbuster drug was under production. He wanted to make sure no crumbs were left to follow his trail.

Steadman came prepared like a Boy Scout. On the passenger seat of his car was a black sling backpack stuffed with $60,000 cash in $20 bills. It was money easily skimmed from his department's bloated budget, disguised as fictitious payments to contractors. Contractors that were shell companies he himself invented. Bonaducci and Marcus commandeered much more to the local politicians through money donated to Allbio's political action committees. There was always money for legislators and regulators to do their bidding. Sewers and water were the big priorities. The senator had created the legislation for all the water Allbio needed. There was no regulation of sewers. Spreading the corporate gold around had benefitted Allbio's work.

But Jo Blair seemed to be on to something, Steadman worried about what Jo really knew. Like an irritating gnat, she needed swatting.

"The Blair's are Commie Pinkos." Borrelia

snickered to Steadman. "Their home is full of Red Russian posters. Communist propaganda."

"Communist workers wielding hammers and sickles?" Steadman gestured with his fist swinging an imaginary sickle. "It figures."

"My partner Decker said he couldn't believe the crazy commie stuff plastered on their walls. He went into their condo the day she complained about a 'break-in'. Wacko stuff about being followed, paranoid shit. She said Allbio was behind it all. She said, "Allbio owns this town!'"

"Really, she said that? Well, all the more reason. She's trouble. She's gotta go."

"Yeah, we'll throw out the trash. Before she points her finger at you." Officer Borrelia pointed at the puny Steadman's head, putting him on the defensive.

Pointing back, Steadman retorted. "Before she and that limey husband of hers decide to go after *you* for breaking her knee." Putting the onus on Borrelia and applying extra pressure," Steadman asked. "So, who do you know that can get the job done?"

"I've got contacts. People in New Jersey. Hit-men are a dime a dozen." Borrelia boasted. "There's all kinds of meat in the sauce."

Steadman hesitated, wondering what meat sauce had to do with hit-men. "Look, how much does a hit cost, if hit-men are a dime a dozen?"

It's negotiable, 40 or 50 thousand, and the problem goes away. Untraceable weapons, no evidence, no body. Just another woman who disappears under mysterious circumstances, maybe she was unbalanced enough to take her own life. See, it will be easy. She'll be fish food probably in the Narragansett Bay. Life is cheap."

"I've got the money with me, $60,000. Whatever is left is your share of the deal. But, not until I'm out of here, at the end of the month." Steadman paused, thinking that he must distance himself from any complicity in the crime. This would be his final dealing with Borrelia. Allbio Security contracted Borrelia to watch after disaffected workers, to keep them on a short leash, to keep them quiet. After today, Steadman would never see the crooked cop again and Jo Blair would be out of his hair. As Borrelia drives away he cannot stifle the laugh "Easy money for me", no trace, and Steadman will be gone.

Goombahs.

Chapter 20 End of Summer

IN THE HEAT and humidity of the New England summer, Jo walked late afternoons down Harrison Road to Main Street. On occasion she would spot the familiar patrol car and license plate...6124. She thought. *I couldn't have done much damage, I'll bet those cops just bent the dog ears back on the license plate.*

Coincidentally or not, she would see the patrol car conveniently parked in the Harrison Road turn-out where they could watch her comings and goings. Odd characters, would cruise the circular dead end of Willow Dean. Jo often complained to Jeremy that they were much too "thuggish", not the typical maintenance crews or garden boys who clipped and mowed. But Jo's mind had played tricks on her for a number of months since the incident. The sound of a wood chipper unnerved her as Jo imagined being stuffed into the orifice with its teeth-like blades; like the movie Fargo, pulverizing her dead limbs into sawdust.

Late that spring, Jeremy and Jo traveled to Lille, France to see "Fantasy", the final ice show of the season. Sofia's fiancé, Armand flew home to finish his studies. They planned to rejoin one another when the show resumed in Germany in the Fall.

It was in Italy, overlooking Vesuvius from the Aminta Hotel in Amalfi, that Jo shared with Sofia the outrageous story of what happened that

140

winter. Sofia was shocked and horrified that her mother would be arrested, beaten, and incarcerated for provoking two cops. Jo stretched the story out in every detail, late into the evening as they lounged in the hotel café bar. She confided with Sofia about the tapped cell phone and Jo's suspicions of Allbio's collusion. Her bashed knee. Her bruised and battered state.

Sofia, confused and without words to describe her feeling, spoke later, quietly with her father. Jeremy reassured her that her mother had been through a rough time, both physically and emotionally. Yes, there was harassment from Allbio which may or may not have been linked with the incident. There were unanswered questions and unresolved outcomes but they would do their best to get beyond the confounding incident.

"I told Sofia enough without telling her too much. Only what she needs to know." Jeremy, the calming influence, placates the unsettling feelings of Jo and Sofia. Everything will go away and fade into the past, confusion cannot last forever.

Later that summer, back in Bayside, Rhode Island, the good looking friendly people seemed to have disappeared. A new element of unsavory sorts seemed to appear.

Jo and Sofia, on their daily afternoon walk to Main Street, were watched, luridly, or was it demonically as they walked through the back lot of the local drug store. Sofia shuddered. She was wary of the sneering, threatening stare from a middle aged, pinch-faced man riding in a late model red

Chevy pick-up truck. Both Sofia and Jo cringed from his unwanted and sinister attention. He was too scary looking to be just the usual creepy sexual predator.

Jo's thoughts immediately turned to her fears that someone, somewhere would try to hurt her, he family, her daughter. Or was this just the usual unwanted attention that too often happened when walking with the young, attractive and shapely Sofia? It is always so difficult to decide and make sense of the confusion that reared back in Jo's mind unbidden.

Jo and Sofia finished their shopping and walked in the opposite direction along Harrison Road. A police patrol car passed them and pulled off into a cubbyhole tucked away among the oak trees. Jo could see the marked car in the distance with its nose poking out from the traffic stop, hidden to capture unsuspecting speedsters.

As they approached the patrol car, it pulled out quickly and raced past them. Jo, avoiding the gaze of the cop, asked Sofia to have a good look at him, "Is his head round or square?"

"Round."

"Good. That's Decker not Borrelia. 'Squarehead' is the really evil one, the one that whacked my legs."

"Scary, Mom." Sofia's big brown eyes widened.

"I know you don't know what to make of all this." Jo didn't want Sofia to fret over Mom's misadventures.

"Don't worry about me Mom, I'll be back at

the show with Armand. *I worry about you!* I don't really understand what happened to you."

"Sometimes Sofia, I'm not too sure either."

Sofia flew back to Europe the following week, much to Jo's relief. From the handsome and beautiful people that frequented the town during the winter and spring, summer brought an influx of odds and sods. Surly, scruffy looking sorts.

As Jo walked to her mailbox one afternoon, a 1990 Ford sedan cruised the circular dead end road at Willow Dean. It was unusual to have any traffic in their private enclave and certainly not the menacing bunch of four scruffy guys that slowed and stared. Jo shirked from their sinister demeanor and toothless grins. The ugliest one with a twisted face caught her eye. He gave a friendly nod as if to socially disarm the gang of four. A bunch of distinctly criminal characters, Jo thought. Not the common variety garden boys who mowed the lawns and clipped the hedges.

People scared Jo, especially anyone who seemed out of place. People who were out of character, not who they were supposed to be. For a while, Jo was suspect of mostly everyone. She yelled at one group of leaf blowers to get the hell off her property, much to Jeremy's embarrassment.

During the winter, Jeremy told her as they lay in bed, "Honey, sometimes not everything you think is true. Perhaps much of what happened, your concerns were valid. 75% may not be real, but 25% is very real. Those FBI guys, they were just doing their jobs. Why you went off on that guy. And

143

Jeremy frowned as if about to cry.

Jo understood. She sadly recognized her paranoid behavior. "But still, that day, I can't help feeling that somehow, *something else* was going to happen that afternoon, with that garbage truck. And somehow, I thwarted what was going to happen by calling the police."

"Yes, I wonder too. What else was planned that didn't happen?" Jeremy mused.

"Something else much worse. Perhaps I would have disappeared? Dumped with the trash? And the cops were nearby. It only took them *one minute* to get here. What were they waiting for? It took the other cop car ages to get here."

"It did? Then why?" Jeremy perked up and paused awhile, thinking. "But things will work out. You'll be fine. We'll be fine. I don't want you worrying. Just concentrate on getting better."

In the days before "What Happened to Mom", as it euphemistically became known between father and daughter, Jeremy told Jo something oddly revealing. He said he told others, "I've known this woman for over twenty years and I've never seen her so scared. I know she says things that are sometimes off the wall. Sure, she's eccentric…and I'm eccentric too. But I know there is something very real happening and that Allbio is very likely to be behind it. They have harassed her…and there is something she knows they want to keep hidden." But who Jeremy told remained a mystery to Jo. *So what am I right about and what am I wrong about?* Jo dwelled on the question.

144

But it was time to move on with life, get a new job, and put everything behind her. Accept the fact that much would go unexplained, unresolved. And "What Happened to Mom" would fade into the past as just one of Jo's many eccentricities.

Chapter 21 Mired in Muck

CONTRACTED FOR THE JOB, their shovels ready, the dump trucks unloaded the charcoal grey biosolid "fertilizer" all over the state. From reclaimed gravel pits to meadows and grasslands in the state parks, to private lawns and gardens and public recreational playing fields. At last they were dispersing the huge mountains of literal crap, the sewage sludge that piled up at the West Bay wastewater treatment plant. Getting rid of it had been such a headache for the string of managers who job hopped from one sewage facility to the next. No one wanted to be buried in the mounds of shit that accumulated over time. Over 30,000 tons a year. What to do with the "biosolids" needed the genius of a creative marketing and repackaging plan. As the marketing agent said "We need to coin a new term, let's call it SuperStuff, something less turd-like sounding than 'biosolids'."

Shovel in hand, rakes lying idle, a short, dark-skinned, muscular man looked out over the two dozen or so four foot high hills that dotted the landscape. "So *now* what do we do with the rest of this stuff?"

The two open meadows, once farmland, now belonged to the state park wildlife refuges. The contracted day laborers were tasked with covering the ground in a thick layer of the newly minted "SuperStuff". It was the cheapest fertilizer money could buy. Claimed to be environmentally friendly, it would transform the landscape into luxuriant

146

green. Touted to reclaim barren land and gravel banks into "Wonderful grasslands where birds and flowers thrive and verdant fields for sporting and recreational use."

It was late Friday afternoon. The work crew boss knew the guys had worked hard at spreading around the fertilizer, combing it through to mix with the soil. He figured they might be sent back to finish the job but he didn't want the piles of the dark thick powder blowing around indiscriminately.

"Gather up some dried branches and twigs." The crew boss pointed to the piles along the perimeter that had been raked to clear the open fields "Cover the fertilizer hills with the dried branches. Maybe we'll be back here next week."

But the next week, more "SuperStuff" fertilizer needed dumping and spreading. The parks and recreation fields would be greened up after a long hot summer. Readied for the start of the school year when the baseball fields of summer are transformed into the football and soccer pitches of the fall sports season.

"I've never seen this soccer pitch looking greener! Wow they really are investing in our community. What a great playing field for the kids." One proud dad congenially proclaimed to the other parents. "In Ireland we would call it a water meadow," he said with a thick Irish brogue.

Another voice commented, "It is a bit close to the river, and there is some standing water on the west end of the field from the recent floods, so the playing field has been shifted east." Heads turned

147

towards the handsome man with his perfectly groomed wavy brown hair. People had just begun to recognize the popular senator who was sitting amongst the spectators. Moments later his 8 year old niece, one of the taller girls with enviable ball skills, scored a goal. The senator whooped a gleeful "Hoorah!" while other chimed in to enjoy the moment.

A sign greeted the arriving parents and spectators. "Remember, soccer is for the kids!" Just in case any of them forgot in the excitement of the game. Some stood watching while others sat in deck chairs. The weather was unseasonably wet and warm; the soil soaked from a week of flooding rains.

The kid's soccer league, a mix of five to nine year olds, brought in primary school kids from the neighboring communities. For today's statewide tournament, a few busloads arrived from all parts of the tiny state. A round robin of short games, girl's teams on the east side of the pitch, boys on the west side, meant that all the kids could play. The philosophy was that everybody played, only some played harder than others. On the west end of the field were miniature machines set in perpetual motion, the littlest of the soccer league, the kindergarten boys. The five years olds ran themselves to breathless exhaustion. They never knew when to stop and they loved every moment chasing that ball.

At the end of the day, the kids would go home sweaty, puffing, and near collapse. But on this particularly damp and balmy day, their soccer shoes and cleats sported a thick black sludgy muck, their socks were hardly visible and their colorful uniforms were splattered like Jackson Pollock originals.

Chapter 22 Poor Little Dogies

Chimera – an ancient mythological character conveying all the rage and madness of our time

LAYING IN BED on a Saturday morning after two nights of mental contortions, Jo's thoughts morphed to images of a writhing child, a seven year old girl. At first demonically un-childlike, she spewed a string of verbal expletives at the nurses and doctors. Then delirium, seizures, coma and an encephalitic, fevered death ensued.

"I haven't slept since we've gotten home from Tucson." Jo exhaled in one breath.

"Your usual worries, I suppose it's the mice in the attic?" Jeremy chided, not masking his sarcasm. He wondered if the deer mice in the attic had finally succumbed to the continuous dosing of green and red poison pellets.

Not reacting to the dig, Jo continued, "Yes, them too, I heard them. But my head, it's been churning over those sick kids... the closing of the schools. You must have read the articles in the local news. What is really strange is the cause of the encephalitis...... not viral, but bacterial, *Mycoplasma pneumonia.* The incidence is *way too high*.....this just *doesn't* happen. Three kids in a neighborhood school with encephalitis, a couple in nearby schools with suspected meningitis and a kid with Stevens Johnson Syndrome."

"What the hell is that?" Jeremy's face

150

punctuated his question.

"Exotic neurologic disease. Very Severe. And today at the hospital I heard about a possible *second* case of the same exotic disease. A horrid rash, inflamed mucous linings. Often deadly. It just *doesn't* happen, and now this clustered outbreak? Not to mention the near epidemic of walking pneumonia. And it is all *mycoplasma*."

"So, what about it? What are you getting at?" said Jeremy

"I remember when I first heard about *mycoplasma*. I was at Gensar biotech, my first time in the development lab. There were a number of small bioreactors. It reminded me of a beer brewery, you called it a dairy at the Allbio tour.... all the vats. The lab also had small plastic tubs full of nutrients with spinners that were constantly stirring. Gensar was growing bioengineered cells, the CHO's." Jo explained.

"CHOs? And your point is?" Jeremy cocked his head, still wondering where the conversation was going.

"You know, CHOs. Chinese Hamster Ovary cells. Mike took me around the lab. We gowned up in white bunny suits, he wore a hair net on his beard. He told me, "*Mycoplasma*, you don't want them to get into your bioreactor. You have to destroy the whole batch of cells!' And then I remembered other things. Right before everything weird happened at Allbio."

"So, what do you remember? What is it you know *now* that you didn't know *then*?" Jeremy prodded Jo to say more.

151

"Batch failures, a bunch of them. When Allbio began producing Quelify in those huge bioreactors, the CHO cell cultures became contaminated. Only the scale of Allbio's bioreactors is thousands of times larger than Gensar's tiny vats." Jo continued speculating. "Allbio was dumping failed batches of cells and drugs. *Huge* amounts! Quite a few contaminated batches, especially when they first started up those gigantic bioreactors. They lost enormous quantities that were contaminated with *mycoplasma*. At the last production meeting I went to, one of the scientists on her power-point slides said *mycoplasma* was the problem. And someone had installed the wrong filters to keep them out."

"And what do they do with the failed batches of CHOs? All the tanks full of contaminated CHOs?"

"Down the drain with those cute, coolie-hat CHOs. They dumped everything down the drain. We were told 'They are just dead cells'."

"So they dump everything down the drain, all the debris left after they make the drug, including the contaminated cultures. The CHOs, the bacteria – the *mycoplasma*?" Jeremy wanted to understand.

"Yes. And the culture media, full of nutrients, amino acids, nitrogen, phosphorous, everything needed to keep those recombinant CHO cells growing. Down the drain and into the sewers. Nutrient 'soup' along with the engineered DNA of the gene that makes the drug. Quelify suppresses immunity in people with overactive immune systems. This man-made immunity suppressing gene churns out a chemical that wreaks havoc with human immunity. It can destroy your ability to fight disease. It can make people weak, especially children."

"Yes, I understand, the CHOs with specialized DNA crank out the drug, Qelify." Jeremy remembered the tour of the new Allbio manufacturing facility before it was sterilized, before they started up production. Jo and Jeremy had oohed and awed over the enormous bioreactors on Allbio family day.

"Remember when we had dinner at Aunty Mary's, when they were just building the sewers? Everyone laughed when I joked about Allbio dumping dead CHO cells, when I described them as little beasts with Chinese coolie hats. Chinese hamster cells with human genes--half hamster – half human."

"Yes, you went on about them using the Chinese for cheap labor!" Jeremy groaned. "But remember, Aunty and your cousins were happy to be getting sewers, they wanted to get off their septic tanks and get connected. They didn't *care* what Allbio was dumping down their drains and into their sewers."

"But I didn't fully understand then. The chimeras." Jo pondered.

"Yes." Jeremy is seeing the light, "A chimera, a mythological character, multi-headed mix of beasts. Head of a goat, body of a lion, and the tail of a serpent. I remember the bronze chimera statue from our holiday in Tuscany. But here we

153

have a mix of human and hamster?'"

"Yes, but let's backtrack. At first, I thought it was all about the water. That the water was dirty, contaminated. Then I thought it was about the bay, when the million fish died -- the menhaden, the "pogies". I thought it was all about the pogies." Jo reflected.

"Pogies?" I like the word 'pogy'." Fishing was one of Jeremy's many passions. "Yes, I remember hearing about the fish kill at a meeting of the salt water anglers. One day in August the menhaden were seen gulping for air at the surface of the water. Within a day, they all died and floated to the surface. A mile and a half stretch of dead pogies. It really fouled Narragansett Bay. The locals were outraged!"

"Maybe the fish died because of nutrient overloading? Maybe Allbio's biologic waste made its way into the bay? And in August, the biologic soup simmered in the bay. Hot days, elevated water temperatures, and run off from heavy rains; there was a whole mishmash of causes. Put them all together and you are left with a bay with no oxygen...dead zones. The pogies suffocated. And the nutrients, especially nitrogen, come from many sources—storm runoff, sewers, pollution."

"But what about all the nutrient media being dumped by Allbio? Was that ever questioned as a possible cause?" Jeremy was incredulous. "You have to wonder."

"Worse still is what *else* they were dumping! Those dead CHOs with the engineered Allbio DNA, the foreign genes that are used to make their drug, Quelify. We know that Quelify suppresses immunity. Maybe that has something to do with the kids getting sick? The newspaper said that the *mycoplasma* bacteria changed into something more dangerous, it somehow mutated and became more virulent. Maybe that's why the mycoplasma now caused diseases, like encephalitis? Think about it. Maybe those humanized-hamster genes invaded the *mycoplasma*?" Jo questioned her conclusion.

"A human-hamster-mycoplasma bacteria? Another chimera? But that is *an impossibility in nature!*" Jeremy excitedly underscored.

"Yes, and the chimera now has a weapon against immunity. It not only causes disease, but also dampens the children's defense against disease. It packs a double punch...a double whammy. The children's immunity is immature, undeveloped; children are vulnerable. These nasty infections overwhelmed the children's defense against disease." Jo riled. "So *now* Allbio has gone from killing little pogies with their 'nutrient soup' to murdering children with 'genetic stew'!"

Jeremy sighed. "Poor little pogies."

"Poor little dogies." Jo sighed too.

"But Jo, you have to tell someone!" Jeremy implored. "Who are you going to tell?"

Part 2 Consequences

Chapter 23   Mutant Strain for Little Dogies

DELIRIUM AND SEIZURES, coupled with outbursts of vile curses from a small child; it was a desperate last act, an uncontrolled cry for help. A spewing forth of vindictive expletives directed against the micro-beast. The foreign invader overwhelmed her young body, took control of her brain and brought on the unbearable pain of a fevered, throbbing head. The young girl mercifully died.

Distracted by the holidays, few people dwelled on the mysterious malady. But then another of the little girl's classmates fell deathly ill. More children living nearby contracted severe neurologic diseases along with an unusually high number of kids with walking pneumonia, so a pattern began to emerge. The health officials and media sounded the alarm. Parents began to panic and asked, "Why is this happening?" There were just too many very sick kids around here.

The unexplained cluster of encephalitic disease infecting the brain defied statistical probability. Jo read in the local newspaper. *Only 0.1% of all cases of walking pneumonia ever progresses this far, where the infection attacks the brain.* It was suspected that the outbreak was caused by a very lethal, virulent strain that had morphed from normally harmless bacteria. It had mutated into an extremely deadly form of *mycoplasma pneumonia.*

159

Pent up with emotion, Jo paced the office of her boss, pediatric surgeon Dr Carl Thomas. Anxious and flustered, Jo blurted out, "I need...I need to ask you something." She stood with her back to him, afraid to show her worried, anxious eyes.

Dr Thomas paused and looked up from the medical chart for his next surgery.

"Yes?" He seemed surprised with Jo's uncharacteristic outburst.

Hesitantly, Jo asked "Do you have much sepsis in recent patients?" Sepsis was medical speak for infection.

Dr Thomas, taken aback, began to anger from what he sensed was as an accusation. He did not respond.

Jo braced herself as she realized the reason for his defensive response. She straightened her shoulders to muster up the courage to ask again. "Swollen joints, like the kid you admitted yesterday?"

The doctor felt confused and surprised at what appeared at first to be a confrontation, Jo was leading the conversation in a different direction. "Why are you asking this?" His glaring stare searched for an answer.

Trying to mollify his anger, Jo got directly to the point. "It's the children, the *mycoplasma pneumonia* and encephalitis in the schools. It should *not* have happened."

Jo paused to think. "Also, joint infections like your patient with joint sepsis, it is not about things that you did."

160

Dr Thomas pensively mulled over what he heard. "I haven't been following the encephalitis that closely." He dismissed any connection with his patient and retorted sharply, still not completely mollified, "I appreciate your concern for my patient. He does not have what you might think."

Jo, concerned that she still wasn't getting her message across, digressed to the past. She looked intently at him to gauge his reaction. Trying to make her story clearer, Jo went on. "Just over two years ago, when I was working at Allbio, things happened, I was involved in a water investigation. In the quality labs, water samples tested positive for contaminants."

"Yes and...?" Jo noticed Dr Thomas' shoulders drop, his blue grey eyes softened, his initial anger subsiding.

"And then people from Allbio started disappearing...they were fired." Jo tried to be concise as she explained. "First, the guy heading up the water contamination investigation was fired. That was followed by two of the microbiologists who were *also* involved with the water investigation. They were fired."

Now following along closely, Dr Thomas picked up on the story line, he added to the story, "Things like this happen. Yes, the company *would* go after the microbiologists."

Jo's voice began to break, nearly tearful but holding back, she whimpered. "And then they went after me". Jo paused as Dr Thomas nodded, affirming he understood the implications. "And I got hurt." Jo's voice faded and broke, but she

161

carried on, "And then another woman was fired, a PhD who investigated the cause of the cell culture failures. Contaminants got in. *Mycoplasma* are so small, just 0.2 millimicrons; they can slip through the tiniest pores. The filters weren't right. The pores were too large, something like 0.5 or 0.6 millimicrons."

Dr Thomas kept nodding, encouraging Jo to go on.

"It's hard to keep the mycoplasma out, these bacteria can easily contaminate the cell cultures batches. Then everything got dumped into the sewage system. The cells that were part of the dumping were Chinese hamster ovary cells. They have a gene construct. They're bioengineered. Allbio inserted a patented gene for anti tnf alpha to make their blockbuster drug." Dr Thomas had written articles on these human chemicals called cytokines, including anti tnf alpha. He knew that they dampen immunity, and that they weaken the body's defense against disease. Those "Chinese coolie workers" carry the gene to make the drug Quelify.

Dr Thomas stared quietly thinking. His head drew closer. "Yes, but how does the gene get out from the sewers?" Dr Thomas wanted to follow its path.

Taking a breath, Jo exhaled slowly, thinking how the new sewers from Allbio ran parallel to the Tuxet River. Putting the pieces together, she surmised, "When it rains, the sewers are breached, and the river....it overflows?" At this point Jo wasn't entirely sure how the immunity destroying

162

gene could have spread through the neighboring communities.

Dr Thomas sat thinking for a while considering Jo's rationale.

Jo, second guessing herself said, "You must think I'm totally off the wall".

"No, these things happen. What else do you know?" Dr Thomas coaxed Jo to tell more.

Jo pulled out a roughly annotated map showing him the cases, the schools, the sewers, the river, the source, Allbio. It all seemed to make sense.

"I wrote a letter to the state health department director, Dr James Morgenthal. He sent the letter on to the CDC to help with their investigation." Still worried about her credibility, Jo tried to punctuate the relevance and impact of what had occurred. "This is the *only* state in the country where this disease outbreak has happened. And the likelihood of a cluster of severe neurologic diseases like encephalitis is very uncommon. Rarely do you have more than one in a thousand that have to be hospitalized. Clusters of kids with encephalitis just don't happen, especially when the infections were in a small area within a group of neighboring schools."

The doctor's pager rang for a second time. "I have a surgery starting." Quickly moving towards the door, he turned back and said, "I won't tell anyone."

Jo returned to her desk and within a couple minutes the phone rang. "This is Dr Thomas. Jo, I left my chart in the office next to the telephone.

Would you get it and bring it to me? I'm in the surgeon's break room". Jo grabbed the patient record and walked as quickly as she could.

Breathless and winded, Jo handed him the chart. "Is this everything?"

"Yes, great." Dr Thomas asked with a tinge of worry, "Are you alright?"

Jo smiled in relief and with a teasing taunt. "Yes. *Are you?*"

Chapter 24 Miasma Mona

WITH MURKY THOUGHTS, Jo arrived home from work on a cold, cloudy day in January. How? Why? Questions needed answers. Hypotheses needed examining.

To clear her head, Jo needed to categorize and sort what she knew. So to shed some light on what transpired, Jo began to write. To chronicle. To emote. To put everything in its place. To compartmentalize. To speculate on what had happened and what was to come. To think about everything and file it away. And later, take it off the shelf and dust it off. To re-think it. Mull it, stew it. Cook it down to a thick and condensed genetic soup.

But then the telephone rang.

"Jo, my name is Mona Sicaro, your Aunt Mary gave me your number." The rapid voice fired on the other end of the line.

"Mona, of course, Aunty has told me all about you. You're the nurse who works with the kids at North County Hospital."

"Jo, can we meet somewhere to talk? How about a drink at Angelino's Bar and Grill in Oceanside? I'm here now if you can get away?"

"Sure, why not. My husband is out playing tennis so I can be there soon."

Angelino's Bar was in North County in the town of Weston-by-the Sea. It had a mixed clientele of blue collar workers and small business owners from the community. Jo knew Mona when she saw her wearing blue scrubs and a multicolored smock printed with the Little Mermaid and Jo's favorite animated red crab, Sebastian. *Just pucker your lips.* Jo mentally grinned as she shook Mona's hand, cold and damp from her scotch on the rocks.

Jo ordered the 'Gansett, a local beer, and another scotch for Mona, thirty something and attractive on a good day. Today was not a good day. Mona looked sleep-deprived. Grey half-circles below her eyes made her look as though she had been sucker punched.

Mona fidgeted with the cardboard coaster. "It's the kids. You know I work with the kids?"

Jo nodded a slow yes, locking in on Mona's dark-ringed eyes.

"The little girl who died from encephalitis that was in the local paper, I was with her the night after she was admitted."

"Yes, I've been following the mycoplasma outbreak closely. I wrote to the state health department about my concerns."

"What I saw that evening scared me to death. I still don't know what to make of it. I've seen plenty of sick kids but what I saw and heard that night just sucked the life out of me." Mona trailed off with a sigh. "I need another drink."

· "Mona, look, I'm interested. I want to know everything you can tell me."

Mona recharged with the next dose of Jack Daniels. "The resident on-call from infectious disease was checking the little girl's IV. She had

166

seizures during the day but she slept a little earlier that evening. Her fever was still spiking and she was now awake. She sat straight up in the bed and began to scream. "Fuck! Fuck! Fuck!" Help me, Help me!" Her face was absolutely dead-pan, as though she had no emotion behind the screams. Her face registered blank, expressionless. You would have thought she was angry and that would show in her face, but it was as if she was unaware of what she was saying. Totally disconnected, speech and emotion." Mona's dark eyes widened and her thick eyebrows arched.

"Please go on." Jo's forehead furrowed with concern and empathy for Mona.

Mona paused to gulp down the scotch and melting ice. "When the resident stepped in closer to the bed, the little girl lunged at him. She thrust her arms out, tried to grab at the resident's throat but he stepped back. I came in closer to help. She pinched my forearm and her mouth bit down hard on my open hand. I pulled it away before she could sink her teeth in and leave a mark. But what happened next was even *more* bizarre." Mona paused and took a deep breath. "She started chewing on the mattress and bedding, like she wanted to *eat* them. It wasn't long before she had another seizure and went into convulsions. The resident added an anti-convulsive to the IV and after a few minutes, she settled down."

Jo listened intently and nodded, encouraging Mona to go on.

"The next morning, I was on my own when the little girl, Brianna, woke up. She threw up, mostly clear liquid."

"Well at least she wasn't spewing up green pea soup!" Jo said, trying to break the tension. "You know, like in the movie 'The Exorcist'?"

Mona smiled weakly at Jo's attempt at humor. "Nor did she turn her head around a full 360 degrees." Mona lost her smile. "The poor thing *could not turn her neck at all*."

"Sorry. I know it must have been harrowing for you." Jo gasped then sighed, shaking her head in dismay. "How very sad for that poor child."

Mona carried on. "The next day, after I left, Brianna shit the bed. The morning shift nurse found her writhing, wiggling in it. Her mouth was smeared in brown. She tried to eat her own feces!" Mona stared at Jo, drained of emotion. She gulped down her third scotch.

Jo took a long swig on her beer, slowly shaking her head. Jo then shifted the conversation to another child; the boy was a classmate of the girl, who had a similar disease. Jo and Mona pieced together what they knew. That the doctors initially thought it was meningitis, but the young boy was later diagnosed with Stevens-Johnson Syndrome (SJS). SJS began with flu-like symptoms, a sore-throat, fever and itchy eyes. The young boy's skin and mucous linings, especially his mouth, nose, and eyes were painfully inflamed painfully and a burning reddish-purple rash spread like wildfire. It blistered within hours. The boy's tongue and face swelled. SJS can often have multiple causes but the boy's bloods tests and throat cultures identified *mycoplasma pneumonia*.

"Yes, he was admitted a few days before the little girl died. The children's parents consoled one another and exchanged updates on their children's maladies. Neither family thought it just an unusual coincidence. The community was well aware that something strange was happening. *These are not the typical childhood ailments!* And there's another two, maybe three suspected cases of severe neurological illnesses. Maybe meningitis or encephalitis. One in a nearby middle school. Nothing viral but all bacterial infections, most likely caused by *mycoplasma*."

"Mona, just yesterday I heard of another suspected *mycoplasma* case of SJS just over the state border. A nine year old girl was brought to Bay State Hospital; she's in intensive care. Girls with SJS get painfully inflamed vaginas!" Jo squeezed her legs together in empathic pain, imagining the searing burning, worse than any vaginal infection she had ever been cursed with. "So what is the likelihood of *that*?"

"About one in a million. It just doesn't happen. No *wonder* the CDC has jumped in to investigate."

"Yes, this is a highly unusual cluster of diseases, and the mycoplasma seems to be the common microbe, but it has somehow changed into a vicious superbug. It's the *only place in the country that this has happened, so it must be a local source.* Mona, I looked at the distribution, plotted out the cases and schools on a map. I included the schools with the ridiculously high number of kids with walking pneumonia. There seems to be a pattern.

169

Let's just hope the CDC's investigation sheds some light on the source. Whatever it is, the kids must have something in common to pick up the infection, the places they visited, or where they played sports in the fall. Think about it Mona, the Health Department told the press that the mycoplasma 'morphed'. It changed. But where did the kids pick up this superbug? Was it at school? Was it at the mall? Was it where they played?"

Mona reflected pensively, "There are other kids coming in. Some through the ER, with other syndromes like painful swollen joints. They're tested for Lyme disease, juvenile rheumatoid arthritis. But nothing is conclusive. Some older kids tested positive for *mycoplasma pneumonia* in their joints. These kids played a lot of sports."

"So I wonder if this is where these kids picked it up. Where did they play?"

Mona just shook her head. She did not know.

Chapter 25 The Purgative

AS THE WINTER DAYS passed, more unexplained syndromes were identified in kids, some were terminal. The children showed obscure symptoms like erythromatoses, blackened bloody rashes, inflamed mucosal mouths and burning immature vaginas. Delirious writhing and pain. Desperate shouts of 'fuck' and 'shit' as though a diabolic presence had taken possession, a demonic psychological disturbance. Pneumonia progressed into systemic weakness, septic joints migrating from knee to ankle, left to right, arthritic swellings, suppurating skins and purulent pustules. Entire schools were infected with noro-virus like bellyaches, vomiting, rapid breathing and gasping for air. Some with skin a purpureus purple. There were too many uncommon manifestations of extra pulmonary symptoms. Not just colds and coughs confined to the lungs.

Jo was haunted. She worried obsessively. She had to know why, where, and who was responsible. It was not an act of nature. How many more will die as the rain and flooding continue and the weather warms and the river overflows. *Did the river carry the untreated sewage, the immune suppressing DNA sludge from Allbio, in the water? Did this chimera filled sludge get into the soil and sucked into the small mammalian lungs and guts? Did the little children who live in the wetlands, play games in the water meadows and fields awash with... chimera?*

The chimera, a stealthy invader, a microbe now made more deadly, more virulent, more pathogenic by virtue of the gene gone wild, with DNA of the immunity suppressor gene. The human-made DNA construct that disarms, it turns a child into a mini-bioreactor to ferment like the small scale bioreactors found in biopharm factories that create the destroyer of immunity. It weakens immunity. It quells immunity. The created DNA enhanced *mycoplasma* ravages small bodies. It breaks down the defense against disease. The Gene Genie is truly out of the bottle.

Jo reread the letter, a reply from the health department head, Dr James Morgenthal, saying that "Mycoplasma is everywhere." Yes, they are ubiquitous. You can't say where something so common has come from. *Mycoplasma is found everywhere.*

True, Jo thought. And then she thought again. *Unless, of course, it is tagged with a genetic marker that clearly shows its man-made origin.* And in this case a newly emergent superbug, a chimera. A mutant *mycoplasma* with a hitch-hiking gene that has latched on and gone for a wild ride. *Who says it cannot be used as evidence?*

Jo muttered to herself, "Those fucks at Allbio have dumped this gene all over the state with the sale and distribution of the SuperStuff sludge from the sewage plants. SuperStuff on the playing fields, concentrated, not some weak diluted immune suppressing DNA from over-flowing rivers! The local paper had recently run an article on how good looking the playing fields and playgrounds were when SuperStuff was applied. Unknowingly they spread the immunity destroying gene-infected mycoplasma creating a chimera, the Gene-Genie."

David Bowie's song is now going through Jo's head "Gene-Genie, Let yourself go!"

Jo read. She wrote. She obsessed some more. She read about the risk of bioengineered bioluminescent bunnies and glow-in-the-dark fish escaping into the wild, but they paled in comparison. Allbio dumped their genetic material. Disposed of the deleterious gene and created an immunity suppressing bacteria, a super-bug. The sewage plants who created SuperStuff and sold it didn't know that genetic material from Allbio represented any threat.

Jo researched about the risks of genes from genetically altered corn turning up in unexpected places. Altered genes can spread around. DNA flows freely in the world. Confinement of the engineered DNA, the genes, is the Achilles heel of biotech. Yet the biopharm industry plays down the risks. Any attempts to safely confine harmful genes would just cost more than the industry was willing to pay. So, just as the oil companies cut costs on safety, so did biotech. And they did so with the dismissive mantra "They are only dead cells. No harm done."

At the end of March, Jeremy took Jo on a much needed purging holiday. A cathartic purgative. A purifying soak in the mineral baths, the geothermal silica laden waters of Iceland. Jo slathered the white kaolin mineral mud pack on her

173

face, careful to avoid her eyes. This mud is therapeutic but is all mud therapeutic? Ghost-like bathers drifting by grinned at the ghouls they had all become.

Jo immersed herself, luxuriating in the feel of silky slime-like sand. It oozed between her toes. A strong smell of sulfur wafted by.

Jo chuckled in jest. "Earth flatulence. It's expelling odors of rotten eggs!"

Jo inspected the crystalline, icy needles growing in Jeremy's buzz-cut hair.

Jeremy told Jo that her facial hairs and mustache "sport the same ice-fuzz".

"I want to know how it will all end," Jo said to Jeremy. Jeremy waded into the mist avoiding her request, trying to get away. Jo pushed through the water, parting it with the tips of her fingers. "Jeremy, how it will all end?"

"And where did that come from?"

"You know, Jeremy, *you know*." Although Jo didn't know for sure *what* Jeremy knew, she thought for sure he *must* know things he could not tell her. She will talk too much. She will worry too much. She will become unnerved...again. If she knows all he knows, maybe someone will try to hurt her. It was just too dangerous until things conclude.

Jeremy again ignored her request, wading past her through the natural hot tub.

Jo persisted, "I don't need to know the precise day---just in general". Is it imminent? Is everything going to plan?"

"It is imminent in cosmic time." Jeremy evaded the question.

"So when?" Jo asked then answered for Jeremy. "When everything is in its place. I understand but it is difficult to be patient."

Chapter 26   Judging Moscow Easter Eggs

IT WAS EASTER Sunday, the big event at the Blair's arrived, the egg competition. Armand was on the telephone talking with his family in Moscow, speaking a mix of Russian and Armenian with his brother and parents while Jo and her daughter Sofia chattered.

"When Dr Thomas called on my cell phone, he had just finished a surgery. He's on emergency call this weekend. His wife and kids are in New York." Jo told Sofia.

Sofia inspected the riotous array of colorful painted eggs. "He knows about the egg contest, doesn't he?"

"Yes, he knows he agreed to be the judge. He'll probably shake hands with you. He likes to shake hands." Jo's attention diverted to the meal cooking in the oven. "I got the recipe for the Yorkshire pudding from grandma, this morning." Jeremy called weekly to check up on his mum and dad in England and Jo had asked her mother-in-law for the recipe.

Armand hung up the telephone. His eyes caught sight of two fruit bowls, one with apples, the other with a banana and two oranges. Armand gasped and widened his eyes at the intentionally phallic display in bowl number two. Aghast at his mother-in-law's naughty sense of humor, shocked and embarrassed, he laughed. "Don't you remember Jo I am not friendly with the fruit," an idiosyncratic phrase which brought all the gathering into fits of laughter.

Jo picked up the banana and waved it around smirking "So what's so funny?" Sofia glanced at her mother disapprovingly. She then returned to inspecting the many multicolored hand-painted eggs.

Jo warned grinning, "Well I *did* have to *censor* some of the eggs. I camouflaged a few."

A car pulled up in front of the condo, Jo recognized Dr Thomas's hybrid van, "Oh, he's here." She quickly darted out the door to greet him. He came bearing an assortment of Easter candies, wine and champagne.

Jeremy had escaped to his computer room while Jo, Sofia, and Armand were in the kitchen. Jo brought Dr Thomas through the French doors to the office. Introductions were in order. A quick "Jeremy" met with an efficient "Carl". Jeremy followed them to the kitchen where Carl unloaded the gifts while exchanging greetings with Sofia and Armand.

Sofia and Jo collected the gifts. "Yum, Cadbury eggs, my favorite." Sofia, the chocoholic, purred like a demure kitten.

"And champagne, for all your work on the publications," Said Carl to Jo.

Carl's eyes scanned the kitchen table, noting the egg baskets and egg contestants on display. His grey-blue eyes poured over the egg-headed soccer team. Each egg sat in cardboard-ringed shirt collar. Their paper arms reached out for a figment of a soccer ball.

177

Jeremy commented, "There are eleven players on a soccer team."

Carl picked up a red player, number 22. "This red one is my favorite," he paused as Sofia handed him a list of hand-scrawled award groupings. "In the funny category."

Armand, an avid fan of international soccer, became animated, "Do you watch soccer?"

Dr Thomas focused his life on traumatic injuries in children. He had little time for sports. "Not much, but this red player looks like he has been bandaged up after hurting himself in the game."

"I hope they played on soft grass. When I played in Africa, Jeremy added, we dreaded falling over and getting infected by bacteria from the raw sewage and mud they used to irrigate the fields."

"Jeremy, I remember your leg when you got hurt in Africa. It took weeks to clear up. I guess all mud is not therapeutic like the stuff in Iceland." Jo added.

Sofia, perusing her mother's egg entries, picked up one that looked hieroglyphic with figurines and symbols. With punctuated shock Sofia reprimanded, "Mom, those are boobs!" On further inspection Sofia's jaw dropped. "And I can see where you scratched out the other thing, and I hate to say what *this* looks like".

Jo replied with a mischievous smirk, "Oh that is the 'biology' egg".

Unable to contain his curiosity, Carl took the egg from Sofia, and colluded. "Well, that is a paramecium," Turning the egg, "And that looks like an amoeba." He referred to a double-glob figure.

"And it is dividing!" Jo pointed to the two blobs with two circular nuclei. Everyone's attention was now drawn to the suggestive egg as it was passed around.

Carl's comment became more cryptic, "Jo often sees things differently than others."

Jeremy nodded in agreement, looking at Jo with pride and love. Armand and Sofia nodded at each other in agreement, all for different reasons.

Carl picked up one last egg, a woman's face with sculpted wavy brown and yellow hair, an eccentric eye and lips seductively puckered into a kiss. "This is the 'fantasy' egg'." Showing the egg to Sofia, who in turn inspected it.

Sofia looked up at Jo in recognition. "Mom, this is you!"

Jo exclaimed in triumph, never shy of letting others know her victory, "So the winner is me! And the Armenian wine is mine! It's very sweet. We will have it for dessert." Gesturing with the bottle as if toasting, "*Nazdarovia*, that is Russian, Carl, not Armenian. Armand's Armenian parents live in Moscow. I think I told you that Jeremy and I were married in Moscow. But we were also married in Vegas."

Carl asked Jo, "And which wedding do you celebrate?"

"Moscow, although it was not a legal wedding, just a church ceremony. Oh, let me show you the pictures!" And Jo darted out to return with a navy blue album full of oversized photographs.

"Watch out! Now she will bore you with the

photos." Jeremy wryly warned Carl.

Jo opened the bulky album on the table, ordered Carl to take a seat, and opened the album to the first page. Carl flipped through. Stopping on the marriage certificate with Arabic lettering, "Johany Aa? Hey, they've written your name phonetically."

In the photos, a high ranking priest clad in green and gold brocade robes resided over the ceremony as the apprehensive faces of the young couple looked on.

Carl is looking at the last photo from Vegas in the wedding album. Jeremy and a very pregnant Jo stood as if lined up at a motor vehicle counter. Behind the counter, wearing a shoe-string tie, was a white-haired Justice of the Peace in downtown Las Vegas, Nevada.

"Jeremy, you aren't smiling in any of the photos." Carl repeated as a taunt, "Why aren't you smiling Jeremy?"

Jo, attuned to the goading, answered for him, "He was marrying *me*. He was *scared*!"

"She only works for me and I admit she can be very persistent and has opinions on everything, as I discovered when we wrote research papers together. Certainly I can see why Jeremy was standing there frozen like a deer in the headlights."

"Don't reinforce his 'poor thing' act, Carl. Jeremy is crafty like a fox and easily gets his way. He made sure I married him, as you can tell from that last photo in Vegas."

Jeremy smiled softly.

Chapter 27 Of Pigs and Men

IN THE SPRING and summer weeks to come, there were more conversations among pediatricians and infectious disease doctors centered on the spate of unusual illnesses. More mysterious maladies were identified that mimicked unusual syndromes. Most were children and young teenagers. A few were adults or very young toddlers. Some common symptoms were swollen, painful joints, especially large balloon-like knees and ankles. The pain and swelling migrated in many from one joint to the next.

A young teenage boy with fevers, delirium, nights sweats, and a blown-up swollen knee. His right knee this time but three weeks ago it was a swollen left knee.

A two year old toddler with unusual septic arthritis in the joints. Could it be juvenile rheumatoid arthritis? Maybe Lyme disease? No. Neither. But what?

An 11 year old girl with a chronic swollen ankle. A sample of joint fluid was drawn by the doctor. Nothing grew out initially but later they found *mycoplasma pneumonia.* A good antibiotic and all would hopefully be well in a few weeks time.

The pediatrician's offices were full of kids. More syndromes, complaints of malaise, belly aches and more respiratory bronchitis. Some had coughs and infections that persisted for months and months.

With the arrival of summer, Jo and Dr Carl Thomas pour over a manuscript they were preparing for publication.

"They edited out my favorite paragraph." Jo complained, pointing to the deleted sentences. "I tried to sneak that in. I guess they don't want anything controversial or speculative."

Jo showed him the paragraph and read it aloud. "New technologies, such as synthetic biology and genetic engineering, could be used to create the next generation of biological weapons. Terrorist groups, through deliberate malfeasance, could construct dramatically more pathogenic bioweapons. Or legitimate scientists could inadvertently release more virulent disease agents with unintended consequences."

Carl shrugged it off. He was busy as usual and looked tired. Jo worried he was too stretched. He looked thinner, tired. Was it the excessive hours he devoted to his practice and in the Operating Room? Not to mention his research, his lectures, his hours teaching medical students, his entourage of tailing residents.

Jo grabbed his arm gently with concern. It seemed thinner than before. "You need to look after yourself." En route to surgery and always in a hurry, Carl wandered off.

Jo thought about her research into the mysterious syndromes. Her serendipitous find on *mycoplasma pneumonia* in swine. How pigs get pneumonia that causes a chronic cough, dull hair, weight-loss, and an emaciated appearance lasting several weeks. How similar man and pigs are. How the evolutionary distance between pig and human genomes, their DNA sequence, is smaller than the genetic distance between mice and humans. How pigs are used in research since they are more similar to humans in their anatomy and metabolism.

Pigs and humans. Similar? Yes, but a lot of things can cause weight loss and a chronic cough. Jo questioned her own deductive reasoning. Was it just her imagination running wild, like when I thought everyone was chasing me? There could be so many other causes, conditions. Still, she worried. But there was editing to do that day.

"Well, they didn't edit out the part about H5N1." Jo pointed at the manuscript draft.

"Bird Flu? Must be what I have!" Carl said, comically screwing up his face with a look of feigned fear.

"No, maybe you have the chimera like the kids?" Jo whispered under her breath.

Whether ignored, not heard or not understood, Jo did not know. Dr Carl Thomas, always in haste, his pager calling, dashed off quickly to get to his next case.

Jo suspected that the "superbug" was still running its course. And it did not go unnoticed by the biopharm companies. When there is an opportunity to treat disease, biopharm comes to the most lucrative rescue. *Not* cures. Cures don't produce a steady stream of income. Treatments are better for those that need them. But vaccines are best. Vaccines are for everyone. Some are required every year, a steady revenue stream for the maker.

That evening, Jo and Jeremy stood side by side at the kitchen counter as they prepared dinner. Jo confided. "Jeremy, Allbio's research group has submitted a patent for a new swine vaccine against *mycoplasma pneumonia*. The vaccine is designed to prevent the disease Allbio unleashed!"

"So you think they have invented a vaccine to prevent the disease they created? That's just like the IT scenario, that anti-virus security software is made by the *same* guys who create the computer viruses. Isn't that scenario just too predictable?" Jeremy worked through the deductive logic.

"So you think my theory is too predictable?"

Jeremy pondered. "Vaccines are often in development, aren't they? But why is there so much current activity, especially for a disease that makes pigs scruffy and stunted?"

"What's the use of skinny pigs? Lousy bacon and ham hocks, yuk!" Jo joked as she stirred the fat, hot Italian sausages floating in a pot of spaghetti sauce.

"But the pigs could be the guinea pigs. Animal vaccine trials usually come before human trials for all sorts of vaccines. Allbio may be working on a human vaccine for *mycoplasma pneumonia*."

"Thank you. Jeremy. That is it exactly. Makes sense, doesn't it? And isn't that a coinkydink?"

"But how did Allbio know that humans would be infected by this nasty new virulent strain?"

"How could they *not* know what happens to

DNA once it is dumped into sewers? When Allbio's deadly genes get loose, DNA doesn't die. It may fragment. But the DNA, the 'Weapon of Immune Destruction', is ready to hitch a ride on the simplest little cells. Just loose, naked DNA ready to latch on to whatever nasty microbe that happens by. Nasty bugs that cause all sorts of exotic diseases are made much, much nastier by a nasty gene."

Jo paused to think. "It gets even more sinister, Jeremy. They have created a cocktail of inactivated or "disarmed" bacteria and viruses. This way big pharma can vaccinate against a whole slew of virulent infections."

"Those opportunities again, fat profits for Allbio – Life we are making it." They sighed in unison.

Jeremy softly sang. "He's so simple minded, he can't drive his module, he bites on the neon, and sleeps in a capsule, loves to be loved, loves to be loved."…Gene Genie let yourself go!"

Chapter 28 Gene Dumping

"IT'S MY RESEARCH. The more I read, the more complicated it becomes. Since when did the life sciences become so fraught with danger?"

Jeremy listened to Jo's monologue that came out of nowhere. He knew it would probably put an end to his Sunday Times crossword puzzle.

Jo went on. "I think the NIH has finally hit the nail on the head. They brought 'synbio' under the national bio-security umbrella. Science advisors are looking closely at the possible misuses of synthetic biology. "Synbio" for short. Constructing new life 'de novo" from parts called 'biobricks'."

"By the Latin 'de novo" you mean making something new, like starting over from the beginning." And Jeremy mused. "And biobricks are?"

"Biobricks… biological building blocks. Snippets of DNA."

"Hell, I remember when DNA was discovered? Well, decoded. Mr. Crick wasn't farfetched when he proclaimed at a Cambridge pub that he and Watson had discovered the secret of making life."

"Yes, life science has changed a lot since I first studied biology. When I went to college, biology was all about sorting out life, placing plants, animals and microbes into categories. Now it's about making life from scratch."

"You told me about how you and one of a *thousand* boyfriends would trap Kangaroo Rats in the California dessert." Jeremy narrowed his eyes as a jab to Jo's promiscuous past. "You wanted to know more about what Kangaroo Rats ate. Oh, and you ended up with a lame Kangaroo Rat as a pet, after you accidentally broke his leg!"

"Poor little guy, I fell on him. He could never hop in a straight line again." Jo whimpered as if genuinely remorseful. "But back to DNA and the new biology. Our genetics experiments in college were limited to fruit flies. *Drosophila*. Curly wings, straight wings, red-eyed, white-eyed. But how quickly biology has evolved....or devolved. What constitutes *life itself* has become increasingly blurred and nebulous."

"And now the possibility of creating new life from scratch?" Jeremy paused and grinned, then sang to the tune of Cumbayah, 'Synbio, my lord, Synbio. Recombo, my lord, synbio' It's the good, the bad and the ugly. The forces of good and evil. But enough with silly songs there is an ethical concern in here."

"Synbio is risky business. Even more controversial than recombining DNA. Some activists warn that synthetic biology is like genetic engineering on steroids. The Pope is outraged at scientists playing God as risky, dangerous, and insanely arrogant."

"Yes, but you are a papist, Jo!" Jeremy teased Jo to wind her up.

"Hey, Mr. Ethics man!" Touché, Jo struck back.

"OK, so this brings a whole new moral dilemma. Will we create life that is something beneficial... or detrimental? Benevolent ... or malevolent?"

"Synthetic biology and recombinant genetic engineering are 'dual use' technologies. The possibilities of intentional misuse are *limitless*." Jo emphasized the harmful intent.

"Ah yes Jo, and the Hippocratic oath. Above all else, do no harm."

Jeremy summed it up. "I've heard about the university kids, a creative bunch bent on building things. They are bio-nerds, not unlike the computer nerds who play with software viruses."

"No way! Computer viruses may be more complicated, but *not* more complex. A software virus cannot reproduce itself, but synthetic-created life *can*." Jo continued, "The universities compete at an annual contest. Past grand prize winners came freakishly close to designing a biologic weapon of mass destruction. A WMD! They designed a cell with biobricks, snippets of DNA, which could be used to interrupt the body's response to infection. All for a good intentions, of course. For people whose immune system has gone out of control. Sepsis is fatal for many. Their defense system just goes haywire. So the university kids designed a cell to intercept immunity fighting chemicals like TNF-alpha. Their designer cell can knock out our ability to fight disease. In essence it becomes a synthetic "Immunity Destroyer.""

"This is starting to sound strangely familiar, Jo."

"Your ethicists talk about the potentially dangerous consequences. This is a new slippery slope for science to moralize about and reflect. Especially if synthetic biology get in the hands of ill-intentioned scientists."

"But what's this got to do with the local mycoplasma outbreak and the kids you have been thinking about?"

"Mycoplasma are the same minimal organisms that some so-called synthetic biologists are playing with. One group in particular uses mycoplasma as their 'biobrick'. They strip them down to just 300 genes and create designer bacteria. And they can design bacteria to do *anything* for them. Make biofuels, drugs, whatever their heart's desire."

"You mean whatever their pockets desire, don't you?"

"But of course. And they are like your computing machines, only these have the capacity to *reproduce* themselves."

"So the genes are like the software controlling the hardware." Jeremy's right-sided brain lit up. "And the ultimate aim of synbiology is to *create life itself!*"

"Yes, custom-designed life. Life created from synthetic, designer DNA." Jo said with the left side of her brain.

Together they pulled the pieces together. The twin forces of good and evil at work. For every Bill Gates paying millions to program cells with newly constructed genes for anti-malarial drugs, there will be a bioterrorist creating lethal superbugs with antibiotic resistance, or worse.

"It is a precarious balance, like being on the

189

razor's edge. Right, Jeremy?"

"Maybe we have already fallen off the edge," Failing yet again to acknowledge Jo's Razor Edge phrase.

Some say that bio-terror or bio-error will lead to millions of casualties in a single event. Those bio-threats could depopulate the planet with distressing speed. Either by organized terrorist groups or by individual weirdos with the mindset of the people who now design computer viruses; they *will* just because they *can* and are curious to see what happens.

"Whether it's terrorists, the kids in the crèche, or the do-it-yourself in the basement bunch, they are all the new global village idiots. Of course, you can never leave out the biopharma industry who could also be the cause of the bio-threat." Jeremy summed up the not so rosy picture.

Chapter 29 Opportunists

JEREMY SHOOK THE newspaper and pointed to an article. Jo read it over his shoulder.

"Look, 'Miracle Grow' for cancer? Lymphoma cancers accelerated in kids? The lymphocytes are the *immunity cells that fight disease, lymphoma cancers in this case!* But in some children who used the new medicines, the TNF blockers like Quelify, the cancer cells began to grow, and grow like the fertilizer for plants that the garden centers sell." Jeremy summarized.

Jo was incensed. "So the treatments now carry the risk of *cancer* of the immune system. Along with all the other warnings like TB and, of course, increased infections."

"But *still*, authorities believe the benefit of these medicines in children outweigh the risks? Jo paused to think about the children and the opportunistic infections that take advantage of their small bodies, unable to fight off disease.

"Jeremy, please don't sing but remember the opportunists?"

"OK, no singing, but the 'opportunists' are the microbes that take advantage of weakened immunity. These bugs cause a shitload of other virulent infections. There are new vaccines that prevent an entire array of these other nasty microbes."

"You remember *Streptococcus*, 'strep throat?' It can also cause pneumonia, meningitis and the necrotic 'flesh-eating' bacteria!"

"Yuk!" Jeremy grabbed Jo's arm and pretended to gnaw on her flesh. "Oh, yummy!"

Jerking her arm back with a giggle. "Oh, let me go on!"

"Now the vaccine wizards have also added other inactivated bugs. Like *Bordeletta*, whooping cough."

"I had that when I was a kid in England!"

"Yes, you English were always behind us in medicine! But also *Salmonella*, and I got the typhoid strain in Mexico City, summer of '73. Chicken tacos nearly killed me! And a last one, *E. coli*, we've seen very toxic strains that kill."

"Yes, the frightening outbreak in Europe last year!"

"And if…what if that nasty gene genie, little opportunists, hitch a ride on one of these other nasty microbes? Just use your imagination of a gene gone wild. Think the unthinkable. The gene that destroys immunity added will make those nasty microbes suppress immunity and make things worse."

"OK, I get it. It's obvious. And the same applies to those viruses too.

"And don't forget *Lactobacillus*, a happy, little good microbe. It's used a lot in making fermented dairy foods like yoghurt and cheese. And that is in the milk that children drink. Also in chocolate." Jo rambled on.

"Chocolate gives me migraines, but that is another good reason to avoid chocolate." Jeremy grimaced.

"And *Lactobacillus* is used in fermenting beer and wines." Jo quipped.

192

"Well you get plenty of them! But if it is so harmless, why include it with this gang of nasty bugs?"

"Good observation. It is absolutely benign. Actually it aids digestion in the GI tract. It's common in your gut......and in my vagina!"

"Let me have a look." Jeremy pushed Jo down on the couch and pried her knees apart, playfully forcing his head up her skirt between her thighs.

The point was not lost. If armed with a weapon, a gene that makes TNF blockers, the harmless *Lactobacillus* could wreak havoc with immunity. Especially in children.

Chapter 30 Pogies

JO'S SILVER SPORT coupe darted and snaked along the river en route to the Amtrak station. It was an unseasonable hot day in October as Jo drove her boss, Dr Carl Thomas to the train station to visit his family in New York.

"What was it you said yesterday about liking global warming?" Carl asked as he smirked, but Jo could not remember her exact words. Both liked irony in humor.

NIN was playing on the CD player which seemed to annoy Carl Thomas. Jo showed him the jacket and lyrics to explain why she liked this discordant techno-noise and lyrics riddled with angst. Jo could see him eyeing the machine gun and bible in opposition; the disturbing message and lyrics made him silent. Jo quickly changed CDs to the less innocuous "Prince" with more uplifting beats, but the same message. They were bantering about how you define musical genius, when the smell of pungent fish hit them as they crossed a bridge over the river. The car windows were wide open on this hot autumn day.

"Fish!" Jo exclaimed, looking right at her passenger.

"Yes, I smell it."

"Dead or alive?" Jo asked.

"I can't tell, but strong." He replied.

"It's the pogies. They've come up the river. Unusual. They usually leave the bay in August, but for some reason they've come up the river into

194

town, as far as the university. Can you see them?"

Carl peered out his window where he could see glimpses of the river. "Yes, I see them, or their motion. I just saw one jump and, oh here is a dead one floating. There seems to be quite a few."

Jo nearly jumped into his lap trying to get a look. Carl, irritated with Jo's distracted driving and concerned about their safety said sternly, "Stay in your seat!" Jo settled back and refocused, feeling reprimanded.

A few moments passed and Carl looked over. As a gesture of reconciliation, he softened. "You can park over there, in front of the fire station...not now!" afraid of her impulsiveness, "but after you drop me off at the train station. You'll be able to walk over the bridge to see them."

To justify her excessive enthusiasm, Jo told him, "Some people fear the menhaden will end up dying once they come so far upstream. If the weather stays this hot, the warmed up water won't hold the oxygen, but at least the river's motion should keep it more aerated than the bay, so maybe they will be ok." Carl nodded as Jo rambled on. "I hope they don't die. The last big fish kill was in 2003 in the bay, when about a million of them where seen gasping and gulping at the water's surface for air. The next day they all died, silver bellies up. That was in August." Jo dropped the good doctor ahead of the taxi line. He never looked back, but waved sideways at her. Jo interpreted the gesture as a disapproving dismissive.

Jo felt she failed again in her attempt to engage him in a meaningful dialogue. But Jo didn't linger on the thought as she was intent on seeing the pogies up close and personal. She parked her car near the fire station and strolled along the bridge where she spent what felt like a daydream watching the undulating rhythmic alternating semi-circles of hundreds of larger than expected, nearly a foot long, menhaden. Their mouths were wide open, as if they were frozen in a permanent scream as they filtered the water for nutrient algae. Their dark backs, a deep gray velvet, splashed a spray of silver as the more playful, or were they just desperate, jumped into the air flashing their glittering underbellies, shining in the brilliant afternoon sunshine.

Jo remembered her earlier droll quip as they stepped outside into the glorious warmth of the golden sun. "Don't you just love global warming?"

The next day, Jo excitedly told Jeremy about the "pogies" how they had come up the river, how she wanted him to see them. She encouraged Jeremy by saying that the blue fish and bass were following the pogies in. And maybe he could go fishing in the river? He reminded her that he hadn't bought a license for fresh water fishing, just for salt water, but he would like to look.

Jo took Jeremy to a spot on the river maybe a half mile from where she walked the day before.

"The pogies are the bread and butter, the meat and potatoes for blue fish and striped bass."

"Pogies? I like that name." Jeremy grinned. Jo explained that menhaden, the pogies, are filter feeders that help rid the bay of algae. Algae that otherwise suffocates the underwater grasses.

196

Without the pogies, the algae flourish and cause dead zones and then the pogies themselves die from lack of oxygen. As they did in the fish kill of 2003.

"They have so many endearing nicknames, sometimes they are called bugmouths, although they don't eat bugs. Also alewives, bunker, mossback."

"Their dark gray backs are kind of mossy looking." Jeremy added. "The menhaden aren't great eating for humans, very boney and oily. But the vulture trawlers in the bay pull them in for fish oil, omega protein supplements. They grind them up and ship them overseas."

"Fats and oils. Maybe that's why some people call them "fatbacks"? Jo questioned.

"You're like a pogy." Jeremy teased. "You've got fat in that shapely butt of yours, plus you like olive oil, like most Italians!"

Jo harrumphed, swiped with her hand and just missed Jeremy's small butt. He flinched and laughed, cowering after his devilishly insulting taunt. Jo saw the "pogies" as a metaphor for what she was thinking, in some way not exactly clear to her.

Chapter 31 Last September

"IT WAS SEPTEMBER."   Jo said to Jeremy. "The day the cops cornered the hit man with the weapons. The guy in the old red truck cruising the drug store parking lot."

"Yes, it has been a while. What ever became of him?"

"I have a theory. That it was all a set-up. Everything seemed just *too* coincidental. That Officer Borrelia should be in the parking lot while this criminal guy is cruising around. And then two *other* cops show up and help Borrelia corner the thug. It's just *too* strange. Way too weird. *Not* a coinkydink."

"Yeah, a very unlikely coincidence." Jeremy said with a bent little finger at the corner of his mouth, mimicking the British gentleman spy, Austin Powers, the international man of mystery.

Jo chuckled at the parody and went on with her suspicions. "But contrary to what it said in the newspaper, I *don't think* someone in the pharmacy called in to report a 'suspicious' guy. I think Officer Borrelia set it up."

"Maybe Borrelia wanted to get brownie points with the police department?" Jeremy's little finger still curled in mimicry, still playing the international man of mystery.

Jo reflected as she stared into the distance. "There was so much going on those crazy tumultuous last weeks at Allbio. But I remember vividly that I passed a 'square-headed' guy who was

198

walking down the ramp of the training trailer; he looked a lot like Borrelia. I figured he was one of the thousand contractors my assistant said were brought in by Allbio Security. It seemed odd that they hired nearly as many contractors as full time employees. But I didn't think too much about it back then. Maybe just in case they needed extra security at the plant? They seemed to have enough for a small private army! But what for? Protection? They certainly had plenty of contract people to draw from."

"So tell me, what do you think was going on?"

"When things first went awry, after that cop Borrelia beat my legs with the police car door and poked me in the eye, I got more and more nervous and began to cough. By the time we got to the police station, the cough became fitful. The other cop Decker also started coughing too!"

"Nervous coughs? You and Decker?" Jeremy wondered why.

"Decker. Maybe he was a plant, and not as *stupid* as he tried to appear."

Jeremy mused. "Yes, that is possible, that he's *not* as stupid as you think. But a *plant planted by who*?"

"Yes. What Decker saw made him nervous, maybe he suspected his partner Borrelia was involved with Allbio." Jo knew that Decker was unnerved by what he saw.

Jeremy toyed with the pieces to the puzzles for a while before asking, "And you think the weasels from Allbio hired the cop, Borrelia, to take care of you?"

"Yes, somebody from Allbio. Perhaps Marcus or Steadman, maybe Bonaducci? *Someone* contracted Borrelia and *he* contracted the New Jersey hit man. But Borrelia chickened out and he decided to make another plan that would benefit him with less risk!"

Jeremy paused to look into Jo's eyes and in a whispered, accentuated breath he said "Steadman, I would bet on him." With a fingered hush on his lips, he tapped out the words of the sentence. "I don't know about the others."

The conversation ended abruptly. Jo was stunned. She paused mutely, mouth opened wide like a pogy. Aghast, she was frozen as she fully grasped that the hit man, with the truck full of guns and knives, was the assassin hired by Allbio to come after *her*. Only Borrelia's change of plan had thwarted the contract.

For weeks, Jo mulled over what Jeremy confirmed. That Steadman and Borrelia wanted to shut her up. Permanently. There were too many questions. Too many connections to keep straight. Once again, Jo wondered what ever happened to the New Jersey hit man with his expired license. She remembered his malleable, twisted face. Was he still in prison? The press said he would not divulge why he was in Bayside, with an arsenal of weapons, in his old Chevy truck. He was just cruising the parking lot, the same parking lot where Jo and Sofia had seen him in his red truck just weeks before.

Jo thought about what the police chief told

the reporters, that a very serious crime was prevented from happening that day. The weapon of choice? What would he and Borrelia have chosen? Maybe the Smith & Wesson snub-nose? All cops love the grip of a snubby. Or something quieter, more intimate. One sharp, quick slice across the neck with a six inch butcher knife. But more likely, Snodland would have grabbed one of the three loaded rifles, or maybe the semi-automatic shotgun in the cab of the truck. It was purported to be within arm's reach.

A few days passed. Jo pondered the thought that she really should "google" this gangster, Jay Snodland, just in case there is something new to know about him. What ever became of him? As she typed into the Google search "Jay Snodland Bayside Police", what came up was in an unofficial court docket report.

"What!" Jo barked. She read on. "Carrying loaded weapon in vehicle, dismissed by judge 3-Mar." Ditto, ditto again. "Carrying weapons while under the influence, dismissed by judge 3-Mar, possession of sawed-off shotgun, dismissed by judge 3-Mar, obstructing police officer, dismissed by judge 3-Mar, driving with suspended license, dismissed by judge 3-Mar."

"Dismissed? What?....now wait a minute!". Jo continued reading. "Case description, Felony, arresting agency Bayside police." Jo thought, it has only been five months since the filing date and the charges are *dismissed*?

Jo flipped to the next page of the docket search. "Ok, ok district court, defender, bail..." And then she froze. "2-Mar *"Defendant Deceased"*.

"Deceased? He died in prison!" Stunned, Jo asked herself what happened, but it did explain the dismissal of all charges? Did he get killed? How did he die? Natural causes? He wasn't *that* old, only in his 40's or 50's, maybe?"

Jo surmised that Snodland never talked after his arrest, or so the press reported. He *never said what* he was up to, and he *never squealed* on *whoever* hired him. So that leaves Borrelia and the Allbio boys off the hook. No incriminating evidence to tie them to the hit man. The evidence for the contract on Jo, buried right along with Mr. Jay Snodland.

Jo was left with one thought, how surprisingly little was known about this "hit man". He had no criminal past. And how *conveniently* he died. Disappeared as quickly as he appeared out of the New Jersey criminal underworld. *What a coinkydink!*

Chapter 32 Jeremy

"YOU MUST HAVE a very high tolerance for pain." The neurosurgeon explained to Jeremy that they could see multiple lesions on the MRI, as he touched Jeremy on the left side of his forehead. "Especially in this region."

"Maybe from my years of playing soccer?" Jeremy quipped and Jo added that Jeremy played a lot of soccer in the 80's.

"No, it looks more recent." It appears that you have had other strokes. You said you have migraines?"

"Yes, many. I inherited those from my mother."

"And what do you take for them?" The resident neurologist continued questioning.

"Advil Migraine, but pills don't always work as I throw up a lot and stay in bed in a darkened room."

"Yes, sometimes up to twenty hours." Jo noted.

"But this was different. I keep veering off to the right, can't walk in a straight line. The neck pain started after tennis. I thought I sprained my neck, twisting it over my right shoulder, looking at my doubles partner."

"We don't yet have a diagnosis and we need to admit you to determine what is going on. It may be an artery dissection that has affected your gait and balance. We need to find out why you're having trouble walking."

"I'm walking like a drunk and I seldom ever

drink."

"Maybe it would be better if you *did* drink." The young doctor humored aloud.

Hours later, Jeremy was admitted to a private room on the seventh floor, overlooking the downtown hotels and white marble state house on Smith Hill.

"You're going to get through this Jeremy, you will be just fine. I love you…very much."

"Yes, I love you too."

"I don't want to lose you!"

Jo remembered the night Jeremy said the same thing to her. When she was so afraid, scared that people would hurt her; hurt her family. When the Noah's Ark of assorted trucks appeared across the road and the ambiguous followings began. Whether imagined or real, whether to inflict harm, intimidate or unnerve, Jeremy would not let on what he knew. But, he too was afraid. Afraid Jo would run; afraid she would be hurt again. Run away. Leave town. Jo feared that Sofia and Jeremy would become vulnerable targets of Steadman's vendetta to stop her in her tracks, before she could do more harm to him. Jo was nearly paralyzed by fear of an impending attack on her and her family.

Jo's repeatedly questioned Jeremy. "Is Sofia safe?"

He would answer, "Yes, Sofia is safe. She is *surrounded* by good people."

"Will anyone try to hurt Sofia?"

"Is my family safe? My sister?"

"Yes they're safe."

"Your parents?"

"They are fine."

"No, no! But please stop. Don't leave. Everyone is safe...I love you and I don't want to lose you!"

Jo reassured Jeremy that he would get well. He would have to take some time off from work to heal and to get better.

"You have to get better, Jeremy." Because you're the only one who knows how everything will end." And with all that transpired, Jo thought only Jeremy had the missing final pieces; he would never say what was going to happen. She worried that all that had happened to them had taken a greater toll on Jeremy than she realized.

When they were in England just two weeks before the stroke, traipsing across the heath, mingling with the New Forrest ponies, Jo commented, "I can't help thinking that things are imminent."

Jeremy answered, "They are."

But what was now imminent had nothing to do with Allbio, a flood of intracranial bleeding to cloud Jeremy's thoughts, his memories, his secrets. What he found out, what he knew. Why Jo was paralyzed by fear. Who he spoke with, met with. What they were doing, so secretly. For much was at stake.

Jo had asked Jeremy "What will come first? Me or the children?"

"You first."

I guess that makes more sense, Jo thought.

The small fish before the big ones.

One little pogy…first.

Ponies, pogies, dogies (Jo's slang for children). Even their names ring of endearing creatures of the earth and sea. Jo and Jeremy walked over the heath, moors, bogs, and gorse. They followed the ponies where they grazed the sweet young grasses, fertilized naturally by the free-range ponies that live and nourish in harmony.

"Keep to the high ground, where the heather grows." Jeremy advised.

"I'll try to find the high ground, Jeremy. I don't want to slip into the bog. And my legs aren't long like yours. Please pull me across and help me!" Jo whimpered and whined, like the woolly Forest ponies grazing on the heath.

"Take my hand Jo, don't be afraid. You won't get hurt, I will make sure of that."

"Is something imminent, Jeremy." Jo's voice trailed to a sigh.

"It is."

"Help me, so I don't get anxious."

"You won't need to; I think everything is coming into its place." Jeremy was matter of fact, quick to change the subject. "Look, there's a fish in the stream. I use to walk along here with my friend, when I went to school in Brockenhurst. We would fill a jam jar with bread and water, wait for the minnows to go in the jar; drag it up quickly on a string, to collect little tiddlers."

Jo looked, but did not see the little fish. She thought it a Jeremy diversion, a ruse, not wanting to continue the conversation of what's to come. And returning to an earlier time for Jeremy, Jo thought, keep calm, as they traipsed across the heath sniffing the assorted dung of deer, cattle, pigs and forest ponies. Drifting off, Jo's thoughts evaporate and condense, like the mist settling on the heath. Thoughts of home again, just days away, and an impending foreboding of events to come, some good, according to Jeremy, and some bad.

Chapter 33 Black Swan

A RARE EVENT, that is what the experts said. Things like this seldom happen. But over the next few years, some of the most athletic and vibrant kids in the community became strikingly weak…unable to elicit a healthy immune response.

Jo kept researching anything that seemed to stem from children catching exotic diseases in the local area. Early infection with chimeric microbes, superbugs that carried the rogue gene, thrived and flourished in those small bodies. Having taken a wild ride on the "opportunes", those opportunistic microbes, those infections that took advantage of those that are immune compromised. The destructive gene churned away, cranking out the blocker, the drug that quelled their immunity. Infection after infection, microbe after weaponized microbe, attacked and invaded. The children's small bodies, as time went on, became baby bioreactors, just like those monolithic large scale bioreactors at Allbio. Their bodies became vessels that churned out the drug "Quelify" that subdued their immune system, making them vulnerable, compromised, and their health assaulted.

Rare autoimmune disease, that's what the fatal condition was generally called for lack of something definitive. The medical community just couldn't pinpoint one type of infection, since multiple germs invaded and attacked, leaving the little ones ravaged and fighting for survival. The opportunes attacked. Over time, more children died. And many more remained chronically ill, exhausting the full gamut of antibiotic and treatments and infusions of elixirs. They too would eventually succumb. Their bodies unresponsive to antibiotics and the usual treatments, poor little dogies.

These kids loved life. They loved sports, in particular field sports, and their greatest common factor was soccer. It was the number one thing these kids had in common; running and playing in the meadows and playing fields. Recreational fields that had been freshly layered with the fertilizer "SuperStuff"; SuperStuff, the sludge and biosolids from the local waste treatment plant that contained Allbio's failed batches of DNA. Superstuff, spread over the patchy playing fields to enrich the soil for lush green grasses to grow.

"Just like mutations are random events, the probability of *nature* creating such an unusual construct is virtually *nil*, Jeremy. Nature would *never* create this monster without human help. The gene construct is foreign, pieced together from snippets of DNA, in this case made by Allbio. It would have never existed in billions of years of evolution. It's a 'designer gene''. They designed it to subdue an overactive immune system. And it can also hamper the body's capability to fight infection and disease. It is also designed to jump into 'hot spots' and insert into CHO's (recombinant Chinese Hamster Ovary cells). As easily as they jump into hot spots, they are unstable and they will easily

209

break away from their recombinant parents, the CHOs. From there they can 'hitch a ride' on other cells or microbes, including the common wimpy mycoplasma microbe. And it already has, Jeremy. Bio-error from negligence saturated by greed."

"Maybe not bioerror, Jo, I would call it a biocrime. And there are kids and parents in the community under a threat of bioterror."

But ultimately, gene dumping is the horror, escape of a synthetic DNA construct. And the mycoplasma are everywhere, as the state's health official said in his letter to Jo. "Mycoplasma are widespread in the community, they are everywhere." But he ended the letter on a different note with a comment disguised as a question. "After all they are only mycoplasma?" His subsequent work on emerging pathogens, the superbugs, went unnoticed by many, but not Jo. Now in DC, Jo suspected what Morgenthal was up to.

Whether or not it was "accidental", inadvertent, or a crime as Jeremy had said, Jo was thinking hard.

Chapter 34 Et tu, Brute?

LIMBO, AN INDETERMINATE state, as if suspended in time. That state of uncertainty, of being kept waiting, or simply left in oblivion. Limbo is where Jo resided for seven years after her impulsive prying of plates, bending them dog-eared. The brutish Borrelia, springing in to action, administered a thrashing disproportionate to the miniscule crime. In brief limbo, Jo sat alone in a jail cell for the first and probably only time in her life. It had to be more than an irrational hissy-fit by a crazed but normally docile pint-sized woman.

Jo entertained the scary thought that the bad guys would someday get her none-the-less. Afraid of what else was imminent, but hopeful that someday, Borrelia would be arrested. Meanwhile, she watched Borrelia moving up the ranks, from patrolman to detective to sergeant. Pulled off the streets and given a desk job, he was quickly elevated to sergeant where he could be watched, encouraged, given the freedom to expand his power and influence over his colleagues, some of whom monitored his every move from internal affairs. Seemingly, he thought he could do no wrong in the eyes of his police chief, especially with the capture of the hit man. He headed up his union local, ready to twist arms, bend rules and eliminate, or at least intimidate, anyone who got in his way.

Sergeant Borrelia, now a detective, was decorated for his heroic actions, most notably extinguishing the flames of a human torch in a parking lot, a distraught soul who apparently lit himself on fire. Borrelia just so happened to be driving by. And another time, the master of coincidence came upon a disturbed fellow hanging from a hotel balcony, just a short distance from where he found the man on fire. Again Borrelia saved the day on Bayside's Main Street where life was rife with precarious goings-on. Whether high-jinks or serendipitous maladies, these unfortunate guys needed a superhero to come to their rescue and Sergeant Borrelia took action.

In short order, Borrelia was elevated and was awarded the highest medal-of-honor for his bravery. A true knight in shining armor in Bayside. He thought himself invincible. He could do no wrong in the eyes of his superiors. And the little people the brute tormented through bullying, beating, bashing, hanging, dousing and igniting, elevated his reputation as intimidator extraordinaire among his elite cohort of corrupt cops. Sid, the Punisher, could extract drug money from dealers and kick backs for territorial protection. He had complete and utter disregard for his victims. They were easy prey. They had too much to lose or they were too scared to talk. He punished and protected, whichever was necessary for whoever hired him. He took assignments from Allbio henchmen with the same zest and fervor as he did from the politically connected, his cronies, and other bent cops.

When his buddies went down in a sting, he nearly gagged on his cake donut and coffee as the press release came over the TV ticker in the police station break room. Four cops were nabbed in a drug sting by the State Police. Only one thought stuck in his mind, "Those fuckers had better not rat on me!"

Sidney Borrelia fretted over how much more would be uncovered. Steadman's money for the contract was gone, spent in the casinos. Would he somehow be linked and exposed? Borrelia had stayed clear of the drug chatter. He just took care of miscreants and delinquent payments, twisting arms and meting out punishment. Sid, the punisher, Sid, the intimidator, scrupulously shielded himself. He knew he was protected by his boss, the chief of police. The Chief watched over his men in blue, or so Borrelia thought. Sidney hid behind the badge for years, toy cop that he was. Little did he know that the chief was just giving him enough rope. Enough rope to hang him.

The thread of his woven illicit dealings began to unravel. The insidious connection between the illicit drug trade and the prescription drugs trade was hard to finger. The corporate drug manufacturers operated in a separate world. But Borrelia, the Punisher, worked in both, hovering between the two worlds following the money. All while projecting an image of superhero Bayside cop. Trusted, respected and venerated for all the good that he did.

Four cops were indicted as part of the drug ring, but one of the cops got off scot-free. He was not charged along with the rest of the drug dealing cops. And Borrelia was quick to figure out why.

"Fucking plant!" Sid seethed with anger. He knew this "disloyal" cop must have been embedded

213

in the drug ring. That this turncoat cop must have been working undercover in internal affairs. He figured this cop *must* have worn a wire and set up his buddies. His fellow cops. What a scumbag, no loyalty to the brotherhood in his eyes. You just can't trust your partners anymore, can you? I wonder what my old partner Decker knows?

Borrelia paced the hallway outside of the break room. Long glass display cases housed the awards, photos and memorabilia of bygone days, validating the good deeds and bravery of the Bayside PD. Borrelia's suspicious, paranoid mind deduced the worst possible scenarios. If a drug detective can't rely on his partner to cover his ass, then loyalty among the men in blue might not be a foregone conclusion. He went through a mental list of his past and present partners. He flashed on his past: busting knees, knuckling eyes, dangling bodies, dousing and igniting, targeting and contracting. He especially pondered the latter, his dealings with the murder-for-hire, hit-man and assassin, Jay Snodland. He pondered for a while about Snodland who conveniently died in prison and never divulged who had hired him. Borrelia began to wonder what ever happened to Lance Steadman, the corporate wimp who contracted and financed the assassination. After all, it was *his* plan to murder Jo Blair.

Borrelia's brain buzzed. And why the hell did Snodland just sit there with two loaded rifles and a shotgun on the car seat next to him? Why didn't he fire one of those ready rifles at the other cops when they showed up unexpectedly in the parking lot? Hell, Snodland had a fucking arsenal, a couple dozen weapons, but the creep never grabbed one, gave up without a struggle! Borrelia questioned things he dismissed before as inconsequential. Was it just coincidence? He could not be sure.

Borrelia's shoulders were hunched over, his squared-off chin buried in his chest. His piggy-eyes peered, scrutinized and mentally ticked off the list of police officers behind the glass in the Bayside PD display case. Borrelia focused on a photo of special police agents in the K-nine force, all skilled in the martial arts. Eyeing each member in the photo, he finally got to his old partner Decker. Decker had always been loyal and seemingly backed Sid without question. Even the strong-arm tactics Sid used to subdue the little squealing Allbio woman were beyond Decker's reproach. Decker never uttered a critical word about the excessive use of force that Borrelia meted out, more than once, on drug dealers and criminal lowlifes.

But Jo Blair was different, no lowlife getting what they deserved, but a high profile, well-paid manager in a powerful biopharma company, Allbio. Decker didn't seem to object to the violent slamming that Borrelia inflicted when the screwy woman, seemingly unprovoked, bent their patrol car license plate. Borrelia was just doing his job as a security contractor with Allbio. He was hired as an enforcer and protector in Allbio's private corporate security. A corporate army of about a thousand; they kept a handle on any little David who might just try to bring down the biotech Goliath.

In the locker room at the police station, Sergeant Borrelia caught Patrolman Decker by the shoulder and startled him with a backslap. "So, how's it going old buddy?"

"Nothing much, just the same old same old." Decker flinched at the aggressive gesture. He hadn't spoken much with Borrelia lately and did not want to now.

"Hey, too bad what happened to our buddy Detective Paisano. Ten years! He was a good cop. Looks like the state police set him up with the others in the group. Ya know, dumped him in the shit."

Decker hesitated knowing full well what prompted Borrelia as he went on. "And being set up by *his own partner*." He grinned with a half-cocked smile. "Now what do you think of that?" Borrelia's twisted smile disappeared as he closed in just inches form Decker's moon-shaped face. Decker could smell Borrelia's cheap aftershave under his coffee breath. Cake crumbs were still encrusted on his lips.

The "Intimidator" was at it again, only this time he was going after his fellow man-in-blue; one he thought he could trust, but one he thought knew too much. Was Decker working on the inside, a rat? Did he have the goods on him? Borrelia angrily suspected a set up, maybe a ruse.

Decker sputtered and began to cough. This always happened when he got nervous; a dry, persistent hack, like the staccato of a handgun. His efforts to suppress the breathless coughing were to no avail. Decker's weakness was conspicuously obvious, his ragged hack a dead giveaway.

As they walked to the parking lot at the rear of the station, Borrelia reminded Decker. "That little plate-bending mouse bitch, you know, Jo Blair from Allbio. What's she been up too?"

"Sid, nothing to worry about. She's working up at the hospital. Not a squeak from her. And she is too far out from the statute of limitations. She can't come after us now."

Borrelia's biggest worry was the disappearing hit-man. He found it pretty hard to believe that the assassin he hired to kill Jo Blair had simply died. "That hired gun never squealed. He could have nailed us, but he didn't. So, why the hell not?" Borrelia kept needling Decker. Inspecting him to detect a falter, looking hard to trip him up, a facial flutter, any sign of guilt. Decker warned himself to get control of the cough, take deep slow breaths, stop the hyperventilating. He took a deep breath. Finally it worked, his cough abated. But just for a while.

"I always thought Snodland would plead no contest to the weapons and firearms charges." Decker tried to convince Borrelia that Snodland would not want to implicate him and Borrelia in a murder-for-hire. "Now would he?" Decker punctuated. One dry muffled cough remained.

"You're probably right, but Snodland never got paid, so there was no trail of money to follow." Borrelia concluded. "There is *no* connecting us. And *you* got your share." Decker had indeed taken his cut, but had handed the share to his handler with the FBI. "That Allbio Steadman wimp never asked for a refund, he was long gone. He didn't want to be

217

here when the shit went down, did he?"

Decker played with Borrelia. "Yeah, we never collected the garbage!" His chuckle comingled with another cough. Both laughed for different reasons.

Borrelia summed it up with a double entendre. "Dead men don't talk." With hit man Snodland seemingly long gone, the veiled threat was not lost on Decker. Perhaps he would be next on Sid's list.

Decker drove towards home and finally caught his breath. He breathed a sigh of relief. He knew that, according to the FBI, Borrelia would soon be arrested, he just didn't know when. He knew it was imminent. He must let his handlers know that his cover, in all probability, was blown. Sid Borrelia suspected him. Sid always was suspicious, and now with his corrupt buddies caught, Sid seemed bent on tying up any loose ends. Maybe he did feel the noose tightening round his bull-like neck?

Chapter 35 Allbio's Gold

JO STARED AT the Visio chart she had worked on over the years.

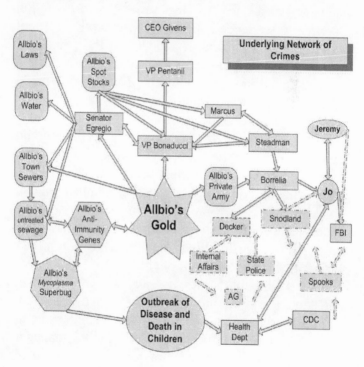

He who has the gold makes the rules. Jo's dead aunt's voice came flooding back to Jo, reminding her of the three rules of how to get along in this tiny state. Allbio's gold bought whatever rules they needed to play the game of drug production. Quelify, the drug, thirsted for a million gallons of water a day. Bags of Allbio gold bought the law guaranteeing an open spigot to clean water, courtesy of the powerful Senator Egregio. More lining of pockets and greasing of palms and Egregio's cronies on the sewage commission would turn a blind eye as Allbio dumped its excrement. Its genetic waste fouling the sewers with mutation creations suspended in rich frothy broth. Piles of viscous black sludge, laden with immunity dampening designer DNA would hitch a ride and create superbugs. Weaponized *Mycoplasma* spread around the state in SuperStuff that made the kids sick, in many cases deadly sick.

It amused Jo to think how people could proceed down the slippery slope. From what appeared honorable, "Life, we are making it!" to menacing and downright dangerous, "Death, we are making it!" Steadman slid from creepy corporate hack to an ominously evil, vindictive bastard who planned to have Jo killed, she was pretty sure in her mind. She gulped at the thought.

For Allbio's big wigs and wannabe big wig Steadman, contracting a dirty cop or two to shut up a noisy incriminating underling was a small price to pay. If CEO Givens or VP plant manager Bonaducci could buy corrupt senators for political and financial favors, Steadman and sidekick Marcus could buy corrupt cop Borrelia as their enforcer to subdue the irritating, whistle-blowing Jo. But mishaps and bungling pulled them deeper into the undercurrent, into the cesspool of conspiracy and murder. Now they were unable to extract themselves from the sewer they were swimming in.

Once the corporate upperworld spiraled downward and met with the criminal underworld, the magnitude of the FBI effort became a comfortable response. There were watchers. There were listeners and data gatherers. For this is where the FBI was at its best…with drugs and murdering thugs.

Some said the FBI effort in the state of RI was monumental. Absolutely mind boggling to the average citizen used to tales of corruption and greed. Certainly, if the scale of their operations was limited to bribery, fraud, and the selling of honest services, it would have been easy to nail a politician for selling his office to the corporate Fat Cats. With the help of Senator Egregio, Allbio set up slush funds, the "spot-stocks", with their brazen manipulations that created backdated stock option grants. They wrote lists of thinly veiled fictitious names that could be changed to the names of loyal employees at the boss's discretion. Options could be cashed in immediately, "on-the spot". The accounts were secretly coded with names like "IM Fantom", referring to fictitious "phantom" funds. Another was called "Fargo", alluding to the darkly sinister movie.

To stuff the corporate Fat Cats pockets even fuller, the law makers, Egregio and friends, helped cut the corporation's capital gains tax so that the execs and their loyal butt-boys and girls could squirrel away most of their money for new cars and toys.

Sweet as candy, addictive as heroin, the bribes and pay-offs linked to agencies, councils, authorities, and officials, were pervasive. The politicos, trusted pillars of society, purveyors of honesty and justice, were transformed from clean to dirty. What upstream was clean water, downstream oozed as raw sewage. Downstream they morphed into chimera, human and monstrous dragons, until their humanity was lost completely. A metamorphosis to mutant freaks of nature.

The corporation of murdering thugs would willingly kill anyone who would get in their way or stem the tide of profits. Anyone who might try to expose them; ready, inhale, aim, fire! Their negligence led to crimes against human health, the spread of disease, and the death of children. A corporation of thugs worse than any in the RI crime family…in some ways more efficient than the Patriarca's Providence mob.

The politicians and corporations were intimately connected. Intricately linked like the Chinese idioms for opportunity and danger. Meanwhile, the FBI was playing parallel games in parallel worlds. No wonder Jo was confused as federal agents mirrored their counterparts. All were bullies and intimidators. All were masters of deception. Or so they thought. As the spooks in the shadows watched the corporate Allbio boys and girls playing secret agents and assassins, Jo's confusion as to *who was who* eventually became crystal clear.

Monumental to say the least, perhaps the actual scale of the federal effort was underestimated, not only that of the FBI but of the other agencies. All worked furiously to piece together the evidence of intentional malfeasance and the unintended consequences of the underlying crimes. It was often said that the FBI no longer rented in Rhode Island. They bought houses and burial plots.

The circle tightened and just like the pogies in Narragansett Bay, the political and corporate big fish would swim in spiraling motion, gulping, gasping for air, silver bellies flashing, unable to breath, suffocating as the temperature got too hot, their lifeline of oxygen depleted. They'd gone too far upstream and couldn't find their way back to the open sea. Pockets full of gold, weighted them down by greed, the downward spiral pulling them deeper into the cesspool that they had created.

The corporation... the biggest and most powerful would be saved for last. Big biopharm Allbio's criminal activities were committed by corporate entities. Those individuals, who influenced decisions, altered the records, cooked the financial books, created fake stock, and dumped deadly DNA. After all, "They are only dead cells. No harm done." But to the prosecutors there is no reason why the underlying corporate crimes couldn't be prosecuted under RICO, the Racketeer Influenced and Corrupt Organizations act. When individuals act, they are corporate agents. Intricately connected, both they and the corporation are liable for the crimes they commit. As one might say, "Corporations are people too."

Chapter 36 Someday 12-21-12

IN AN AMAZING feat of synchronicity, Jo and Jeremy watched the FBI sting operation "Razors Edge" underway. Jo still thinks Jeremy had some prior knowledge, but he would just smile. "See, I said something would happen." The roundup began and ended within a matter of days, some within hours, and others only minutes apart. From Rhode Island to Texas to California, each in succession, starting up the corporate ladder of Allbio, down the chute to Detective Borrelia, and on to the dark, dank corridors of the state house. Most were taken into custody by federal agents arriving in black SUVs. They surrounded their homes in the early dawn and caught up with them at their most vulnerable time.

Arrested at his home in a dawn raid by the FBI in Rhode Island, was Detective Sergeant Sidney Borrelia. They indicted him on a plethora of criminal activities; illicit machinations in his past and present lives. There was helpful Sid "the smurf" who laundered money that ended up in the hands of the Columbian drug cartel. Years later, he helped deranged individuals; torched them in broad daylight and dangled them from balconies. As intimidator and punisher, Borrelia slammed and thumped the legs of little Jo; knuckled her eyeball and left her with bruising blue armbands. Just some of the many punishments he doled out. He relished in inflicting pain and suffering, but now the rope had tightened.

With the help of the FBI, the State Police, and internal investigators in the Bayside police force, undercover agents Decker and Snodland gave damaging testimony. Borrelia's schemes and meetings with Allbio's henchmen Steadman and Marcus added conspiracy charges. His contract work with Allbio went beyond the pretence of special event security. He was accused of arranging to meet and deal with the planned assassin, hit-man Jay Snodland, not knowing he was an FBI informant. Snodland was now living elsewhere under the witness protection program. Snodland, working undercover for the FBI, wore a wire to record their encounters. Borrelia's old partner Decker, also working with the FBI, corroborated Borrelia's involvement in the failed contract and the cash he got from Allbio's Lance Steadman in the hit man plot. Borrelia was indicted on 37 charges, all felonies. Given enough rope, he hung himself, along with the indictment of others in his particular cohort of crime.

Arrested by the FBI in the state of Texas, Lance "the Chihuahua" Steadman and Gary "Jabba the Hutt" Marcus. They had paid $60,000 to then patrolman Borrelia with Allbio money, allocated ironically from Jo's training grants. Jo's state grant money was used to hire her own assassin, an irony the prosecutor in Steadman's trial could not resist pointing out. Steadman and Marcus were convicted in separate trials for bribery, grand theft, and conspiracy to murder, which meant they faced sentences of over 20 years each.

Arrested by the FBI in the state of RI, Senator Sam Egregio was charged with bribery and selling his honest services to Allbio. He had brought new legislation to the state house guaranteeing Allbio an unprecedented million gallons of water every day. A huge amount of water for any manufacturer.

"I can introduce bills to the state house and you *can not* use my vote as evidence against me!" Senator Egregio countered. He was shielded by a constitutional hangover that protected "speech in debate". Allbio's CEO and their lobbyists had courted the Senator at the dinner meeting in the mansion and Egregio twisted the arms of the water authority. In the end, he had left a smoking gun. Smoldering white envelopes full of cash that Senator Egregio and his buddies slid across tabletops and under dashboards to people on town councils or water boards. The rats gave him up and broke loyalty with a now failing and impotent politician. Egregio exchanged his financial services to Allbio for commission fees in the guise of *investment advice*. The FBI auditors found he set up the fictitious "spot stocks" for Allbio, which CEO Givens was subpoenaed to testify about as a hostile witness for the prosecution.

Town councilmen, in collusion with Senator Egregio, had pushed the sewage commission to allow the disposal of biological wastewater from Allbio. They let them dump the deadly genes untreated into the sewers. They bribed the city managers to turn a blind eye to the dumping of enormous amounts of Allbio biological waste, DNA debris and cell culture nutrients. "After all, they are only dead cells." They kept saying, repeating what Allbio had told them.

Senator Egregio convinced environmental regulators that the sludge from the sewage treatment facility could be used as "fertilizer" or "bio-solids" called, ironically, SuperStuff. Tons were applied to land near schools, playgrounds, residences; some just feet away from some private drinking wells. The trial was a media circus rich in lively colloquy and name calling... mostly scatological. The senator was surprised when several of those he had bribed or strong-armed decided to rat on him, breaking one of the three Rhode Island rules. Out of office in a surprise defeat, the ex-senator could not help or intimidate as he could before. The rats turned, seeing a chance to save their own skins on the sinking Allbio ship. The Senator was convicted and sentenced to jail for crimes that went far beyond the selling of his "honorable" services.

Henry Givens phone lines lit up like a digital billboard. "Mr. Givens, there are six SUVs with federal agents at the security hut. They have search warrants. And I have our Security Director on another line from Texas. I'll conference him in," gasped Henry's assistant.

Breathless and in a clear panic, the Texas Security Director told CEO Henry Givens that Bill Bonaducci had been handcuffed by federal agents and marched away to a black SUV. Rumor had it that a roundup of Allbio senior people was underway. Three helicopters hovered over the corporate offices in the Allbio compound.

On hearing that one of his trusted VPs had been arrested, Givens looked up at General Custer hanging on his office wall. "Is this my last stand? My demise?" Givens looked to General Custer both for inspiration and as a warning of the consequences of hubris. But now General Custer became a fatal reminder to Givens that he reached the end of the battle.

12-21-12 was a day Jo and Jeremy Blair waited for. But justice for some of the dead children would never come.

CEO Givens' deserter VP Ferris Pentanil, the chief Allbio scientist, fled Allbio a few years before, suspecting he would be held accountable for his part in the raw disposal of engineered genes. Pentanil pulled out before the sludge was disposed of, as he knew trouble lay ahead for Allbio. But the FBI pulled him into their net. He had spent the years since Allbio seeking his own personal fountain of youth through bio-aesthetic medicine. He hoped the next new gene would make him immortal.

Bonaducci, former New England plant manager, moved to the Allbio Texas drug plant. He left Allbio New England afraid his fraudulent indiscretions with the spot stocks and his failure to tell the health authorities that there was a remote possibility of trouble with what he had dumped into the sewers, would catch up with him.

CEO Henry Givens, VP Bill Bonaducci, and Ferris Pentanil were indicted by a Grand Jury and charged with gross negligence, crimes endangering human health, and crimes against the environment.

Chapter 37 Trials and Tribulations

TIME PASSED AS Allbio pushed to extend the trial date. But it would be 219 days of court proceedings with testimony from 177 expert witnesses from law enforcement, academia, government agencies and public health. FBI, CDC, EPA, DOH, HHS, NIH, NBFAC and USAMRIID were among the agencies, the acronymic alphabet soup of experts presenting their opinions. National Laboratories, university researchers, agency officials, and law enforcers were intent on piecing together the mammoth jig saw puzzle.

Jo and Jeremy's anticipation of "U.S. vs. Allbio, et al" finally shifted to the tense drama unfolding in the ornate courtroom of the U.S. District Court. The trial judge, Ilda Carvallo, called to order a courtroom packed with lawyers, federal agents, and Allbio executives. Judge Carvallo, a striking white-haired matriarch, went through the formalities before stating the charges against Allbio. She was speaking about the inevitable motion by the Allbio lawyers to dismiss the charges.

"The prosecutor's theory is that Allbio has negligently released biological agents, deadly genes, and DNA. That these deadly genes have caused disease and destruction to human health, in particular to the health of children, is a *serious* accusation. Allbio and three senior executive managers stand accused of federal crimes against human health and the environment. Expert opinion from law enforcement, scientists, public health, and government agencies will be heard. I have actively screened all expert witness and opinion using the Daubert standards… and what that means …."

Judge Carvallo paused and looked sternly across at a group of six lawyers for Allbio, who were shuffling papers, disturbing her train of thought. She continued.

"According to the 1993 landmark case, Daubert (pronounced Dow-bert) vs. Merrell Dow Pharmaceuticals, the Supreme Court held that the Federal Rules of Evidence govern the admission of scientific evidence. As trial judge, I act as the gatekeeper to determine whether the proffered evidence is scientifically valid. So, as not to confound the jury, I have vetted each scientific expert…their knowledge, their experience, their skills, their publications. I found them qualified to testify on the scientific facts. They will help answer the questions: Who? What? When? Where? And finally Why? These scientists are particularly qualified to point out both the benefits and dangers of advances in science and technology. Therefore, the defense motion for dismissal is denied."

During the trial, most of the witness testimony was narrative, using science exhibits to explain cause and effect. Since the offense was considered a "biocrime", it was assumed that the outbreak of disease and the cluster of cases could be traced back to its source. Much of the forensic evidence would be biological, microbial, and genetic DNA.

The first expert witness called to the stand

was the special agent in charge of the FBI investigation and forensic scientist, Dr. Edward Charles.

Prosecutor Reznor began. "Could you state your name and position for the court?"

"I am Dr. Edward Charles, the head of the FBI criminal investigation and an expert in forensic science."

"For the jury Dr. Charles, would you please explain how a "bio-crime" differs from traditional crimes?"

Dr. Charles looked towards the jury, "Biocrimes are very similar to traditional crimes where people are harmed. In traditional crimes, the weapons are usually things we are all familiar with, like guns or knives or even a chemical poison. They can be used to inflict bodily harm or commit murder." Taking a breath, he continued, "Biocrimes, on the other hand, are caused by biological agents. Biocrimes can be an act of bioterrorism. They can also be a hoax. They may be an intentional, unintentional, or an inadvertent release of biological material."

"So the cause of biocrimes are biological agents. Would you please explain what biological agents are for the jury?"

"As defined by Title 18 of the U.S. Code, a biological agent is a microorganism or infectious substance. It can be a naturally occurring, bioengineered, or a synthesized component that is capable of causing death, disease, or other biological malfunction in a human being. Biological agents also include animals, plants, and other living

232

things, they differ from chemical poisons."

"So, all living things?

"No, not *only* all living organisms, but also the *components* or parts of living things. They can be structures inside of cells, or material such as DNA. The structure can occur in nature or they can be synthesized, man-made. They can be created or bioengineered in laboratories. We often hear about genetically modified foods, like corn, or bio-fuels, or bioengineered medicines. The basics of the science are explained in the jurors' notebook. Your notebooks will help you understand the biology that is fundamental to this case which deals with a designed gene created by Allbio."

Prosecutor Reznor prompted, "The FBI investigation surrounding operation 'Razor's Edge" was integrated with other investigations. Would you please elaborate on these collaborative investigations?"

"As head of the FBI investigation for operation "Razor's Edge", my colleagues in the joint investigation will present expert testimony and evidence along with our collaborators in law enforcement, science, and public health. The forensic evidence will rely heavily on science. Biological, microbial, and epidemiologic evidence are connected to the outbreak of disease. The relatively new field of microbial forensics has been rigorously tested, but not yet presented in a court of law, whereas DNA has been used extensively in murder and rape trials."

Prosecutor: "Would you explain how DNA and microbial forensics will be proffered as evidence in this trial?"

Dr. Charles: "Many pieces of microbial and biological evidence have been brought together by the CDC, Public Health Departments, government laboratories, academics and scientists. You will hear expert opinion from law enforcement, scientists, epidemiologists, microbiologists, public health officials, and many others. Each will bring key pieces from their investigations. Each has been vetted thoroughly and approved as experts by the honorable Judge Carvallo."

Dr Charles nodded at the trial judge. He was well aware that the experts offering evidence from microbial forensics had to now withstand the scrutiny of the legal system. Would the techniques and methods of biological forensics be deemed legally defensible? The opportunity to test that capability in a prior case had passed, when the suspected perpetrator of the 2001 anthrax attacks committed suicide. The anthrax pathogen, a microbe genetically unique and identifiable in its origin, could not be proffered as evidence in a trial that ended with the death of the scientist thought to have released the biologic agent.

Defense attorney Burgsdorf had his expert witnesses too.

"Dr. Morris Minor, you were intimately involved at the 1975 Asilomar Conference where scientists debated the opportunities and risks of experiments involving recombinant DNA."

"Yes, I was involved with experiments myself, inserting genetically engineered genes. We

234

were concerned that, perhaps, the introduced genes could turn ordinary microbes into human pathogens. Those are microorganisms that cause disease."

"And what were your findings?

"We assigned an estimate of risk to the type of experiments we anticipated in the scientific community. We then set up safety guidelines. The lowest level of experiments required physical containment. For higher levels of risk, biological containment was suggested to reduce any dangerous consequences from the release of engineered organisms into the environment. The U.S. Guidelines for recombinant DNA research were first issued in 1976."

"And have there been any incidents with dangerous consequences reported?" Burgsdorf asked the spectacled elder who looked the stereotypical image of the mad scientist.

"For over thirty years, many experiments have been performed with recombinant or as laymen would say 'engineered' DNA. Recombinant DNA experiments have *not* been implicated with any threat or danger to public health."

"And can you comment on the benefits of the technology?"

"Genetically engineered drugs, foods, crops, vaccines, and therapies have enhanced life, medicine, agriculture. Just to name a few of the benefits. The technologies have created successful industries, wealth, and jobs."

Dr Minor's testimony continued to extol the effectiveness of the safety precautions in producing quality controlled therapeutic drugs. They were important medicines for debilitating diseases.

The prosecuting attorney had a few questions too for Dr. Morris. "Dr. Morris, what is your involvement with the biopharma industry?"

"I have disclosed that I have served as an advisor or board member for various pharmaceutical and biotechnology companies."

"Including Allbio's board of directors?"

"Yes, I have disclosed all industry affiliations, past and present. Many academics have ties to pharmaceutical, biotech, and medical companies."

"So, when you said that "Recombinant DNA technology has created successful industries, wealth, and jobs you included yourself in that assessment. What portion of your wealth has come from the industry?"

"I realize you are alluding to a 'conflict of interest', but you would be hard pressed to find a reputable scientist that does *not* have ties to industry!" Dr. Minor waggled his thin, goose-skinned neck in an angry headshake.

"That will be all, your honor." The prosecutor felt comfortable he had discredited some of the rosy picture that the renowned scientist had painted.

Chapter 38 Dual Use, Misuse

ANOTHER WEEK OF expert testimony; for the defense, more scientists touted the benefits that bioengineered medicines brought to patients. Other scientists, for the prosecution, warned of the dark side of such "dual use", benefit and harm, technologies. The dueling banjos of biotech and bioethics played on.

Jo and Jeremy were relieved to move past the acrimonious academics, each trying to vilify the work of the others. Jeremy reminded Jo about the British scientists. When the Watson and Crick model of DNA was first published, they did not credit the work of Rosalind Franklin. Franklin, at age 37, died from ovarian cancer. Her "dual use" tools, and probable cause of her death, working with an extremely fine beam of x-rays lead to her discovery of the crucial double helix. The Nobel Prize in Medicine would never be hers.

"In academics it is all about recognition and attribution. They like a good fight in their ivory towers to discredit colleagues and pump up their stature in their chosen fields." Jeremy reminded Jo.

"Your honor, we will now hear expert testimony from the state health department's epidemiologists and public health officials," Reznor told the court. "They will give us their insight from their investigation." The prosecuting attorney introduced medical epidemiologist, Dr. James Morgenthal, who used to be the top state health official before moving to Washington. He detailed the local outbreak of disease in children he had seen in his former job.

"Outbreaks of pneumonia are common occurrences in communities. The causes may be viral or bacterial, but it is *uncommon* that they are reported. But we were confronted with unusual diseases that were *not* the garden variety of ailments that normally afflict school children." Dr. Morgenthal had the looks of a basset hound but a surprisingly high-pitched voice. His high pitched yelp was persistent, aggressive, and unfortunately annoying. But he knew he was on the side of right and he was not going to let his idiosyncrasies get in the way of the facts.

"Dr. Morgenthal, what was the first indication that something unusual was occurring?"

"It wasn't until four children in the same school were diagnosed with encephalitis-like diseases. All were reported to us within a two week period. We were alarmed to find that two of the children were in the same third grade classroom. Statistically, *mycoplasma* leads to meningitis or encephalitis in only one-tenth of 1 percent of cases. And clusters just *don't* happen. This is the only place in the country where it *did* happen."

Dr. Morgenthal gazed alternately at the judge and jury, pausing to emphasize the impact of the anomalous events. Unlikely. Unusual. Did the jury get it? He wondered if he made his point about how *unlikely* all of these infections were in such a small area.

He went on to elaborate his point. "The

238

state's incident command system was activated and the CDC sent in their Outbreak Investigation team to collect samples from the children and their family members. The team took swabs from the nose, throat, mouth also sera, blood specimen, plus chest-x-rays. Nurses interviewed the families, looking for patterns of infection. What places had the children visited? Where were the kids playing in the weeks before, when they were first exposed to this unusually virulent superbug?"

He emphasized the point that mycoplasma are generally not a major health concern. "Annoying but wimpy, they are seldom a killer. And ubiquitous, they are found everywhere."

He pointed out why they quickly called the CDC to investigate. The high mortality, the high morbidity, and more severe syndromes presented that had prompted the CDC's actions. The outbreak started early on with pneumonia and progressed to debilitating skin and nervous system diseases. Initially, they contacted infectious disease doctors, neurologists and pediatricians. Over time they began to notice syndromes in the older kids 11-12 year olds, 14 and 15 year olds. There were fevers, night sweats, rashes, swollen joints migrating from ankle to knee, right to left, lasting for weeks. Was it Lyme disease or rheumatoid arthritis? No, the tests for these were negative. But when the joint fluids were needle aspirated, the samples grew out *mycoplasma pneumonia.* Different diseases, but the same cause. And all the children and teens lived along a corridor ten miles long and four miles wide. Like the tail of a comet.

"Could you explain more precisely the "corridor"? What does it mean?"

"Yes, the schools, cases and communities, when plotted on a map appeared to follow a swath across the state. On the timeline, the cases of bacterial 'walking pneumonia' actually began weeks before the cluster cases of encephalitis-like diseases. The pneumonia seemed to occur in waves, every five or six weeks. The number of cases increased over time, beginning in late August and ending in February. You can see the numbers on the 'EpiCurve'. That's what we call the charts we use."

"The charts are also in your juror notebooks." The prosecutor reminded the jurors. "Please continue."

"The infections persisted in the children and teens. Their bodies just didn't fight off the infections as well as they should have. There were too many sick kids with protracted illness. The syndromes just didn't go away until treated aggressively with antibiotics. What was *really* surprising was the unusually high rate of infection for pneumonia in the nine neighboring schools. The infection rate was at least five times higher than you'd expected in a normal outbreak."

"What was the source of this deadly mutant strain of *mycoplasma pneumonia*?" The prosecutor prompted.

"Our challenge was to find out *where* this uncommon mycoplasma came from. The mycoplasma that caused this outbreak of *unusual* diseases: encephalitis, meningitis, Steven Johnson Syndrome, rampant pneumonia, migrating joint sepsis, and other mysterious conditions." Dr. Morgenthal counted with his fingers as he enumerated the list. "As a medical epidemiologist, we look at the What, Where, When, Why and How of an outbreak of disease."

George Burgsdorf, lawyer for the plaintiff, did what he could to cast doubt as he cross-examined Dr. Morgenthal, who was now subdued and acquiescent. Had he become unnerved?

"How can you be sure that this was not a natural phenomenon? Mutations happen in nature, don't they, Dr Morgenthal?"

"Well yes, but.."

"Other outbreaks of mycoplasma are not uncommon, are they?"

"Yes they are common…"

"It is not all that unusual for disease to occur in clusters?"

"No, diseases can occur in clusters."

"Children contract encephalitis and die. And the child who died tested negative for mycoplasma in her spinal fluid and brain tissue? Correct?"

Dr. Morgenthal paused and answered softly. "Yes."

"The girl who died had a cough and cold. But *mycoplasma pneumonia* was not the definitive cause of her encephalitis."

George Burgsdorf dismissively summed up his defense. "It could just be coincidence. Our expert epidemiologists will now question your statistical analysis."

And they did.

Chapter 39 Burgsdorf and Fitzpedro the "safety" guy

DAYS LATER, DEFENSE attorney Burgsdorf called his witness, Jerome Fitzpedro, a rounded plump tomato of a guy, to the stand.

"Mr. Fitzpedro, you have worked in biopharma for over 20 years including three years at Allbio New England?"

"Yes, that is correct. I am a Bio-Safety Officer, a specialist in the safe confinement of recombinant organisms." Fitzpedro beamed with a self-congratulatory grin.

"Please explain your expertise with respect to bio-safety, specifically in reference to the safety of recombinant Chinese's Hamster Ovary cells. I believe they are called CHOs."

"For over twenty years, CHOs with recombinant DNA have been used to produce therapeutic drugs. Recombinant DNA molecules are made from snippets or pieces of DNA. They are "recombined" from these tiny segments."

"To your knowledge Mr. Fitzpedro, what are the bio-safety risks of these recombinant genes being transferred to other organisms?"

"Studies have shown no transfer of DNA to lab workers or biopharma facility workers. Nor has there been harm to humans from gene transfer to bacteria. There has been *no* harm to the environment."

"So Mr. Fitzpedro, are you saying that

biopharma companies using CHO cells are considered a low level of risk?"

"Yes, they are the lowest level of risk; Level 1 on a scale of 1 to 4. In the environment, CHOs die rapidly and do not raise any safety concerns."

"So from your experience, is there a risk of DNA transfer from CHO cells to microbes in the wastewater from biopharma companies?"

"DNA degrades very rapidly, so the probability that DNA would transfer to bacteria or other microbes is extremely low and any ill effects would be negligible. I would say it was a very remote chance, if any."

"Thank you Mr. Fitzpedro."

Federal prosecutor Reznor proceeded with his cross-examination. "Mr. Fitzpedro, when biologic waste is disposed of from a Level 1 facility, where does it go?"

"Well that depends, the risk of DNA persisting in the environment is low. Some companies treat the wastewater with heat. Sometimes acid is used. The cells can be deactivated."

"Does Allbio use these methods?"

"Sometimes, it depends on the facility. When I worked for Allbio, heat and acid were used at the west coast facilities, but not on the east coast. In Germany and the United Kingdom, heat inactivation is required."

"And while you were at Allbio New England, what was the practice in disposing of the biologic waste?

"Wastewater was disposed of in the sewers. How it was treated was up to local and state government. They make the laws and regulations."

"So the bio-wastewater is deactivated before putting it in the sewer system in some European countries and on the west coast of the US, but not treated on the east coast at Allbio New England?"

"CHO cell cultures are a Level 1 risk. They are exempt from Level 2, 3, and 4 requirements for inactivation, according to guidelines. Rhode Island did *not* require that we deactivate the wastewater."

"The biologic waste was not deactivated."

"We called it wastewater. The CHO cells are dead. They have been lysed, which means they were broken up prior to disposal."

"Mr. Fitzpedro, did Allbio do any monitoring of the local environment for genetic material?"

"No. DNA does not persist in the environment. It breaks down. There is no need for monitoring."

"So the wastewater was *not* deactivated before it went down the drain, into the sewers that Allbio and the town built."

"Not while I was working on the Allbio site. No. The sewers provided physical containment of the wastewater. That is the requirement for a level 1 facility."

"Were there any breaches of the sewers?"

"Breaches? Not to my knowledge." Fitzpedro was a cool tomato. He was used to grilling by the FDA.

"Weren't there reports of sewage discharges

during construction of the sewerage pump station in town?"

"Yes, there were reports, but there was no evidence showing a breach at the pump station. It was confirmed by the dye methods used. The state environmental department did the testing."

"Was Allbio concerned that their wastewater containment was breached?"

"That was beyond our responsibility. The liability for any breach did not belong to Allbio. Allbio may have helped pay for the sewers, but regulating the waste is the responsibility of the local and state government."

"Mr Fitzpedro, if there *was* a suspected breach of containment, a release of biological wastewater from this massive, large scale facility, would Allbio have tested the environment for genetic material, for DNA fingerprints? Do they have polymerase chain reaction (PCR) testing in their labs?"

Fitzpedro was visibly reddened from the grilling, the prosecutor thought he looked ripe to pick. "This was a low risk, Level 1 facility. The local environment does *not* need to be monitored and nobody asked Allbio to do that."

"Is there a significant risk that bacteria in the environment could be transformed by recombinant DNA? I believe you would call it by 'horizontal gene transfer'?"

"That's unlikely. It hasn't happened. It would be a very rare event!"

"But not impossible." Reznor pressed. "Could the wastewater with the foreign DNA transform or "infect" bacteria at the West Bay Sewage Treatment facility?"

Adamantly, the pompous Fitzpedro retorted. "The transfer of recombinant DNA would have already happened *somewhere else* over the past 20 years."

"How certain can we be that diseases did not come from something in the biological wastewater of a genetic engineering plant? Could the disease's cause have gone undetected?"

"It is possible, but I think it would be unlikely."

"But you said that other companies and even Allbio's other plants use heat or acid to *kill* their cultures before dumping them. Didn't you?"

"Er…yes." Leary-eyed, Fitzpedro half-anticipated what line of questioning was coming.

"How rare would it be for Allbio's designer DNA, the immunity suppressing gene they create, to transfer or "jump in" to a mycoplasma?"

"I don't know. I'm not a specialist on mycoplasma."

Prosecutor Reznor looked pleased with the response. Especially since he had an upcoming expert, a mycoplasma specialist, who could answer the "horizontal gene transfer" question.

"Who in West Bay had oversight over permits for sewage disposal from the Allbio plant? Who enforced the rules and regulations?"

"The regulatory agency would be the sewage commissioner for the town? "Maybe the city manager? I don't know their names. That was all negotiated with the higher ups at the company. It would be the head of manufacturing and Allbio New England site VP, Bonaducci, probably with Allbio corporate. That was not part of my job, I only was responsible for making sure things were safe in the plant." Fitzpedro was quick to cover his bulbous butt.

"Your honor, I have no further questions."

Like Pontius Pilate, Fitzpedro had washed his hands of any responsibility.

"The 'tomato' looks a little stewed!" Jeremy whispered to Jo.

Chapter 40 Never in the natural world

THE MEDICAL DIRECTOR in charge of the CDC investigation, Dr. Janice Stickle, looked uncomfortable in the witness stand. Her tiny shoulders crouched, arms folded across her chest, obviously tense, she was anxious to get all the facts out and tell her story.

"Yes, we had been notified by the state's Department of Health. We were concerned that the confirmed cases of encephalitis and other related diseases may *not* have been a *natural* or *normal* occurrence. We at the CDC's Respiratory Disease Intelligence Service notified the FBI of our suspicions. Together the CDC and FBI initiated simultaneous epidemiologic and criminal investigations."

The prosecutor encouraged the narrative, "So could these cases of disease have indicated possible crimes?"

"Yes, there was a suspicion that the cause was not a familiar pathogen but that the bacteria morphed into something more virulent. There were various hypotheses as to the source."

"Please continue Dr. Stickle. What more can you tell us?" Prosecutor Reznor encouraged.

"The state medical laboratory is part of a network of U.S. laboratories. The lab confirmed *mycoplasma pneumonia* as the source of infection but its extreme *virulence* was highly suspect. It was deadly. In particular, the cluster of encephalitis and neurological diseases were an *exceedingly rare* event. In only one-tenth of 1 percent of the cases does *mycoplasma pneumonia* lead to encephalitis. Walking pneumonia seldom ever leads to encephalitis. And this was the *only* place in the country that this happened."

"So what did the CDC do in your investigation?"

"We sent in our team of medical personnel to collect specimens: nasal, oral, throat and blood. Orthopedists and neurologists collected synovial, cerebral and spinal fluid. A multitude of tests *ruled out* other pathogens and other communicable disease agents. CDC found mycoplasma in nearly all the children's samples. So we then began looking for the local source. We interviewed many people, school nurses, officials, families living in the small area where the diseases were detected. We wanted to know *where* the mycoplasma originated. We did not know at the time if it arose naturally or not. And we needed to know just how much danger there was to the public, especially the young."

"And then what did you do next?"

"Well, this lead to an environmental investigation. We began testing our different hypotheses. Where did the mutant come from? We took samples from the schools, residences, indoor places such as the malls, and in particular the outdoor activity locations. The children's playgrounds, parks and playing fields: baseball diamonds, soccer fields. We looked at the soil that the children played on. We wanted to know, *where* did the kids pick up the "superbug"? We wanted to know *why* such a normally insignificant infection led to so many very sick children in a narrow geographic area."

"Had the bug mutated into something more dangerous, Dr. Stickle?"

"Yes, we suspected the diseases in the nine schools were caused by an unusual, deadly form of a common microbe. Perhaps a genetically engineered DNA construct, *not seen in nature*, was the cause of the increased virulence. We suspected a gene that destroyed the children's ability to fight the disease. A gene that disrupted and destroyed immunity, perhaps?"

"So is the question, what made the disease more infectious and more deadly? Or is the question, what made the children more vulnerable? Can you help us in our understanding Dr. Stickle?"

"The answer to the two questions is *both*. A gene could make the disease more deadly and affect a child's immunity. The children became more susceptible to the disease because they could not fight the diseases off. This superbug was also highly resistant to antibiotics. The bacteria became more deadly and infectious because it now carried a weapon to break down the children's natural defenses."

Dr. Stickle explained that the FBI and CDC worked together to collect evidence. The evidence was tested at multiple labs throughout the country. The Laboratory Response Network, the country's public health laboratories, received the original samples. Tests were verified in other medical, university and national laboratories. *The results agreed that this was the first and only time we have seen this specific mutation."*

Dr. Stickle was perfunctory and direct as she explained how biological evidence differed from physical evidence. "Forensic investigation involves the crime scene and the collection of evidence. Microbial and DNA testing were used to test samples. But it was the DNA sequencing that gave us the needed evidence, a type of DNA fingerprinting. The method called real-time PCR (Polymerase Chain Reaction) will be explained to you in detail by another CDC expert. But I am telling you the facts; that PCR testing is fundamental in identifying unique genes. PCR identified the "DNA signature" that made the ordinary mycoplasma so deadly. It carried the same DNA fingerprint that Allbio dumped into the sewers."

"So Dr. Stickle, you are saying that DNA evidence is more accurate than other physical evidence?" Reznor prodded for more.

"We looked for very unique and unusual DNA. And we can identify unique DNA with a level of confidence unheard of before from any other physical or forensic evidence. We do this with a higher degree of accuracy than any hair, bullet or human fingerprint could ever have."

"And what you are saying has been corroborated by the FBI?"

"Yes. There are flaws in matching fingerprints, ballistics, voiceprints, bitemarks, footprints, handwriting, tiretracks and ummm... bloodstain splatter. The FBI investigative team has confirmed that *all* physical evidence suffers from

251

confounding variables. Human fingerprint evidence was once thought to be infallible, but errors have happened. There have been cases where an incorrect fingerprint match put innocent people behind bars. But the identification of *unique* DNA, DNA that has *never occurred in the natural world*, could be the lynchpin that ties this case together."

Chapter 41 *It's all in the sludge*

NEXT TO TESTIFY was Peter Scrutare, the expert consultant and undercover agent with the FBI. He gave witness to what he observed first hand. He was hired to run sewage treatment plants and hopped, skipped and jumped from the West Bay treatment plant to Allbio's wastewater facility.

"Mr. Scrutare, for the jury please explain what sludge is."

"Well sludge comes from human waste, household and industrial sewage. Heavy sludge settles in the tanks at the sewage plant. It is dried, mixed with wood ash. It sits for at least 60 days, generating high temperatures that kill off bacteria."

"All the bacteria are killed?"

"No, not all. But most of the pathogenic bacteria die."

"And where, Mr. Scrutare, did the sludge end up once it left the treatment plant?"

"There were mountains of it, labeled safe Class A "biosolids". There was an attempt to sell it but few were willing to buy it. In the end some local residents were offered the "SuperStuff" for free, and they took it. The Fishing and Wildlife management identified a lot of sites that could use compost. Thousands of cubic feet of dried sludge compost was spread in parks and playgrounds near the rivers and streams. Some was spread near the local schools. Sometimes it was mixed with the soil. The town made no attempt at figuring out the required 1 to 2 inches of spread, instead they dumped it up to 2 feet deep in different locations. In one location, SuperStuff was spread just a thousand feet from a private drinking well and even closer to residential dwellings where children played. The town and the owners of the land were fined by the State Department of the Environment."

"Mr. Scrutare, explain your understanding of how the Clean Water Act defines sewage sludge." Reznor wanted clear meanings, not just someone's interpretation.

"The Clean Water Act defines sewage sludge as a pollutant. In 2002, a National Academies of Science panel warned that sewage sludge is an unpredictable and complex mix of biological and chemical wastes. You just cannot adequately assess its risks. And sewage sludge can have high levels of pathogenic organisms, bacteria, viruses."

"So are you saying that we really don't know what is in the sludge or how bad it is for us?"

"Yes. But the EPA, the Environmental Protection Agency and companies that manage the crap... sorry your honor, waste...promote land application of sludge as safe and beneficial. They have for decades."

"So is the EPA saying that the safe control of sewage and sludge is the responsibility of the State?"

"Yes, they are."

"Under the code of federal *regulations*, Title 40 Protection of the Environment, the state must regulate the use or disposal of sewage sludge to protect public health and the environment. But is the State also responsible for the deadly DNA that was dumped in the sewers by Allbio?"

"It is, but only if they had the knowledge that the DNA was potentially deadly. They had to rely on the knowledge that Allbio shared with them. Allbio said their DNA was only a Level 1 hazard and therefore not harmful."

Chapter 42 Anywhere, Everywhere,

"OUR NEXT EXPERT witness is a CDC specialist in Mycoplasma. This group of microbiologists call themselves mycoplasmologists. Would you tell us about your work with the respiratory disease section?

"Mycoplasmologists are intimately familiar with mycoplasma, the simplest basic form of bacteria. The fragile cells have a minimal amount of DNA, small genomes and no nucleus. Until fairly recently, mycoplasma were *very* hard to detect because they did not grow easily in cell culture."

"And how has that changed?"

"During the recent outbreaks of mycoplasma we used new tests to detect certain "markers". We used what we call "real-time PCR" to test respiratory specimen. Using PCR, we can amplify, that is, we can multiply just a tiny amount of DNA into millions of copies for analyzing. The test then targets gene sequences to positively identify *mycoplasma pneumoniae* as the cause of multiple diseases."

"And do you have evidence that the mycoplasma came from Allbio?" Reznor knew that the defense would relentlessly attack with this question if he didn't ask it first.

"No. The mycoplasma could have come from *anywhere*. Microbial forensics can *not* prove the source of the mycoplasma. Mycoplasma are found *everywhere*, they are as common as muck. But we do have evidence to show that the deadly

DNA that *attached itself* to the mycoplasma could have only come from one place. And that place is Allbio."

Gasps and choking guffaws from the defense attorneys were quickly silenced by Judge Carvallo's dart-throwing gaze.

Unfazed, prosecutor Reznor continued with his line of questioning. "So if mycoplasma are found *everywhere*, what proof do you have that *deadly DNA that attached itself* to the mycoplasma came from Allbio? Could it have been a mutant?"

"Using DNA forensics, we used the same type of evidence that would be used to convict a rapist or murderer. Just as humans have very *unique* DNA, so do engineered genes that are used to produce recombinant drugs."

The CDC specialist didn't stop, he was almost there. He lunged forward as though he would jump from the witness seat like the Allbio gene jumped into the mycoplasma. Excited, charged up like the laser-beam in the palm of his hand, he exclaimed, "And so did our culprit! The engineered DNA *owned by Allbio*. The naked DNA that came from Allbio's CHO cells!"

He calmed down. "Allbio lysed the cells, broke them up, but the unique DNA was not destroyed. The naked DNA, whole pieces and fragments remained."

"Naked?" Asked Reznor with an uncharacteristic raise of his eyebrows? A glimmer of naughty humor from this otherwise serious, unemotional hardball.

"It may be 'naked', that is, *not* in cells, but it

can persist in the environment. And there are specific markers. And identifiers such as control signals and vectors."

"OK, slow down. One thing at a time. Tell us about markers."

The CDC expert was young, handsome, focused. He directed his laser pointer at the specifics on markers on the projection board. "Exhibited here is the marker sequence, pFCR-FHDV-ruTNFRh-AC. Do not let it baffle you. This gene was designed to make or 'express' the anti-immunity TNF blocker produced by Allbio. Our testing determined this marker sequence in many gene testing samples. The identifiable gene is owned by Allbio."

"And control signals and vectors? What are they?"

"The control signal, the "FHDV" in the sequence, helps the gene "jump in" to the CHO's, and the control signal could help it "jump in" to mycoplasma.

Excited with the science and the mystery it would explain; the pieces of the jigsaw revealed the entire picture. The CDC expert could barely contain himself.

"Vectors are like shuttles. They are constructed to break the species barrier. The vectors help genetic material "jump in and out" of one species and jump into another. They carry the foreign DNA into all sorts of organisms, and in this case, Allbio's immunity suppressing gene into an unintended target, the mycoplasma. They hitch a ride *wherever* they can, *whenever* the opportunity arises."

Jeremy whispered in Jo's ear "Opportunes!". Jo elbowed Jeremy lightly in the ribs and glared at him with an amused and cheeky 'I told you so' grin.

"Samples from the Allbio's working cell banks were subpoenaed. Using PCR testing, the gene marker in the Allbio cell bank samples matched the gene markers in environmental samples. Sadly, the marker was also in the nose-mouth-throat samples taken from sick children.

Reznor recalled Dr. Stickle to the stand and she confirmed. "At our labs, we analyzed the oral-pharyngeal specimen that were positive for mycoplasma. The children's samples carried the Allbio genetic marker in 80% of the specimen tested by PCR."

Next, 'Sludge-man' Scrutare was recalled to the stand.

"And what did you find out about the genetic markers, Mr. Scrutare?"

"We looked along the identified path of the disease, the ten mile stretch that roughly paralleled the Tuxet River. We tested in the newly built sewers from Allbio to the town's sewage facility. And we found Allbio gene marker fragments. We also found the same gene markers in the soil where the children played soccer. Finally, we tested and found the same Allbio gene marker in the unprocessed sludge piled up at the sewage facility, and in the bio-solid compost sold as SuperStuff and deposited throughout the area."

"Gene marker fragments? So what is the significance, Mr. Scrutare?"

Mr. Scrutare amplified. "We found the genes, the DNA, in the settlement tanks; in the percolating filter beds at the sewage treatment plant layered in with living cells in the "bio-film". And this led us to conclude that the genes linger. For days. For months. Perhaps for years if frozen. If they linger in the sewage plant water, then they linger in the SuperStuff."

"Yes, but where is your corroborating evidence?"

"Samples from the different locations were sent to the various agencies and academic institutions. We amplified, multiplied the DNA in the samples using the PCR method we have testified about previously. The samples were compared with the known - the unknown, the foreign - the familiar, the constructed - the deconstructed. Again using PCR all the labs confirmed that they found the same DNA fragments of the Allbio gene, pFCR-FHDV-ruTNFRh-AC."

"So the proof was in the proverbial genetic pudding?" Reznor punned with a faint glimmer of a smile.

"Yes, the proof was in the sludge pudding." Scrutare answered, poker faced and matter of fact. Having worked convincingly undercover, he was skilled at divulging nothing. Like Sergeant Joe Friday, "Just the facts, ma'am."

Finally, testimony from the last scientist Wordsworth, a syntho-biologist turned ethicist, described how designer bacteria could be created from the minimal organisms, in this case the mycoplasma.

"We know those mycoplasmas are normally quite innocuous. But there are scientists, both legitimate and illegitimate, using *mycoplasma pneumonia* as building blocks in genetic engineering experiments. They strip them down of any extra DNA, create a basic cell and then insert all kinds of designer genes."

Wordsworth reiterated what other experts had said, that synthetic biology could be used for purposes of good and evil, a "dual use" technology. "In this case, Allbio is guilty, your honor, of inserting their designer label, a deadly gene, into the lowly mycoplasma. It went for a wild ride, through the wastewater, the SuperStuff spread on the fields and eventually ended up attacking the children of our smallest state. They clearly were warned about the dangers of releasing an immunity suppressing gene without making sure it was inactive. At Allbio New England, they went against their own processes, to do as they did elsewhere."

Defense lawyer Burgsdorf countered. "But surely this amazing science is in the hands of well-intentioned scientists who design new medicines?"

"Amazing science? Certainly." Wordsworth nodded his head. "Potentially dangerous? *Without a doubt!*"

Wordsworth peered over at Ferris Pentanil who couldn't stop reacting and burst out. "But it was *unintentional!*"

"Order in the court, Dr Pentanil! Please keep your remarks to yourself." Judge Carvallo sternly retorted. "You will have your day to defend yourself on the stand!"

Jo and Jeremy drove home from the courtroom proceedings that day in contented silence, until Jeremy slipped a CD into the player. Guitar strings strumming, and Bowie began singing...... "Small Gene Genie, she took off to the city, E E E A E E E A. Strung out on lasers and slash-back blazers, Ate all your razors........" The evidence from this day's hearing suggested Allbio's little genie had indeed journeyed around the city.

Chapter 43 The Last Testament

THE TRIAL MOVED from the experts to the defendants and, as the judge had promised, Dr. Ferris Pentanil would have his turn on the stand. Federal prosecutor Reznor went for the heart, gut, and soul of Ferris Pentanil. "Dr. Pentanil, when the Allbio New England plant started producing its drug in the summer of 2005, were there many batch failures from contamination?"

"Yes, there were some, but that was expected in the start-up phase, after all it was a new state-of-the-art facility."

"The largest of its kind in the world, yes?"

"Yes, Allbio New England is reputedly the leader in…"

"Just answer the question please, Dr. Pentanil."

"And did Allbio have a "Bio-safety" plan for containment procedures, to make sure that no dangerous materials were release into the community's environment?"

"Yes, it did." Pentanil's back was bunched up, arched in a cat-like defensive posture.

Pointing to the document he held as evidence. "Your signature on the plan says you approved of the plan, Dr. Pentanil. Is that correct?" Reznor asked.

"Yes, but .."

"Let me paraphrase from the CFR, the Code of Federal Regulation Title 42: Public Health, that a written bio-safety plan, one that is commensurate with the risk of the agent, is required?"

"Yes, Allbio New England is a Level 1 facility."

"In your Bio-Safety plan, the biological CHO cells were released into the sewers. Dr Pentanil, you were responsible for that decision, weren't you?"

"Yes I was, but we did *not* release living cells. The CHO's were lysed, broken up *before* they were discharged from the plant. They were dead cells!" Dr. Pentanil was adamant, self-righteous and obviously pissed-off.

"Hmmm, dead cells, only dead cells. Is that correct?"

"Yes!" Pentanil snapped back, terse and annoyed.

But the lysed CHO cells contained an engineered gene that disrupts immunity. Reznor did not pause for an answer. "You are a scientist Dr Pentanil, what is your PhD in?"

"Microbiology." Pentanil looked as though he was holding his breath.

"As Vice-President, you were considered the "Top Scientist" and manufacturing expert at Allbio?"

"Yes." His V-shaped eyebrows pointier than ever, chest expanding, his broad red tie puffed out like a red-breasted robin.

"I will read from the employee "Values Clarifications" manual. "Allbio Value #1 "Be Science-based….apply the scientific method, collect and analyze data and make rational decisions." Is that the value you promoted, some say *created* at

Allbio?"

"Yes, that is Allbio's credo. I take great pride in designing our 'Values Clarifications' course for employees."

"So you would say that if your manual were scrupulously followed, you should have investigated the wastewater risk before you put it in the sewers?"

"I suppose so, but the plant was considered a low risk Level 1 site."

"Surely you are familiar with the National Academies of Science reports: the Fink Report, Biotechnology Research in an Age of Terrorism and the National Science Advisory Board for Bio-Security; their report on Dual Use Sciences and their Potential Misuse? Dr. Pentanil, have you read any or all of these reports?"

"I do not see what *bio-security* has to do with biotechnology. Allbio is *not* a *terrorist* organization!" Pentanil smirked and grinned deviously, eliciting sniggers and snorts in the courtroom, especially amongst his Allbio compatriots.

"Order in the court! Dr Pentanil, the defendant will answer the question!" Judge Carvallo directed.

"Yes, sorry your honor." Dr Pentnil cowered.

"You are also familiar with the science academies report on Biological Confinement of Genetically Engineered Organisms? It warns of the unknown consequences of releasing recombinant or engineered genes?"

"Yes, possible unclear consequences. There is no scientific proof. The cells that Allbio released were dead!"

"Biotechnology has two potentials, either for great benefit or for tremendous harm. It is a dual-use technology. Do you agree with that statement Dr. Pentanil?"

"Yes." Pentanil answered quickly to avoid the wrath and another reprimand from the judge.

"Dead cells I agree, but the genetically engineered DNA, the fragments remained. We have heard the Allbio markers in their manufactured gene were found in the samples in the environment. Do you agree to that fact?"

"Yes."

"From the National Science Advisory (NSABB), scientific experts in dual-use technology presented guidelines to the National Institutes of Health. The board drafted seven categories of dual-use experiments of concern for the NIH. Are you familiar with their guidelines? They listed seven genetic experiments of concern?"

"I don't remember."

"Let me refresh your memory Dr. Pentanil. Of the seven experiments, # 2 is DO NOT disrupt immunity. Immunity is *key* to our defense against disease. The national scientists are concerned about inserting immunosuppressive genes into bacteria, viruses."

"But Allbio does NOT conduct any experiments where the genes are inserted into bacteria or viruses!"

"Perhaps then, it was experiment #6 that

Allbio conducted by enhancing the susceptibility of the children to disease? By compromising their immune system? Allbio transferred the engineered gene, the TNF blocker, to the children affecting their immunity by stealth. The hitchhiking gene went for a ride on the common mycoplasma. It created a biological weapon of mass destruction."

"Allbio did *not* experiment with children. How *dare* you!" Dr. Pentanil repudiated vehemently.

"Maybe not experiments at the Allbio site, but, *Allbio's experiments took place in the sewers, in the water, in the soil and on the playgrounds, and in the sick children.* The Allbio DNA was spread around the state through the SuperStuff. The children became Allbio's experimental test tubes, Allbio's unwitting "mini-bioreactors". The weapon-carrying mycoplasma evaded the children's normal defenses against disease. The small bodies of the children could not make enough vital immune protectors. Allbio supplied the TNF blocker, the weapon that destroyed the children's first line of defense."

Dr. Pentanil reiterated, "The genes are unstable, they do NOT persist in the environment!"

"But Doctor we have heard testimony that the genetic material does linger, have we not?"

"Yes, but anyway someone *else* could have taken those genes. A disgruntled employee could have stolen the CHO cells."

Deep furrows now accentuated his punctuated eyebrows as he continued to futilely refute the evidence, "Even if the DNA is 100%

identical, does it prove it was ours? Someone *else* could have created the same gene and released it!"

"According to the evidence we have heard, you are grasping at straws, Dr Pentanil? It is a stretch of the imagination to think that *someone, somewhere* could have made genes that duplicated Allbio's gene as an act of terrorism. The expert evidence the court has heard clearly showed the anti-immune gene is owned and produced only by Allbio because your company has a copyright on that immunity suppressing gene."

"Has there been any evidence of others creating your gene with the marker that is unique to Allbio's marker?"

Dr Pentanil eyebrows flattened into a linear scowl "Not as far as I know."

"Had you done your due diligence, followed your own manuals of good practice, read the reports sent to you from the National Academies of Science, you would have known. You *should* have known. You said you were familiar with the recommendations on Biological Confinement of Genetically Engineered Organism. Is that correct?"

"Yes."

"Then, you are aware that.." and Mr. Reznor continued to read from the text. "The decision, *whether* and *how* to confine the Genetically Engineered Organism (GEO), must be made. Who has the responsibility to decide? The responsibility and commitment must come from Allbio management. We must question their *Judgment, Values and Instincts as the report recommends.*" Reznor scowled over his glasses, pronouncing emphatically each and every word.

"The nation's top scientists told you, the decision must come early. It cannot be an afterthought. Any ill-effects, negative consequences, cannot be undone, can it Doctor Pentanil?"

Ferris Pentanil would not look up from his fixed gaze on the floor boards.

"If the decision is delayed until *after* product development, the need to receive ROI, return on investment, could cloud *Judgment.* Dr. Pentanil, the court must question your *judgment!*"

"You need to ask the witness a question," the judge quickly interjected before the defense lodged an objection. Silence permeated the courtroom like the thick cloud that enveloped Ferris Pentanil.

"Yes your honor, Dr Pentanil, *was it you who decided to dispose of the DNA with the immunity suppressing gene, to dispose of the "failed" pre-production batches of genetic material?*"

"I advised on bio-safety guidelines for recombinant DNA based on what was known at the time. In nearly thirty years, there has been no incidents, no harm to humans. We abided by the NIH guidelines for level 1 laboratories; facilities that posed a low risk to health and the environment. Many companies release DNA wastewater into sewers. The regulations vary from state to state, from country to country. Some companies deactivate, other don't. The local and state governments issue the permits."

"Dr Pentanil, were you responsible for the decision to dispose of DNA from the bioreactors in Allbio New England facility?"

"I *advised*. The final decision belonged to the Allbio CEO, Henry Givens."

Jeremy looked at Jo and gave her a hug, "You *did* know what was going on, as Courtney, our lawyer, told you. There was something *you knew* that worried Allbio and set in motion *all sorts* of events. You tried to set up something that would find the root cause of the failures. But you, and anyone else at the plant that could do that, got fired instead. As it turned out, it took years to put together, but as usual your scientific instincts were impeccable." He whispered. Jo simply sat there, basking in the glow of vindication, as gasps of disbelief, horror and amazement could be heard throughout the courtroom.

The unexpected twist of Pentanil giving up CEO Givens caught even the prosecution team off guard, the defense team was trying to absorb the accusation they had not anticipated. Pentanil had spoken off the company's carefully crafted defense script, incriminating the top dog. Henry Givens nearly burst in anger as his tanned cheeks and ears reddened a fiery crimson.

Proceedings were abruptly halted by the defense, a shift in strategy for the unexpected finger-pointing that prosecutor Reznor provoked. The next day's headlines read "Expect the Unexpected" as the media honed-in on what was to come, in what had rapidly become a sensational trial.

Chapter 44 Corporate Capo

HENRY GIVENS WAS NOT a man who allowed others to alter his fate. His aggressive style and intimidating gestures made other's wary and deferential. Even the self-assured Ferris Pentanil cowered under the enormous ego and self-confidence that Givens exuded. You did not want to anger Henry. He who must be obeyed. He who knew all things. The unflappable, imperturbable leader oozed confidence. Only underlings saw the blustering bully, who shaped the world the way he saw it, and made sure the opinions he received reinforced his thinking. Profits at Allbio motivated him, and he made sure he got a substantial share.

Before Givens took the stand, his defense team prepped him impeccably. His mantra became "Expect the Unexpected". He not only had to defend himself against the charges against him, but against the accusations by the 'traitor' Ferris Pentanil that Givens had signed off on what had been a dangerous effluent in West Bay sewers.

"Mr. Givens, what is your background?" The defense attorney for Henry Given set the stage for what was to come.

"My background prior to Allbio was in the military, many years in leadership roles. My expertise was naval and aeronautical engineering. I have an MBA from the Wharton School of Business. My job as CEO is strategic leadership of the Allbio Corporation. When I joined Allbio over ten years ago, I was assured that the company was

271

flush with scientific expertise and that was *not* what was needed from me. I depended on Ferris Pentanil and other scientists for their leadership in manufacturing and science. I had no science beyond high school, but I studied the biotech industry and knew I could lead and grow the company into the world leader. Allbio today is *exactly* that." Givens was the epitome of cool; his eyes narrowed, his nose elevated in smug arrogance as he glared at the prosecution team. He had followed the script perfectly.

"And what was the role of Dr Ferris Pentanil at Allbio?" Defense attorney Burgsdorf asked.

"Dr Pentanil provided the leadership in manufacturing and science. He had over twenty years with Allbio and led the manufacturing organization. He oversaw the production of the drugs and he made decisions on regulatory compliance." So Givens delineated, he drew the line in the sand. "I make decisions on strategic planning; Dr. Pentanil made manufacturing and scientific decisions."

Attorney Burgsdorf lead the narrative towards a predetermined conclusion. Givens was the dynamic leader who delegated power. The world he created, his leadership and guiding strategy, built confidence in his employees. Pentanil was the scientist. He built the biotech factories; reliable, efficient factories.

Givens knew what he wanted. The biggest, the best. He was very clear on his strategy.

Prosecutor Reznor took advantage of the momentum building up and the tension between the dueling senior executives. Who then *was* responsible for corporate decisions? Who made the decisions, good or bad? Not getting a quick response, Reznor reiterated using a different line of attack, "Mr. Givens, the sheer scale of Allbio New England is unprecedented in its size. Is it not?"

"Yes, it is the largest facility of its kind in the world." Givens assumed his pompous and impatient demeanor.

Both played at mutual intimidation. The prosecuting pit-bull versus king-pin of the corporate upperworld.

"Yes, Mr. Givens we have heard that, but wasn't there a problem with obtaining enough water?"

"Yes, but we worked with local people to get the permits."

"Who specifically did you work with, Mr. Givens?"

"I cannot recall the names of everyone, we worked with so many."

"Maybe, Mr. Givens, but didn't you work a lot with the disgraced and convicted "fixer" and then state senator Sam Egregio?"

"I don't recall."

"Strange, Mr. Givens, seeing as you were forced to testify at his trial on corruption and other crimes. Are you sure you forget sitting in that court?"

"Maybe I did, but it was some time ago."

"Do you not recall the 'spot stock' scandal that Allbio got involved in with Senator Egregio?"

"I thought it was a simple book-keeping

error."

"A simple error that Mr. Egregio is now serving prison time for?"

"I cannot be held responsible for the actions of a corrupt official."

Reznor took a different tack "Mr. Givens, why were all the people investigating the problems with the pre-production batches fired?"

"I don't recall. I am not micro-managing plant managers about personnel issues."

"But weren't you curious that a group of people, some who had only been at the plant for three weeks and all having some part in investigations into the problem, were let go?"

"No."

"But simply *dumping* the failed batches did save Allbio money, instead of using the process to make sure the immunity suppressing gene was inactive?"

"Yes."

Reznor felt he had established some credibility problems for Givens and returned to matters in hand.

"Who signed off on Pentanil's recommendations about Allbio New England's failed pre-production batches?"

"I signed off on the recommendations because I believed Dr. Pentanil was trust worthy."

"But you said you were not a scientist, so you could not have the expertise to understand all the points in the advice given?"

"I suppose so," Givens was still thinking about how he had been linked to the corrupt senator.

"So you signed off on a dumping of genetic material at Allbio New England even though there was evidence available that there could be a problem. And their process differed from disposal processes at other plants. Isn't that the truth, you relied on a single source, Dr. Pentanil, and did not ask anyone else *why* we treated the DNA waste different at other Allbio plants, *before* you signed?"

Givens took an age to answer, "Yes, I guess I made a mistake, just a simple human error."

"I see, like the simple book-keeping error that you played a part in. No further questions for this witness."

Chapter 45 Bioterror, Bioerror, Biocrime

DEFENSE LAWYER BURGSDORF made his final argument to the jury. He asked and answered, "Do you believe that individuals in a corporation can be responsible for what occurred inadvertently? Surely they *can not* be held culpable."

Attorney Burgsdorf adamantly stated his final words. "There is *no evidence* that Allbio designed a mutant mycoplasma strain. Statements to the contrary *can not* be used as evidence."

In his closing argument the federal prosecutor, Reznor, emphasized Allbio's negligence. "Negligence in *not* taking responsibility for decision making, clearly the CEO Givens did not take his responsibility for decisions he signed off on. Allbio's negligence to assess potential risks led to disregard for human health and human life. In fact this was actually gross negligence. What is the difference between negligence and gross negligence, members of the jury? Some say it is the difference between a fool and a damn fool. But gross negligence is the reckless disregard for the rights and well-being of others."

The prosecution hit hard on Allbio's corporate responsibility. "Can the corporation be held liable? Or must a corporate agent have allegedly defrauded? Behaving fraudulently in denying the knowledge that he or she had? Dr. Pentanil clearly denied his scientific knowledge.

276

This represented fraudulent lying about what *should* have been known, and *made* known to others in the corporation. CEO Givens signed off on a process, to dump immunity suppressing genes, based on poor risk advice from Pentanil. It *may* be a bioerror." Reznor reiterated.

"CEO Givens was vague on certain details regarding his relationship with the state senator Egregio. It is a fact, established in another court, and public record that he personally played a role in getting water and having sewers built for the new plant. Money was paid out by Allbio's Political Action Committee to the disgraced senator. Beyond that, he colluded with the senator to create a stock scheme that, in similar cases, has been clearly shown to be illegal. Fictitious stock holders and revised dates brought advantage to the recipients by 'choosing' a day when the price was high."

"There can be dangerous consequences as we have seen here. DNA disposal practices at Allbio New England differed from other plants. This drug producing plant of a legitimate corporation released engineered genes. Dr. Pentanil was correct, Allbio is not a terrorist organization, but by dumping the genes into local sewers, ill-intended terrorists could have taken advantage of Allbio's material. Homeland Security has recently issued warnings of interest, by al-Qaeda, in bioengineering and recruiting sympathetic scientists. Bioerror or Bioterror? Their disregard for the risks of putting that engineered gene into the community looks like more than error. Nobody can deny the nature of the deadly consequences for the children who were sickened or killed. The crucial evidence is that the corporation clearly *did not* follow its regular practices for disposal of engineered genes."

Prosecutor Reznor asserted, "Playing around with DNA is an entangling dilemma. And the Gene Genie is out of the bottle. And, *in this case the court has heard, Allbio Corporation left evidence*. Samples traced the genetic markers. Using DNA fingerprints, scientists from around the country isolated the recombinant, anti-tnf alpha gene construct, the immunity destroying gene owned by Allbio, in the sludge and soil samples in the community. They found it in the playgrounds, where the children played. The evidence was in the soil on the playing fields. And the same deadly DNA material created by Allbio was in the children. Allbio has to take responsibility for the dead children and irreparable damage their product created."

Jo and Jeremy both broke out in audible sighs, for Jo this was validation long postponed. There were tears in Reznor's eyes, and shock in the eyes of the judge and jurors.

Prosecutor Reznor, calmed his emotions and caught his breadth. Dramatically he queried, "What did the defendants *not* understand about the risks of disposing *dangerous genes*? Dr. Pentanil, as the scientist, clearly should have understood. Mr. Givens should have queried *why* Allbio New England did not follow company practice in other plants. *Other* regulators in different jurisdictions had made Allbio dispose of their material properly.

It is disingenuous of Pentanil and Givens to claim it was not a problem for them to solve. The testimony here shows malfeasance by company and state officials. Allbio used the lax regulation as an excuse to let the lethal gene hitch a ride on the mycoplasma bacteria, creating a virulent, deadly mutant pathogen. The company stayed silent even as the publicized outbreak occurred, and they made no attempt to rectify the situation. It is strange that, only years later, the company built a processing plant that no longer allows their waste to flush untreated into the sewers. It clearly shows they knew the risks they were taking.

He clearly had prepared for the moment. He continued to summarize the impact that Allbio's transgressions had inflicted on the small state. "An ordinary bacteria that caused common but nonfatal diseases, like walking pneumonia, became a weaponized "superbug" that attacked the brain of a child, causing encephalitis and death. *Nature would never create this monster. But Allbio did, thoughtlessly dumping immunity suppressing material.* Without Allbio's help, the ordinary bacteria would have caused little harm."

"Allbio has indeed committed a biocrime, not a bioerror."

Chapter 46 Underlying Crimes

FOLLOWING A 17 MONTH trial, the jury convicted three senior executives on 49 of 58 counts which included: 5 counts of making materially false statements to state and federal agencies; 6 counts of obstructing FBI investigations; 16 counts of violating the Clean Water Act; 13 counts of violating CFR title 42 the Public Health and Welfare Act; and 9 counts of violating CFR title 40 of the federal Environmental Act. Prosecutor Reznor and the prosecution team had reason to celebrate the success of their colossal undertaking.

But appeals were already in progress before the three senior executives could be sentenced. The press speculated that former VP Ferris Pentanil would get seven years. No one could refute the fact that the senior managers had repeatedly violated the Clean Water Act. They acted badly. They blatantly discharged hazardous biologic agents into the sewage system. Their offenses lead to crimes against the environment and public health.

The outrage in opinions, editorials, blogs and commentaries fueled a volatile, vindictive public. The public wrath ensured that Allbio Chief Executive Officer, Henry Givens, former Vice President Ferris Pentanil, and Vice President Bonaducci, who managed the Allbio New England plant, would pay for their crimes. As Judge Carvallo summed up. Together, they destroyed human health. Together, they killed children.

Judge Carvallo in her final instructions to

the jury reminded them that the defendants were charged under the RICO statutes. Evidence in a RICO conspiracy does not have to be direct. It can be shown through circumstantial evidence, as it has been in this case by the prosecution.

During sentencing, the judge stated if "corporations are people too" then the Allbio Corporation too has been found guilty by the jury of negligently dumping hazardous substances into the sewers. The corporation violated the Clean Water Act. The corporation acted knowingly. The acts were voluntary, intentional and *not* the result of accident or mistake of fact. The facts, according to Judge Carvallo, were validated by the expert witnesses. But the facts provided by the expert testimony were ignored by Allbio's senior management.

In cahoots, Allbio officers failed to investigate the risks associated with Allbio's contaminated waste, filled with immunity suppressing genes that they created. They disposed of the biological agents, the unnatural genes. They dumped the Killer Gene and hid their sins against human health. They put the lives of children in serious jeopardy, all for money. They bribed the legislators to do their bidding and public officials to turn a blind eye. They fired the wary underlings to silence disbelief. Allbio employees hired the contractors, including at least one crooked cop, and contracted a hit man. Those who committed the crimes. The jury found Allbio guilty of willful blindness and gross negligence. Worst of all, they

281

are guilty of the murder of unseen victims. They were the bosses, the corporate officers, who orchestrated the *underlying crimes*.

Needless to say, ramifications for the corporation and its officers were very serious. But RICO? Was the corporation guilty of conspiracy? Guilty of violating the Racketeer Influenced and Corrupt Organizations Act, RICO. Were Givens, Pentanil and Bonaducci responsible for the underlying crimes? Leaders of a syndicate like the Mafia, they lead their own private corporate army. Were the leaders responsible for the crimes they ordered others to do? Or were they exempt because they did not actually do it?

"So it is all in the knowing?" Jeremy asked lawyer Courtney Hill as they met around the familiar well-worn conference table. He and Jo both wanted some clarification of what was to come. Could the Allbio Corporation and its agents be held responsible for the underlying crimes, including the conspiracy to murder Jo?

"Since they were knowingly a part of the plan, they *don't have to be found guilty of committing any actual crime they had got others to perform on their behalf.*" Courtney explained.

"Even if they are *unaware* of the crimes that were committed?" Jo stare wide-eyed at no one in particular. She wanted to be perfectly clear.

"Yep, you got it. They *do not* have to be aware of the details of the criminal activity."

"So the big bosses are *still* guilty of conspiracy." Jeremy smiled wryly.

Still not totally satisfied with the explanation, Jo asked "But how do you *prove* it?"

"Despite its harsh provisions, a RICO-related charge is considered easy to prove in court. It focuses on patterns of behavior as opposed to criminal acts."

"How is that?" Jeremy's interest piqued.

"The jury's belief of what the bosses knew. Their links to different people. Their *connections*. The jury would have to believe that all that went on, even the individual details, went on *without* the knowledge of the big bosses. The senior officers would have had to be oblivious of what went on right under their noses. Remember, Capone and other gangsters were charged with tax evasion. The prosecution showed that as a result of criminal activity, large infusions of undeclared income accrued to Capone. He may not have known where every dollar came from, but he could not be oblivious to the mountains of cash the gang's activities created. "

Jeremy smiled.

Courtney smiled.

Jo smiled.

Clear as mud? Jo hadn't got her prosecution of the brute who beat her up or her former boss Steadman, but overall she felt validated. She and the world now understood the *underlying crimes*.

Chapter 47 Postscript

"CAN YOU BELIEVE what they *did*!" Jack punched Hong lightly on his arm to punctuate.

"Foolhardy, but fun, fun fun!" Hong was excited by the news that ran rampant through the synbio bloggers and microbio gene hacking networks. The so-called 'stupid' experiment created a dangerous airborne strain of bird flu. The experiment had now been replicated in a number of university labs. The newly created bird flu virus could be transmitted in the air from human to human. This experiment was even more frightening than the gene swapping used to reconstruct the 1918 "Spanish flu". The 1918 flu killed 2% of the population. Bird flu, designated H5N1, had a kill rate of over 60%, but contagion was limited to direct contact with birds. It had not been airborne.

Ever since the synthesizing of the polio virus, any virus could now be created from scratch. But the H5N1 virus was even more dangerous because it didn't *need* to be constructed. Its worldwide availability made its destructive power immense on a global scale. It could create a potentially lethal pandemic.

Jack Ashbell and his buddy Hong Min Chan had been bio-hacking since the earliest advent of do-it-yourself science. Even as kids, they would hang out in Jack's basement lab where they toyed with chemistry sets and microscopes back in elementary school. Jack inherited the family home in rural southern Rhode Island where he had grown up with his grandparents. His unmarried mother had died in childbirth. Jack grew up with few constraints and little guidance.

Jack was a tinkerer in more than one sense of the word. He had gone about his scientific tinkering with wild abandon. He still had his barrels of Tinkertoys that he used to model his molecular creations.

Recipes and genetic concoctions had been their two main diversions. With their DNA synthesizer, the pair replicated relatively innocuous genetic sequences. Mostly they design harmless but bizarre bacterial creations. Scented bacteria like *E.coli* that smelled like bananas or wintergreen mint. Jack had thrust the flask under Hong's nose who at first objected. "Oh, it doesn't smell like shit!"

Fluorescence genes, from a glowing green jellyfish, had been added to bacteria. The glow-in-the-dark bacterial flasks lined a shelf above the lab bench. The lab was littered with second-hand lab equipment: a microfuge for test tubes, thermo-cycler incubators, microscopes, chemicals, glassware galore. For growing cells and microbes, there were fermenters and roller bottles full of opaque custard-like orange media. In the dim light, the four bioreactor spinner flasks lined up side by side looked like Pokemon toys, their double barreled inlets resembled ears. Against the far wall, for heating, cooling and freezing, stood an old autoclave, kitchen refrigerator and a large freezer stacked with centrifuge freezer boxes. Jack and Hong indulged themselves with a PCR machine, a DNA synthesizer that made targeted copies of DNA sequences. They also had the essential gel box that looked like a shallow flat Jello mold. It was used for making short strands of proteins and separating DNA and RNA with an electric current.

Jack was the scientist. He read about the nation's scientific advisors who cautioned about the "seven experiments of concern" that could cause a biologic threat. Together he and Hong would pull out the Tinkertoys and construct models. They were hell-bent on usurping the legitimate scientists. Neither was rule-bound. Both were frustrated on their mundane day jobs. And they wanted to create the next generation of bioweapons.

Jack had the right background, a PhD in microbiology. He explained to Hong, "Yes, do no harm with biologic agents or toxins…..or microbes, especially bacteria and viruses. The seven 'commandments' as I interpret them are, DO NOT make microbes 1) that are more deadly, 2) that disrupt immunity, 3) that are resistant to antibiotics, antivirals or vaccines, 4) that are more contagious and easily transmitted, for example in air, 5) that can infect more hosts, i.e. other animals, 6) that can make their animal hosts more susceptible, and 7) DO NOT generate a new or novel pathogen, a 'de novo'."

"So, the 'commandments' said, do not create new or altered lifeforms…that will destroy us." Together Jack and Hong constructed their Tinkertoys. They were like kids playing in a crèche with building blocks, the synthetic biologists called "biobricks".

They sat back on their lab stools to admire their Tinkertoy creations that modeled the "seven experiments of concern".

"Anything is possible, and I am sure we have the right materials and ingredients to concoct the right cocktail. After all, it's not rocket science, is it?" Jack exclaimed as the two buckled over in paroxysms of laughter.

Hong managed the Animal Colony holding rooms where the university's research animals were segregated by species: mice, rabbits, gerbils, guinea pigs and ferrets. On Hongs next trip home to China, he would collect samples from chicken that died from bird flu, H5N1. They already had a freezer full of H1, H2, H3 flu viruses along with the E. coli and other common microbes. They had their sources.

You don't need animals and nature to resort and reshuffle genetic material, like in the Allbio case. Just a lab, somewhere, with rogues idiotic enough to play with death.

The college animal facility on the university campus in Rhode Island housed mammals for research: mice, rabbits, ferrets and other rodents. Basic science; that was all the animals were used for. But that didn't stop the two colleagues, a would-be-scientist and an animal technician, from playing on their own. The two buddies were partners in invention. Hong tended to the animals needed for experimentation. He supplied the college scientists with research animals. At the same time, he bred ferrets and mice for an ill-conceived project, a "stupid science" project that would

287

surpass the newest variation of bird flu H5N1. They would tinker and produce an airborne H5N1 more *deadly* than variations already concocted in a few university labs.

Hong and his friend Jack would ensure that their newer, fully weaponized breed of H5N1 would be invincible. Not only easily transmitted by air droplets from human to human, but it would be laden with every possible gene of destruction and death. In addition to being passed easily between humans, it would also attack the victim's immunity, render vaccines totally ineffective, and warrant the newest antiviral drugs useless. There was no cure. 100% lethal. Fatal to humans, few if any could survive. There would be certain death to all exposed. Perhaps some island dwellers could survive, in places isolated from the rest of the world. Maybe in a far away island like Tristan de Cunha, over 1700 miles from the nearest land, the two friends would escape together and live in splendid isolation.

Hong Min Chan controlled and managed the Animal Colony holding rooms where the animals were segregated by species. On his annual trip back home to China, Hong collected samples from chicken that died from the non-aerosol form of bird flu, H5N1. A virulent virus, but it was easily contained in plastic vials encased in triplicate hard plastic containers, like cocooned Russian matryoshka dolls. The cultures went undetected by x-ray and sniffers dogs. Hong housed the H5N1 samples along with the H1, H2, and H3 virus cultures in Jack's old but dedicated freezer. He was not stupid.

Hong's buddy and cohort, Jack Ashbell, concocted a mix of nucleic acids. Jack had access to the nucleic acid synthesizer in the University lab in a nearby town. He used it to construct an array of nucleic acids, the building blocks of DNA and RNA. Together Jack and Hong mixed the viruses and nucleic acids, played with gene vectors as if they were transporter toys, and hoped they had compiled the essential genetic mix to create the most deadly superbug ever know to man. It would surpass the lethality of the lab created superbug, airborne H5N1, that had been kept under lock and key at high security BSL-3 labs.

The first of the ferrets died. It was the tenth generation of ferrets infected with the cocktail of transfected viruses. Hidden away in the ceiling cavity of the "dirty" room, the ferrets went undetected. Hong climbed through the HVAC access each evening during his usual shift.

Hong called Jack on his cell phone. "The uninfected ferrets in the next cage are dying. We have to be careful! If this new mutant H5N1 gets out, it could cause the plague of the millennium!"

A remote controlled plane flew just above the campus buildings of the rural college. It was 2:45 AM when the 12 foot wingspan neared the animal housing facility. You could hear the slight whir of its electric engine. The plane's wings and entire body had been painted black. The initials SLAC (Stop Lab Animal Cruelty) were painted in green lettering on the top side of the wings. The forward part of the fuselage contained a built-in drop box large enough to hold several pounds of explosives. A central pan in the drop box allowed the contents to be released. Candy was often the usual cargo. Tonight it was packed with C4 and a detonator. The plane's nose dropped, aimed directly at it target, the animal colony unit.